ACTING UP

LIBBY PURVES

ACTING UP

Hodder & Stoughton

First published in Great Britain in 2004 by Hodder and Stoughton
A division of Hodder Headline

1 3 5 7 9 10 8 6 4 2

A CIP catalogue record for this title is available from the British Library

ISBN 0 340 82630 4

Typeset in Plantin Light by
Palimpsest Book Production Ltd, Polmont, Stirlingshire

Printed and bound by
Mackays of Chatham Ltd, Chatham, Kent

Hodder Headline's policy is to use papers that are natural, renewable and recyclable
products and made from wood grown in sustainable forests. The logging and
manufacturing processes are expected to conform to the environmental
regulations of the country of origin

Hodder and Stoughton Ltd
A division of Hodder Headline
338 Euston Road
London NW1 3BH

To Emma, Madame Galina and Tina C
who, between them, have every
quality a woman could ever need

While I am grateful for all the advice given to me
by the entertainment industry and by members of
H.M. Forces on Operation Telic, all incidents in this
book are fictitious and no character is intended
to represent any real person.

The exception is the Duckie cabaret, which is beyond
reinvention and therefore appears as itself: by kind and
unanimous permission of its producer and performers.

I

'It's not much of a trousseau,' said Marion Anderson, gazing down at her daughter's bed. Her eyes filled with tears. 'My poor baby. All winter I've been praying this wouldn't happen. I thought, somehow, they'd call it all off.'

She was a neat, darting little woman, her dark hair barely streaked with white. She pushed a stray lock behind her ear and sniffed, looking across the room to a stout grey-headed woman who was fiddling with a hairbrush at the dressing-table. 'I mean, look at it all! I should've got used to the Army by now, God knows, but all the same, Pat . . . she's a young girl!'

'I know,' said her friend in soft Scottish tones, putting down the brush and moving across to join her. 'But I'm exactly the same about Callum's kit, and he's a boy. Every time it's laid out like this, I wish he didn't bring any of it home. The uniform's fine, it's the small things that make you ache at the sight of them.'

She put out a finger and touched the skein of DPM webbing, neatly threaded with tools and small pieces of equipment, as it lay across the quilted pink footboard of the bed. 'Bless her, she's found a slot for the sewing kit we gave her! I hoped it would be useful, it's such a neat wee case.'

'Yes, but it's different with a daughter.' Marion persisted along her own line of thought. 'You sort of *expect* boys to go off to war. We've all got the basic grammar of that, hard-wired into us. The band in the street, the recruiting officer, the King's shilling in the bottom of the tankard . . .' She sighed. 'It can't ever be the same sort of shock with a boy. But the idea of Susie going . . . I wouldn't ever say it to her, but it just seems all wrong. And I hate that – that – thing!'

This time she reached out, and touched with a horrified finger the stiff, powdery charcoal lining of what her husband and daughter had taught her to call an 'NBC suit'. *Nuclear, biological and chemical.* The two mothers shuddered, and contemplated it in silence for a moment.

'I know,' said the Scotswoman at last. 'I don't like to think about it either. Or the vaccinations and the pills they give them. I know it's for protection, but it's a horror to think about.'

'Especially when you and I thought we'd be in the throes of a wedding this week.'

'Ah, don't.' Pat's eyes filled with tears, and she shook her head vigorously. 'We just have to have faith that it'll all be over soon and we can drink their health in the garden when summer comes.' Then, with a brisk return to practicality, she pointed at a pair of standard army boots on the floor and said sharply: 'Susie's never taking those! She ought to have proper desert boots. I know they haven't got the desert trousers and things yet, but boots! She can't wear those!'

'I told her that,' said Susie's mother. 'She said desert kit wasn't issued yet. Boots go with the rest of the kit.'

'Callum bought his own.'

'I know,' sighed Marion. 'She told me they had a bit of an argument about it. He was going to get her a pair just the same as his, but she said that with all the shortages, and the fact that she's taking a Softee sleeping bag and quite an expensive jacket for cold nights, she can't. She says it's wrong to have all her basic kit better than her soldiers'. The boots are fifty pounds or more. Squaddies probably couldn't afford that, especially the young ones. Some of her men are very new, and from families on benefit, she says. Really rough lives they've had, that's why they joined.' Marion shook her head with sorrowful affection. 'Her father backed her up, actually.'

'I suppose the girls have to be all the more careful about that sort of thing,' said Pat, vaguely. 'Proving themselves. All that.' She prodded the heavy, useless boots with her toe. 'But you can always send her a pair of desert boots out after a week, she'll be glad enough of them then. Feet do matter. The men always go on and on about them. Callum fusses over his toenails, like you wouldn't believe. Ach, goodness, it's odd seeing things the same as Callum's, but smaller!' She reached down to touch a pair of mottled combat trousers, designed more for hiding in woodland than in desert, which were laid out neatly next to a pile of folded T-shirts on the bed. Then she started guiltily as the door burst open.

'Got it all, I think,' said Susie Anderson, without preamble. Her arms were full of plastic shampoo bottles, and a sleeping-bag puffed exuberantly from her shoulder, retained by a thin strap. She looked startlingly like a younger, nimbler version of her mother but her dark hair was cropped as short as a boy's. Her sharp gaze instantly registered the glimmer of moisture on her mother's cheek. 'Oh God, oh God, you two! You're not sobbing over my Bergen, are you? I knew I shouldn't have left you here alone.'

'Got us bang to rights,' said Marion. 'But there is an excuse. It was just looking at the NBC suit and thinking about the wedding dress that set me off. And your lovely hair, I do miss it, darling.'

'I'm an army officer,' said Susie flatly. 'Not a model. And the dress is perfectly safe in its plastic bag in the wardrobe, as you well know. I'll fit into it all the better when Callum and I get home.' She shrugged the sleeping bag off her shoulder on to the floor. 'I'm a soldier, Callum's a soldier. What would we be like, the pair of us, poncing around in striped trousers and big white dresses with everyone else heading off to Iraq? And what do you think my old hair would look like, after a couple of weeks in the desert? It grows bloody fast anyway.'

She threw a cascade of bottles and bags down on to the only remaining clear patch of bedspread, straightened up with her hands on her hips and surveyed the two mothers. Something in their aspect must have made her feel that they were unconvinced, for she spoke to them again firmly in her high clear commanding voice, softened by an almost imperceptible but constant edging of humour.

'Mum, you know the score. I'm an officer. You can't expect me to spend my whole career driving Green Goddesses to fires in carpet factories, and arseing around on Salisbury Plain.'

'I know,' said her mother. 'I've been a soldier's wife for long enough.' Then, with deliberate brightness: 'Oh, that's a good idea. Shower gel you can use on your hair too.' Mother and daughter looked at one another with identical grey-green eyes, and finally, reluctantly, smiled.

'Try it out first,' said Pat MacAllister, fingering the shampoo bottle. 'Some of these combination shampoos really dry your skin out, and that's something you don't need, not in the desert.' Then her composure seemed to crack again as her eye fell on a paper bag which had burst open to reveal six neat blue-and-white packets. Susie followed her gaze and pressed her lips together for a moment before saying, with a visible attempt to curb her annoyance: 'Dear mother-in-law-to-be, please, no Catholic headshakings. It's not that I reckon I'll get lucky with some passing Gurkha. All the girls are going on the Pill full-time, no breaks. It's only so we don't get periods. It's going to be a pretty grim environment as far as hygiene is concerned. This,' she picked up a drum of wet wipes, 'is likely to be the nearest to a shower I get, once we're over the border.'

Pat seemed appeased, but Marion looked away, more shocked by the number of packets on her daughter's bed than by their contents. Six months? she thought. Six? No! This would be a quick war, surely, like Afghanistan the year before? She blinked, and focused with unnecessary intensity on a green puffy nylon jacket which, alone of the items on the bed, had no military look to it at all. It was, as Susie would have said, far too nice to be army issue. Pat followed her gaze and after a moment said with forced cheerfulness: 'That's quite a nice wee coat. Do you think it'll be cold? I thought it never was, in Iraq.'

'Cold at night, they say,' said Susie. 'And now, if you don't mind, ladies, I need to get the Bergen packed. I have to concentrate.'

'We just came up to bring the socks you wanted, and see if there was anything . . .' began Pat, but Marion took her arm and led her towards the door.

'Nothing we can do here. See how organized she is. Proper Sandhurst-style.'

'Well, anyway, I've a last few tapes to sew on for Callum,' said Pat. 'I'll sit in my room with them for half an hour, then it'll all be done by dinner and we can enjoy ourselves.'

'That's right,' said Susie. 'Callum texted me, by the way.

He'll be here around eight. Thanks, anyway. The socks look perfect.' She turned away, and began rolling T-shirts into tight tubes.

When the older women had gone, and the complexities of her packing absorbed and distracted her, Susie began to hum and then sing a wordless little song, blithe and lilting, and the tune was 'Soldiers of the Queen'.

The house was old, broad and comfortable beneath its blackened beams. Downstairs, padding around on beautiful uneven flagstones, General Sir Richard Anderson was filling decanters and laying them out on a silver tray whose curly engraved inscription vouchsafed that it had been presented in 1925, by the mess of the Hampshire Regiment, to an eponymous General Richard. A sharp eye might also have noticed that the silver collar on the glittering whisky decanter was a further witness to history, bearing the rose and tiger arms of the Royal Hampshire and the date 1938, pre-dating its assimilation into the Princess of Wales' Royal Regiment some half-a-century later. On the wall the portrait of the earliest General Richard glowered in full and elaborate regimentals, and on the table by the heavy silver cigarette lighter stood a small, rather ill-cast bronze bust of Colonel Gerald Anderson, presumably the recipient of the whisky decanter, and the inscription '1920–1944. Gone to Glory'.

It was a very military room, though it is fair to say that none of the family actually noticed any of these items any more, and it was only first-time visitors who found them-selves transfixed with awe, curiosity or stifled hilarity at its trappings. The hilarity was generally well-contained, although it had not always been so in the case of the General's eldest child and his friends.

'It looks like a corner of the Imperial War Museum,' Francis had once drawled, throwing his unmilitary limbs into a faded chair. 'No, not even that. It's like the back stairs at the In and Out.' His father had taken him to the renowned Naval and Military Club on Pall Mall once, and Francis had never forgotten it.

'Well, I don't care,' said Richard brusquely, on this and several other occasions. 'It's my bloody drawing-room and my bloody ancestors. Yours too, if you had the slightest respect for them.'

'I suppose their manly influence got diluted,' the boy would say. 'Mummy, I blame you totally. Bad blood. You must have brought nasty rude civilian genes into the family.'

But Marion Anderson had been in the Services too, a Wren in dapper navy blue when she met Richard. He was manning a recruiting stand at a country fair near Salisbury. It was 1975, and against the backdrop of fluttering hippy dresses and fantastical frogged mock-military jackets his eye fell on her neat uniform with pleasure and relief. So when the unfruitful day ended, the young officer had come over with two of his soldiers to help her and the spotty young sea cadets under her command to dismantle their tent. That had been the beginning of it, and the beginning of the end for Marion's Navy career.

Perhaps, though, Francis was right and she did have an incurably civilian streak, because in the event she did not mind leaving at all. 'I only joined the Navy to annoy my dad,' she told Richard, after six months of slow, courteous courtship. 'He was CND, and a big union man.'

'Better you leave anyway,' said Richard, already a Captain at twenty-seven. 'If we're getting married. Two Service careers in one family is complicated.' And Marion had stared with her big eyes and blushed and said, '*Are* we getting married, then?' and the rest of the evening had been the happiest either of them could remember. Marion handed back her uniform, did a proofreading course and rang all her old schoolfriends in the publishing trade; thus she kept herself discreetly busy and intermittently earning during her husband's postings to Belfast, Bosnia and the Rhineland. The only clash caused by her work occurred when she was sent the proofs of a fat, ill-tempered novel called *Smashing the System*, and the package was opened and an alert raised by a security-conscious clerk in Balkan Command.

She bore their two children in army houses, packed them off to boarding-school at thirteen, and drove cross-country to collect and reassure them on exeat weekends during the first Gulf War, when Richard was out of contact for five alarming days. Marion became, and ever after remained, a perfect army wife: optimistic, cheerful, unobtrusively kind to less seasoned wives, a saviour of threatened service marriages and a skilfully tactful companion when her own husband returned from a hard posting to go through the first, dis-located days of resumed domesticity. Only the outbreak of a second Gulf War and her daughter's sudden involvement managed to shake her equanimity at last.

'I can't believe,' she said now, descending from the bedroom, 'I just cannot believe that it's another Iraq War. Same place, same Saddam Hussein, only this time Susie's in it.'

Richard poured her a drink, and took his own to the window to look down the darkening avenue of chestnut trees. In the middle distance he could just make out the white marble glimmer of the sundial (presented by general subscription to Colonel Sir Anthony Anderson, on his leaving

Poona in 1873). He said nothing. Marion sipped her drink and continued, musingly, 'She was such a child last time! What, fourteen? Nothing on her mind but horses. Though of course she did like to play at cavalry charges. Dear little Susie . . . who'd have thought it . . .'

The General spoke then, with a certain uncharacteristic obliqueness. 'Francis rang,' he said. His tone was abrupt.

Marion threw a sharp glance at her husband, understanding his train of thought perfectly.

'Is he coming?' she asked warily.

'About ten. Said not to wait supper. He'll see Susie for long enough in the morning, he's driving her to Brize Norton to the plane. She had the choice of him or Callum for her lift, and she told Callum to sleep in.'

'Couldn't Francis get the earlier train and join us for dinner?'

'Said he had an audition. Some new management possibility.' Richard turned, and put down his drink. 'Darling, it wasn't me. I said nothing. Nothing. I'd have liked him to be here. Pat's got to get used to him.'

'I know,' said Marion. She moved over to him, and put her arm round his narrow waist and her face against the wing of badger-grey hair that curled behind his right ear. 'You're a man in a million, you know that?'

An arm came round her shoulder. 'I've got on with Francis a lot better,' said the father, 'since I bloody well gave up on him. Pat's just going to have to learn to do the same thing.' He dropped a kiss on the top of his wife's head. 'And anyway, I think it was a real audition. He sounded very lit up. Talking about a television chance.'

'Oh, God,' said Marion, pulling away slightly and glancing round for her drink. 'We'd better brace ourselves, then. It's a terrible thing, being nervous of your child making the big time.'

Richard drained his glass and moved back towards the decanter. 'Do you know,' he said thoughtfully, 'I was actually rather looking forward to him singing at the wedding. That's how mellow I've got lately.'

'That,' said his wife, 'was because he agreed not to do it in fishnet tights, and you vetted the song.'

'I think Susie was grateful,' said her father primly. 'Callum certainly was.'

'Susie loves her brother,' said Marion. 'And if he had *really* wanted to dress up as Marlene Dietrich and do "Underneath the Lamplight" at the reception, she'd have stood for it. Whatever Pat and Callum said.'

'Gallant girl,' said Richard. 'Saddam Hussein isn't going to know what hit him.' He refilled his glass, a third time.

2

⬥•◆•⬥

The small, dented Renault rolled uncertainly alongside the village petrol pumps in the dusk, and stopped just short of the nearest one. A lithe figure jumped out and put its shoulder to the inside of the driver door, pushing and steering for the last few feet. From the little garage a figure in oily overalls emerged and watched this manoeuvre with an air of phlegmatic amusement.

'Thought it'd be you,' said the *garagiste*. 'Nobody else got buttercups 'n' daisies round his bonnet. You run right out, have you?'

'Literally just here, on this blessed spot,' said Francis Anderson. His eyes were huge under the neon forecourt light, made bigger by traces of mascara and smudged grey eyeliner. 'I should have stopped on the bypass, but I thought I'd make it here. I hate using those self-service machines, they swoosh it out so *fast*, I always get petrol on my shoes and then security men take one *sniff* when I go into producers' offices, and assume I'm a human bomb and I get frisked. I should have filled up earlier, but you see I do have a can, Susie gave it to me, and having it makes me all the more reckless. Like a tight-rope walker with a net, there's not the same terror.'

'It's cheaper on the bypass,' said the man, who appeared well-accustomed to this torrent of words from his customer and able to block it out at will. He unhooked the nozzle and deftly unscrewed the gaudy little car's petrol cap. 'Not that I'm not glad of the trade. But I do shut at eight really. You're lucky. I was working on the bike.'

'I never thought of that,' said Francis. 'I come from the City that Never Sleeps. Ooh, Sam, can I use the bog while you do that?'

'Help yourself. Not locked yet. You want her full up?'

'Erm – well, perhaps not. Stop at twenty quid,' said Francis. 'Times is hard.' He vanished round the end of the building, and a moment later a dim light came on in the breezeblock lavatory. A small, cracked mirror hung from a nail on the wall, and Francis peered into it, with careful consideration, before pulling a case of moist round pads out of his trouser pocket and dabbing determinedly at his long lashes. When they were clear of smudges – though hardly less striking for that – he threw the blackened wipes into the oil-can which did duty as a bin, and went back out to the forecourt with his twenty-pound note.

'Thanks, Sam,' he said, proffering it. 'Personal service, all amenities, cheap at twice the price.'

'Petrol price'll probably go up again with this Iraq War,' said Sam, wiping his hands on his overalls and accepting the money. He glanced at the mound of plastic clothes-carriers in the back, and slid his eyes away from a tousled blonde wig in a net bag. There were, after all, limits. 'Vicar says your sister's off there soon.'

'Tomorrow,' said Francis. 'I'm driving her to Brize Norton early. She's going in a troop carrier, can you imagine? Like a war film. It's terrifying.'

'I thought they used charter planes these days.'

'Well, same sort of thing. Lots of raucous squaddies with huge feet. Rather her than me.'

In the gloaming, Sam the mechanic looked curiously at the young man in front of him: dark, big-eyed, darting in his movements, quick to smile and apparently unembarrassed by the remarkable circumstance of his little sister going off to fight with the British Army in the desert while he stayed at home and messed about with his wigs and his show-business and his daft flowery car. Took all sorts, though. That was what the vicar said. And the boy was always friendly, give him that; Sam remembered him as a child, coming to have his bike mended and always saying thank you.

'Well, wish her luck from me too,' he said finally. 'Lovely girl.' He watched the little car's tail-lights dwindling down the lane.

When Francis put his head round the dining-room door, dinner was all but finished. A cheerful uproar greeted him, Susie leaping to her feet to hug him, Pat and Marion exclaiming in variously pleased tones, and big Callum swivelling in his chair to raise a comradely fist with slightly exaggerated heartiness.

'Late as usual!' he said.

'I had an audition,' said Francis. 'Went well. I think.'

'I tell you one thing,' said the Scotsman, 'I'll not rely on you for my stag night. You'd never get me to the church on time.'

'You do me wrong, you cruel dragoon. I'm never late for gigs, and the wedding is the gig of gigs, and the stag night is the overture. Rely on me to cling-film you to a lamp-post, or confiscate your trousers and put you on the train to Aberdeen in a mini-kilt. Or whatever custom demands. I will be there! Blokesse oblige!'

'Have you eaten?' asked Francis' mother, running her eye

over his thin frame. 'There's some beef left, it's beautiful, and the potatoes would heat up.'

'Mmm, but don't move, I'll get it.'

'I will,' said Pat decidedly, rising from the table. 'You sit down and talk to your family.'

'What *was* the audition?' asked Susie, but a warning frown from her brother lowered her voice to a mutter. 'Oh, I see. *Pas devant les parents?*'

'*Plus tard, chérie,*' said Francis, with a wink.

The General had moved to the sideboard to carve more beef, and Pat returned rapidly from the kitchen with a plateful of vegetables. Between mouthfuls, the newcomer shot out questions, chiefly at the engaged couple.

'Why can't you go out on the same plane?'

'Different regiments, Callum's lot goes the next day.'

'Won't you be in the same place?'

'Might be, in Kuwait. To start with. But there'll be hundreds and hundreds of us, and there's more than one camp.'

'When do you go over the border?'

Richard flinched, Pat glared, Callum looked at his plate; but Susie was amused.

'For God's sake, Francis, how do I know? Even the Prime Minister doesn't know that yet. Even *George Bush* doesn't know.'

'God, you mean you've got to sit in Kuwait, Ku-waiting? Till they blow the whistle?'

'Obviously! Not everything's scripted and staged, you know, with lighting cues! Welcome to our world, luvvie!'

Callum glanced at his fiancée with pleasure and relief. He often wanted to make a joke of his future brother-in-law's theatricality, but never knew quite how far to go. Beneath the surface bonhomie of their relations there still ran a thread of uncertainty. There was goodwill between them, but they were too young and too different for there ever to be ease.

'Are you looking forward to Iraq?' asked Francis, this time directing his question more at Callum than at Susie.

'Fran-cis!' This from his mother. 'It's not a *party!* It's not a *show!*'

'No,' said Callum. 'It's a fair question, though. And if you think about it, the RAF always used to talk about war as a show, didn't they? Wizard prangs, all that?'

'I suppose so,' said Marion.

Callum continued: 'Anyway, the answer's yes, isn't it, Suze? It's a war. We're trained for war. It's what we're for. You can't help looking forward to it a bit. Hope it's quick, and no civilian casualties and all that – but it's our job. We're up for it.'

'That's right,' said the General. 'I was over forty when I went out for Gulf One, and I counted myself bloody lucky to get out there. In my generation, a lot of soldiers never saw anything but Belfast and exercises on the Rhine. Our fathers fought in World War Two and our grandfathers in World War One, and for a long time it looked as if we'd be the generation which never saw a real campaign. Callum and Susie wouldn't be normal officers if they didn't look forward to it a bit.'

Susie looked from her father to her fiancé, and her dark eyes shone. 'The other thing,' she said, 'is that if you're a woman, it's the same only more so. We've never been allowed this close to a war before. We don't fight in the front line, but Signals will be crucial, and I know the job, and I'll be doing it. So the answer's yes.'

'And are you scared at all?'

'No,' said the pair together, then Callum added, 'It's

the wrong word. Apprehensive. Keyed up. Hopeful. Not scared.'

The conversation, spurred by Francis' naive questioning, had taken an unexpectedly earnest turn. Pat looked at her son with love and pride, and Marion, contemplating hers, thought that he had after all arrived in time to perform a real service for them all. These simple questions were never asked aloud in this military family, but the presence of an outsider to their world had spurred both her daughter and her future son-in-law to unexpected openness. She was suddenly ashamed of her emotion in the bedroom earlier, and glancing at Pat, saw that Callum's mother felt the same. Of course the children were right to call off the wedding until it was over. They were who they were, and in latter years at least it was the Army which had made them that way. It was up to their mothers to be proud of them.

Oblivious of these glances, Francis took a swig of his wine, speared the last roast potato, and said: 'Well, that's great. You get out there, have a lovely war.'

'Bless you both,' said Pat heartily. 'And here's to coming home safe and happy, and a summer wedding.'

'We'll keep the home fires burning and pass the time away in absolutely *perfecting* our hats' said Francis, and this time even the General laughed.

The Anderson family's acceptance of their children's diverse foibles was not a plant of quick or easy growth. It had taken years – decades, thought Marion – for the differences between the two of them to become a cause more of merriment than difficulty. As a small boy, Francis had wriggled from his mother's arms at military parades and tattoos to tap-dance abandonedly to the beat. Susan, from the age of two, had stood solemnly to attention at such occasions, eyes bright, drinking in the splendour and ceremonial of her father's calling. Small Francis had no taste for soldiering, patriotism or decorum of any kind: bugles left him unmoved, and he would even move to the National Anthem – a hip-swivelling, toe-pointing, hand-flapping set of moves at that. At his cousin Edwin's passing-out parade at Sandhurst, Marion had to hold him down, by force, when the bands began to play.

At school Susie concentrated gravely on her work, acquired rows of solid A and B grades and took A-levels in Politics, History and French. She rode her pony fearlessly, joined the local rifle club, and was clear from the age of twelve that she wanted to join the Army. At university she studied Politics and led the officer cadet corps; at the Royal Military Academy she never put a foot wrong and emerged fit, focused and determined, with the highest of commendations.

Francis, meanwhile, idled through three schools in between expulsions, only settling in the final one because its Theatre Studies department inspired him. He taught himself guitar, piano and harmonica after alienating and insulting various professionals hired to instruct him in their use. He played in a series of bands, and left half-way through his first year at a minor university because the course was 'dull'. Just as his father was despairing of him, however, he passed an audition for the Guildhall School of Music and embarked to general surprise on an arduous vocal and theoretical training. For a few halcyon years it was possible for the Anderson elders to refer proudly to their daughter at university and their son training at Guildhall.

By the time his younger sister moved on to Sandhurst, however, Francis had graduated and it became apparent to his parents that he was not, after all, going to be an opera singer or concert pianist or school music teacher. ('Though he's so marvellous at getting on with children,' Marion had said sorrowfully, when she realized that this particular daydream was never going to come true.) They learned, by gradual and oblique means, that during his student years Francis' surprisingly modest demands on their support had been supplemented not by income from bar work or busking, but by a flourishing and distinctly louche career performing in clubs and pubs. There were not the type of pubs and clubs his parents had ever entered. By night he was no longer Francis Anderson the serious music student, but Madame Fanny Fantoni, chanteuse and vamp, with a stinging line in repartee and the most remarkable falsetto top C in Clapham.

It was evident that this was no mere student pastime. During the summer after his graduation Francis spent long hours on his computer, writing and designing flyers advertising Madame Fantoni to arts centres and pubs. He took open-microphone sessions at comedy clubs, and sang in costume in the Covent Garden Piazza until the police demanded to see his licence. His success was admittedly limited, although the act was polished and refined daily, so his fame did not rapidly spread to his parents' tranquil backwater. But a guest spot in the Salisbury Festival led to a memorable encounter between his mother and one Marjorie Hampton, the wife of her husband's old friend Colonel Jack Hampton.

They were sitting in the stands at the Royal Military College at Sandhurst, watching Susie's intake of young officers in their passing-out parade. Marjorie Hampton – whose own nephew was also parading – leaned forward from the bench behind and hissed: 'Marion dear, I was shopping in Salisbury yesterday. Was that your son I saw outside the

Guildhall, wearing a grass skirt and some feathers and singing? In an *accent*?'

'P-probably,' stammered Marion, drawing her mouth into the shape of a smile. 'Yes, I think so.' It was, she knew from various garments left lying round the house at weekends, the height of Francis' hula-girl period ('South Seas Sadie').

'Oh,' said Marjorie Hampton, and it was the most eloquent monosyllable Marion had ever heard. That evening, at the passing-out ball, the Hamptons seemed to be steering clear of the Andersons, although Rupert the nephew took one dance with Susie and patted her on the shoulder when it ended, with something confusingly like pity.

'What on earth is his problem?' she asked her mother, as the young man strode away.

'His mother saw Francis in Salisbury, advertising his hula show outside the Guildhall.'

'So?' Susie bristled defensively.

'Oh, darling, you know!' said Marion. 'It's a generation thing.'

'He patted me on the shoulder, the little creep—' Susie glared at the retreating Rupert '—like he was sorry for me! Poor little Susan with the dodgy brother! Well!'

'Don't make a thing of it, darling.'

'And he dances like a lame hippopotamus! And he's a rotten shot, too! At least Francis can do what he does, and do it *well!*'

It was all Marion could do to smooth her daughter's temper; but with her, as with the General, Susie's unswerving partisanship for her wayward brother acted as a brake on any awkwardness or embarrassment of their own. She went to Francis' performances, valiantly tried to like his associates on the club scene, and occasionally even advised on his costumes. Her taste, however, was soberer than his, and Francis listened only out of politeness before sneaking off to add another ruffle or expose another inch of his legs: which were, it must be said, a touch slenderer than Susie's with their sturdy marching calves. After a couple of months at Sandhurst she found herself, reluctantly, giving him her narrowest pair of high-heeled leather boots for an experimental new rock character entitled Kelly Kinko, loosely based on Suzy Quattro. Kelly proved an unsatisfactory creation, as Francis rather disliked rock; still, she let him keep the boots. 'I never could have zipped them up again anyway.'

But when Callum came on the scene, and it became rapidly apparent that this was serious for both of them, Susie was careful to inform her lover of the family's black – or, at least, colourful – sheep, in a tone that brooked no disagreement.

'My brother sings and dances and does an act as a drag queen. Well, we don't actually say that; they like to say they're 'character comics with skills'. Drag queen sounds too seedy.'

Callum had taken it on the chin, though he affected an exaggerated Sandhurst drawl as camouflage for his surprise. 'Character comic with skills? Right-oh. Will remember that.'

'You'll really like him.'

'Will I? Will he like me?'

'I'll tell him he'd bloody well better.'

'Anything you say, ma'am.'

Susie punched him. The one aspect of military life she had difficulty accepting was the appellation 'ma'am' for female officers. In every other way, though, she and Callum were of a mind: the Army was the best, the bravest, most ordered and excellent and adventurous of places to be, wherever in the world it might send them. They were happy in their work, and in one another. For the moment, they had everything their simple, straightforward and energetic natures needed.

3

Callum and Susie did not share a room in the parental home. Marion would have happily tucked them up together, but Susie was delicate about her father's old-fashioned feelings, and accordingly on that last night was to be seen gliding down the corridor and creaking up the winding attic stairs to the little wedge of a bedroom where her fiancé was usually billeted.

'You awake?'

''Course I am.' The dark figure in the single bed stirred, roused itself and opened wide his arms to her. 'Come here.'

Susie eased into the narrow bed and into her lover's arms with a little 'Ohh!' of pleasure. They had been together for eighteen months, but the hard muscle of his arms, the soft triangle of skin at his throat, the utter rightness of every part of him never failed to fill her with a deep peaceful sense of homecoming. The young man held her close for a moment, in equal wonder at her supple softness and the fresh smell of her short curling hair, then said: 'Wonder when we'll do this next?'

'Shhh. Don't wonder. Let's just do it now.'

Later, when Susie slid from the bed, Callum fought against sleep to watch her pulling on her dressing-gown, and said: 'I could still drive you to Brize in the morning.'

'No,' whispered Susie. 'We agreed. Goodbyes now, while

we're alone and it's quiet. You lie in, have some time with your poor mum, and Francis will get me to the plane. I'm making him leave two hours early and he's definitely got a toolkit and tyre. And a petrol can. I went out and checked in his boot before bed.'

'I love you,' said Callum into the darkness. Susie came rapidly back to his side, kissed him and said, 'I love you too. We'll talk. Send e-blueys."

'Good luck, sweetheart.'

'You too.'

A few hours later, in an unpromising wet dawn, Susie Anderson threw her Bergen rucksack into the back of Francis' little car, which slumped visibly under its weight. It lay, an uncompromising military lump amid the tangle of clothes-carriers, wigs, and plastic bags from which poked an assortment of male and female shoes. Francis, pale and yawning, climbed into the front seat and said: 'You'll have to navigate, Suze. I can't find it on the map, even. P'raps its an Official Secret.'

'It's near Oxford. I know the way.'

They spoke little at first, but after they had stopped at a petrol station for coffee in paper cups, Francis began to tell her about his audition for a production company putting together a late-night cabaret show on Channel 5.

'It's a bit rude,' he said. 'More than I like, really. Hormonal teenage stuff, to be honest, with that dirty-minded Irishman anchoring it. But it's a lovely showcase. Three new acts a week, and two regulars. I'd be a regular.'

'Telly would be good,' agreed Susie. 'I suppose any telly. It's the main way people get known these days, isn't it?'

'Unfortunately,' said Francis. 'It bloody well eats up material, that's the problem. That's why you don't see Ken

Dodd on telly much, or any of those wily old buggers who've been on the circuit forever. But it's a bit less of a problem if you sing, like I do. You're not burning up jokes at five a minute.'

'Well, it's character stuff, isn't it? Not stand-up comedy, not really. More like Edna Everage, but with music.'

'Yeah. You are a darling, bracketing me with Edna Everage.'

'Who did you do the audition as?'

'Fanny, obviously. And South Seas Sadie. And I just put on a leather jacket and your boots and did a little bit of Kelly Kinko. Fat creepy producer liked that. Dirty beast! Leather fetishist. He'd be awfully disappointed that you lady soldiers go off to war with that horrid webbing these days instead of a lovely Sam Browne.'

Susie laughed. 'Oh, Francis, thank God for you. You have no idea what a safety-valve you are. But look, we'd better switch on the eight o'clock news. Listen to another half-dozen reasons why I shouldn't be going to Iraq at all.'

'Radio doesn't work,' said her brother apologetically. 'Someone bust it breaking into my car a couple of weeks back. Trouble with South London.'

'Mine works,' said Susie, and pulled out from her tunic pocket a tiny button radio with a single earphone. 'Could be my last UK news bulletin. Ought to hear it.'

'Tell me if there's any earthquakes,' said Francis, and lapsed into a considerate silence as the car wound through the Oxfordshire by-roads towards the military airfield. So much did brother and sister take one another's trades and natures for granted that it did not occur to either of them to fore-see that the security guards on the main gate would take against the car on sight. Although Susie showed her pass, they found it impossible to accept that a bona-fide officer might travel towards war in a battered red Renault festooned in garishly painted buttercups and daisies. Lieutenant Anderson, after a few minutes' arguing, was forced to walk the last few hundred metres to her assembly point with her Bergen, while Francis turned back.

'I suppose I do look like a Greenham woman,' he said as he tugged at his stiff gearstick to reverse away from the guardhouse. 'I never thought of that. 'Byee, sweetie. Go safe. See off Mr Saddam. Send us messages.' He blew her a kiss, and one for the sentries.

'Will do,' said Susie, and shouldering her pack, she walked briskly into the base and into the next stage of her life.

Callum heard the car depart but lay unmoving in his bed in the little attic room, obedient to Susie's wishes that there should be no farewell. It was almost light; gazing up, he could make out the eccentric pattern of the dark, sloping roof beams. The wall opposite the bed, the only flat one, was papered with a faded Victorian design of roses and blue love-knots and the other walls sloped upwards to become a ceiling in comfortably flaking white. It was like sleeping in a cosy, ancient lobster-pot.

He loved this house, and had done so ever since the first time Susie brought him home after an evening out in Salisbury. His own home in Glasgow was in a long handsome terrace, a solid little merchant house with square rooms and no imagination or nonsense to it. Pat kept it with equally unimaginative neatness, exclaiming in real horror over any blemish. In his teens he had painted his own room dark purple and strung fairylights around it to make a private disco cavern; Pat had been unable to set foot in it for two years, merely pushing the Hoover in through the door with,

'Och, away! You clean up, I can't bear to look at it!' Under
Pat's rule walls were pink or cream, skirting-boards repainted
annually, useless items stored out of sight or given to the
charity shop, and broken or tattered furnishings firmly
thrown out. The only item whose daily purpose was unclear
and illogical was the big Bible on the dining-room sideboard
(not that they ever dined there, not after his father's death).

When he announced his engagement, it had been
necessary for her to come down to the Andersons' and
confront a very different style of housekeeping: venerable
faded curtains, ragged but truly Persian rugs, cat-shredded
upholstery, and in every corner the useless but resonant
trophies and regimental insignia of a military past. Nobody
could have called it a dirty house but: 'The dust!' exclaimed
Pat MacAllister to her friend Morag, when she was safely
back home. 'They've a woman who comes in, but nobody
watches her! Still, Callum's happy, and she's a nice wee
creature, Susie.' Callum, well aware of his mother's reaction,
quietly resolved that once he was married he would make
very sure that Susie was not persecuted beyond reason by a
duster-wielding mother-in-law.

For himself, he loved the house and the Anderson parents.
He liked Richard's gentle, cultured ways and deep knowledge of military history, Marion's warmth, and the ease they
both seemed to feel with their ancestors. The latter quality
was a particular balm to his soul, for the MacAllisters had
little ease with theirs. The late Ian, his father, had been a
roaring Ulster Protestant, who decamped to Scotland in
disgust at the start of the Troubles when it seemed clear that
the Catholic minority was going to make its voice heard.
With bitter irony he was ambushed by love (and not
inconsiderable lust) for Patricia Cronin before he discovered

that she was a Catholic herself, and not willing to relinquish her faith. They married in a Catholic church after a series of stammering 'instruction' sessions with a nervous young priest, during which Ian spoke not one single word. They produced Callum, and for a while lived in reasonable accord, going to their separate churches on Sunday and leaving the baby with a neutral minder. When Ian, after six months, mooted the matter of the child's baptism, Pat told him that she had herself baptised him, into the Catholic Church, within five minutes of his birth. 'While you were out of the room when they did the stitches. Ye'll see that I had to do it.'

The marriage lasted another five years, but the gulf between them was too great; the news from over the water, from Belfast and Londonderry and the black wicked border villages, ate into their uneasy, inarticulate love and corroded it from within. Every bomb, every shooting, every hunger-strike and Orange march on the news drove them further apart; the slow fury of the father at having a Papist son soured every moment that they had together. Pat took to bringing Callum to church with her, after which every Sunday lunch took place in a heavy, threatening silence. There were good moments, happy snapshots of family life: Ian took Callum sailing on the Clyde in a little brown dayboat, taught him knots and read him *Treasure Island*, and once or twice the family took a holiday trip to Orkney and watched the seals on the rocks. But on the day before Callum's sixth birthday, after no apparent provocation, Ian MacAllister left the house with two suitcases, never to return.

In his teens, embarrassed but urgent in his need to know, Callum asked Pat what had actually happened in the weeks he remembered with childish confusion. She merely said, 'It

was brewing a long time. Rest his soul.' For not long afterwards, the absent father died, abruptly, of a heart defect
which the doctor later told his wife could have carried him
off at any time. There had been no divorce; Pat took Callum
to the funeral, to throw a flower down on the coffin and pray
in a Protestant church.

The result of this start in life was that Callum developed
a quiet but sincere detestation of all things churchy or
religious, and that Pat, with unspoken guilt of her own to
contend with, never felt she could impose her Catholicism
on him again. Nor, despite the continuing trouble in Ireland,
did she raise one murmur of dissatisfaction when he joined
the British Army and went on patrol in the still-turbulent
streets of Londonderry. Such forbearance was the last debt
she owed the dead Ian, and she paid it faithfully.

Despite all this, Callum had willingly agreed to Susie's
desire for a full church wedding and had suggested to his
mother that she might like a Catholic priest to be present as
well. It seemed to Pat that the beauty of such a moment
would somehow heal the past. Its postponement, in honour
of this Godless war, wounded and terrified her more than
she could admit to any soul alive.

So Pat was lying awake too, in the grander guest room at
the far end of the house, hearing Francis' little car crunch-
ing on the drive and seeing its headlights arcing away, up
the hill and off towards the north. In the grey dawn, lying
neat in her high-buttoned nightdress on the sagging old
Anderson bed, she crossed herself and murmured a 'Hail,
Mary' for the soldier girl, and another for Callum. 'God
preserve them! Bring them safe together!' she murmured aloud.

When mother and son met at the breakfast table, though,
they had little to say. The Andersons were increasingly

withdrawn, politely distrait; the General retired into his study and Marion into some complex and probably unnecessary baking. The day became uncomfortable, intolerable almost: swollen and distended with the fullness of unspeakable meaning. By lunchtime Callum had had enough; collecting his last pieces of small gear from his mother he hugged her briefly, gave his thanks to the Andersons, and set off half a day early to rejoin his regiment. In the car he switched on the one o'clock news bulletin. When it reached the usual report of a passionate protest against the war, he reached out and clicked it off.

He thought for a moment that he might listen to some music, but abruptly discovered that he had no heart for that, either. Thus Callum, in his turn, fled towards the security and brotherhood of his regiment and turned his thoughts resolutely away from home.

4

'Who'd have fuckin' thought,' said Staff Sergeant Miller in heavy, sarcastic Scouse tones, 'it'd be so fuckin' cold!' He flapped his arms, shuddered, pulled off his shirt and hauled his sleeping bag up to his armpits before falling, with deliberate comedy, into his slot in the narrow tent which skirted the group's vehicle. 'Freeze the nuts off a brass monkey, once the sun goes. Wasn't anything about that in *Desert Song*, was there?'

'Settle down,' said his young officer without heat, speaking from the depths of a puffy bag further along the ground-sheet, half-hidden behind an inadequate veil of sacking. 'Got to get a bit of sleep before the next Scud alert.'

'Scud alert!' said another voice from the corner of the tent. 'Ten a bloody day!'

'You'd be sorry if there wasn't one, and then there *was* a Scud,' said the officer.

'More scared of the Yanks, me,' said another voice, deeper and harsher in tone. This time Susie sat up sharply, shivering a little as the cold hit her bare neck above the khaki T-shirt.

'Enough of that!' she said firmly from behind her sack. 'There's always going to be blue-on-blues. Don't make a song and dance about it. You heard what the Colonel said. They're accidents, they happen.'

'Sodding Yanks, sodding ragheads, sod the lot of them,'

said the voice again, churlishly. A murmur of agreement went through the tent: there had been several rumours of friendly fire or US Navy error on the grapevine during those scrambled early days of preparation. The men and women still confined on the Kuwait side of the border were sore, nervy, suffering a kicking, restless sense of helplessness and searching for someone to blame.

'Save your cursing for Saddam,' said Susie Anderson firmly. 'Keep your mind on that. He's the enemy. We kick him out, we free the Iraqis, let them live a decent life, then we push off home. It's our job. If you carry on like that, Corporal, I might take it as a signal that you're pining to clear out the latrines.' She grinned, softening the rebuke with a murmured '– on curry night', and there was a gurgle of laughter from the men. She took her duty to morale seriously; there had been a powerful briefing on the subject.

'But remember, soldiers need to grumble,' the Colonel had added to the group of young officers afterwards. 'Great tradition of the British Army: grumbling about the food, the allies, and the idiot officers. Just keep a balance. Feel your way. You'll know when it's going too far.'

The group settled, comforted by one another's quiet breathing. Soon the snoring would begin; behind the exiguous piece of hessian which symbolized her separateness as an officer, Susie closed her eyes and willed herself to sleep before the nasal thunder grew too loud. A sentry's feet crunched on the grubby sand beyond the line of vehicles, and Susie slept among her soldiers as she had done for weeks now in the enervating, dusty heat and cold of the desert region.

At first she had nightmares every time she slept, brought on – so the more seasoned campaigners informed her – by the much-mythologized side-effects of army vaccines and malaria tablets. Often she felt less than well, and had to hide her weariness during the sessions of fitness training, digging-in, and training with the NBC suits. She was buoyed up, though, by daily wonder at being here at all: a soldier among soldiers in the ancient land of Abraham, with a real job to do on the edges of a serious and vital war. The marvellous-ness of her situation struck her every time she woke, often four or five times during an interrupted night. This was real. This was living. She thought with pity of those who had not been chosen to come to this hard place.

This particular night was interrupted twice: once by a SCUD missile alert, and once by a jangling, terrifying but ultimately unfounded rumour of a chemical-weapon dis-charge. These alerts about invisible death, more frightening by far than the fear of bombs, set the chilly, alarmed soldiery hauling themselves awkwardly into their NBC protective suits, shuddering as the cold fabric touched bare forearms fresh from sleeping bags.

In the morning, walking through the camp in a sandstorm towards the waterless showers and the grim row of field latrines with their flapping hessian curtains, Susie met her Major. She had learned by now to curb her instinct to salute: saluting was banned in the Gulf lest it give invisible snipers a clue as to which were the officers, the prize targets. He acknowledged her with a smile and a surprising instruction.

'You're moving,' he said. 'Divisional HQ. Just for a while. Transport at eleven hundred.'

'Yessir. Sir . . .' His smile, and his failure to move away directly, gave her the courage to go on. 'Does that mean I won't be going over the border?' An edge of mutiny was kept well-suppressed in her voice. The sand was howling sideways across the featureless grim terrain, and tugging at the dull green army-issue *shamagh* which she wore wrapped around her nose and mouth to keep the grit out. She turned sideways for a moment to unwind the muddled cloth and then, wincing at the sting on her face, looked straight at the senior officer (who himself affected an absurdly colourful orange-and-purple scarf which gave him the air of an exotic parrot). She was wearing the invaluable pair of ski goggles which Callum had given her on their last evening. Dark glasses, he had said, would not be proof against flying sand. Susie had entirely forgotten she was wearing the goggles, which partly accounted for the senior officer's smile. With her curly dark fringe, flapping crest of *shamagh* and yellow-tinted goggles, she looked like some rare reptile.

'No,' he replied. 'You'll be going, all right. This is just for a couple of days. But they want another gir—another hand on the Bird Table in the last stages of the Plan. Someone quick and bright. And it won't do you any harm to get the geography of Southern Iraq firmly into your head. I think I'm going to want you running one of the rebroadcasting stations we're setting up; it's out of the action, but crucial. Best if you have a solid picture in your head of where everybody's going to be.'

Susie stared, astounded, her heart hammering. 'Yessir.'

'Meanwhile, Lieutenant Thompson's going to look after your lot while you spend a few days in HQ.'

'Sir.' She turned away, wrapping the cloth back round her glowing face as she left.

A day later, in the big tent which formed the centre of Divisional HQ, Susie found a group of very senior officers indeed, huddled in conclave with mugs of tea in their hands. A little apart from their conference stood a large makeshift table with a map on it. This apparatus seemed to be under the charge of a harassed but cheerful girl of her own age and rank.

'We had to pinch the wood to make it, from a Kuwaiti woodyard,' she said. 'And I nicked the cardboard from the reprographics cell, and this roll of Sellotape from my favourite Yank. And there aren't enough icons – I wanted to borrow some of those sweet little metal thingies from the Americans, but for the armour and the recces and stuff I've had to make the icons myself. Could do with some help.'

She indicated an upturned ammunition-box on which lay a pair of scissors, a roll of Sellotape, a few pencils and some sheets of paper. Susie saw, to her amusement, that the young woman's recent task had been cutting out neat little wafers of paper representing tanks and artillery, labelling them in a small even hand, and looping inside-out Sellotape on the back of each so they could be stuck on to the board and, with a certain amount of ripping and easing, moved around when necessary.

'Bloody hell,' she said reverently. 'It's one thing running out of bog paper and having to eat American rat-packs, but I never knew things had gone this far.'

The girl grinned, suddenly seeming ten years younger. 'Yeah, it's cool, isn't it? But the good thing is, any Iraqi militia give us any trouble, we've got the scissors of mass destruction.'

'You look as if you've got all the stuff you need,' said Susie, pointing at a neat rank of home-made brigades ranged down the margin of the map.

'Need spares. The trouble is that the officers lay everything out, then they lean over it to point things out, and the Sellotape means they get the icons stuck on their jacket sleeves. I had to run after a Brigadier yesterday with a whole armoured division stuck to his elbows. I think that's why you're here. They've started to enjoy having beautiful women race up to them and interfere with their clothing.'

'Any idea,' asked Susie in a low voice, 'when we go in?'

The blonde looked at her, leaned forward and muttered, 'NAPS issued tomorrow. I heard, anyway.'

Susie's mind was hazy from the heat, for the wind had dropped and the temperature soared. For a moment the word failed to register, then she remembered: Nerve Agent Protection tablets would be issued, they were told, forty-eight hours before any movement across the border into Iraq. A tingle of horrified excitement moved through her. 'Right,' she said. 'Right. So I'll probably only be here a couple of days at most.'

She looked down at the map, with its scatter of markings and symbols, and a thought struck her.

'I don't suppose you can tell from that where the regiments are headed?'

'Yeah, some of them,' said the young woman cautiously. 'Not supposed to chatter about it.'

'Fiancé,' said Susie, and named Callum's regiment.

The girl grimaced. 'They'll be moving faster than most. That's Basra.' She pointed. 'I'd guess he'll be taking Basra, yeah. Look, I'm not supposed—'

''Course not,' said Susie hurriedly. 'Anyway, what do you most need? Armour, transports?'

'Both, pleeease,' said the blonde. 'And since I knew you were coming, I thought you could take over for a few hours. The chaps are no trouble, sweeties really. Just keep things tidy and try to stop them wandering around covered with paper infantry. I've wangled a trip to Doha with one of the lorries, I haven't had a break for a fortnight. You want anything? Soap, sweets?'

'I'm out of deodorant,' said Susie gratefully. She delved for her money.

'Doha-dorant. Righty-oh. I'll pick you up some wet wipes too. They've got great drums of them in 'specially, cunning little bastards. At least the war's doing the Kuwaiti pharmaceutical stores some good.'

'No news lately?' said Pat, down the line to Marion. She had resolved not to ring constantly, but every two or three days the urge became overwhelming, and it was tacitly understood between them that this was a reasonable interval.

'Nothing for a week now,' said Marion levelly. 'We don't expect it. We send her notes on the e-bluey system every day or so, but I can't tell whether she gets them. They took their cellphones off them ages ago, before they crossed into Iraq.' She glanced down the hallway towards the rectangle of dancing green light at the garden door. 'Anything from Callum?'

'Well, yes!' said Pat. 'That's why I rang. They've got an embedded journalist, a Canadian, travelling with them. He lends his satphone to the boys for a minute or two each. I don't think it's really allowed, but God bless Canada.'

'Ah, what it is to be in a glamorous regiment!' said Marion. 'So how is he?'

'I spoke to him on Wednesday, and again last night: he's fine, he couldn't say where he is, but it sounds as if it's Basra. He's in high spirits, anyway, so it's somewhere that things are going well. Och! Oh, dear, I shouldn't say that down the phone, should I?'

'It's hardly a secret,' said Marion. 'It was on the news yesterday that we're in Basra with not too many problems.'

'He wanted to know about Susie, he's sent her a couple of e-blueys but no answer lately.'

'She'll be pretty busy. Richard says that now the first fighting's gone so well, setting up the desert communications nets is a huge priority. Signals will be worked off their feet, and you know how conscientious she is.'

That night, at least part of the two mothers' anxiety was allayed. In a brief moment of the television news from Basra, two Scottish soldiers were shown fraternizing with Iraqi children. They had their guns slung on them but were helmetless, displaying the plumes on their berets with insouciant gaiety. One turned his face unknowingly towards the camera for a moment, alight with amusement and mischief, and a moment later was heard singing to a solemn little girl and boy who stood warily before him near a bombed-out building.

'Ally ally, ally bally bee,' he crooned,
'Settin' on yer mammy's knee,
Greetin' for a wee bawbee
Tae buy some coulter's candy.'

Marion leapt from her chair and ran to the telephone, although she knew even as she hurried that it was too late, the moment would be gone and the newsreader's face back on screen before Pat had time to tune in. But the voice which answered the phone was breathless with excited pride.

'You saw him! Callum!'

'Yes! Singing to the children – isn't he something?'

'I sang that to him in his cradle! But, daft boys, they weren't wearing helmets! Or flak jackets by the look of them . . .'

'I know!'

'Och, Jesus preserve them!'

'Amen!'

Susie was thirty miles from Umm Qasr in a spot with no name and no landmarks bar the distant oil wells; she was in her element. Home, family, Callum, the wedding, her whole previous life had receded in the past days. All that mattered was the exhilarating effort of bringing order out of confusion, setting up her signal post, holding her vital place in the network of desert communications. Staff Sergeant Miller had finally proved a tower of strength and morale. Under her direction, and with his tactful advice, the humped encampment of vehicles, trailers, antennae, generators, and camouflage nets took shape and became her first lone command, her little empire. Everything worked. The seven men worked well and proved the quality of their training.

Her own curious situation as both the only officer and the only female proved, to her secret relief, to be hardly a drawback at all. These men were technicians: there was little machismo about them, and as Susie respected their competence so they respected her understated authority and level cheerfulness. Once the rebroadcasting job began, grumbles about allies had stopped. News filtered through about the Americans' fast push towards Baghdad, and the little team rejoiced. Grumbles about food, however, continued, and vital though their work was, it was essentially very boring indeed. The universal hobby was ticking off the charts which each man kept showing his time away, each day representing nine pounds extra in the pay packet.

'Six months,' said Miller, 'and I reckon I'll be on the way to that little MG.'

'Why stop there? Stick around for a year and you can get a Ferrari.'

'A year? D'you really think . . . ?'

'They'll replace us.'

'With what? Reservists? Boy Scouts?'

'Enough of that,' said Susie, returning from a discreet scrub behind the flapping camouflage net of the latrine area. 'I've known some very useful Boy Scouts in my time. Is that aerial fixed?'

'Was all right all the time. It was the power.'

'Good.'

'Anyway,' said the man who had advocated the Ferrari, 'we won't be here long. I reckon they'll move us to an HQ in Basra somewhere.'

'We'll obey orders, that's all,' said Susie. 'I want my dinner.'

'Did you see the provisions they dropped off?' asked Miller. 'We're back on MREs.'

The American ration issue, 'Meals Ready to Eat' or MREs, had had a mixed press from the British troops to whom they were issued when UK rations were short. The curry was voted excellent, the stew tolerable, but the burgers were universally loathed. 'Gristleburgers!' the men said. The tiny Tabasco bottles that accompanied them were collected by their senior technician, Corporal Harrison, until he had six or seven which he could squirt all at once on to one of the gristleburgers before eating it with much yelping and many cooling gulps from his water bottle. The American high-tech heating system was much admired for its ingenuity, although most of the time the soldiers made use of the built-in BVs, or Boiling Vessels, in the vehicle. Traditionalists, however, liked to talk fondly about the old system of heating food in a billycan balanced under the bonnet of a running lorry. 'That sweet tang of diesel,' said Miller dreamily. 'Happy days!'

Susie ate her stew without much enjoyment, thinking wistfully that she had never really appreciated the miracle of getting fresh salads and rice at Camp Rhino, or even the chicken-and-sweetcorn pasta in the British ration packs.

'It's funny,' she said to Miller, 'how you start thinking about every meal in advance. My mum and dad went on a cruise once, and they said it was the same thing – you just lived from meal to meal.'

'Funny fucking cruise, this is,' said the Sergeant amiably, and began humming under his breath a rude little song whose refrain was: 'Groundhog Day, Groundhog Day, hardly worth it for the pay, Iraq is the arse-oh of the uni-varse-oh!'

Susie's expression stopped him. The soldiers' favoured grumble was the sameness of their routine, and the Groundhog Day joke was one which rapidly wore thin with their officers. It had reached the point when even humming the tune while working was calculated to grate on an officer's nerves.

'Sergeant . . .' began Susie, but he was now innocently rooting in his pack for the caramels to which he was addicted. 'Want a sweetie, ma'am?'

'Don't mind if I do,' said Susie, accepting the spirit of apology in which it was offered. 'I'll save it for bedtime.'

The air was still that day; beyond the little group the desert spread, quietly shimmering, the skyline broken only by a distant structure which they had learned to call a GOSP, or gas/oil separation plant. There had been no firing or bombing in their sector for some days: a sense of relaxation blessed them now, a conviction of a job almost finished. Not one of them really believed they would be in Iraq six months on, let alone twelve. Sunset came, magnificently coloured by distant sandstorms, and a cool starry night unfolded majestically overhead. The news from the north was good. Statues had been toppled amid scenes of jubilation.

Susie smiled in the darkness, and chewed her toffee, and looked with pride on her men: the sentries motionless against the stars, the rest settling down with the wary, economical competence of experienced soldiers. What a place to be, what a life to live, what a story to tell, what an adventure! To crown it all, she knew Callum's regiment to be in Basra, and she was aware from messages passing all that day that Basra was well under the control of the British Army. He had succeeded, too. They might meet before long.

It was on an early April night, just after dusk, that a thin angry boy called Atif wriggled clear of a prisoner-of-war party as it was transferred to a lorry outside Basra. Alone, he made his way back towards the town, and on the way possessed himself of a can of petrol from a damaged garage along the bleak roadway. He was walking towards the unquiet city with death in his heart. He cared nothing for Saddam Hussein, but every human being he did care about – mother, father, twelve-year-old brother, crippled aunt and baby nephew – had died together on the first day of the attack on Baghdad, when a heavy shell ripped through the house. He knew this because he had managed to telephone his uncle's office; now his uncle had apparently fled northward and Atif was the only son left, the strong man of his family. But he was a militiaman and a prisoner, long miles away from his green home, trapped in the dry and horrible south. He could do nothing to help them. He could not even gather up their bodies from the filth and the rubble and give them decent burial.

So Atif took his petrol can and gathered rags and matches to damage the enemy. His hatred warmed him and blurred his grief: alone for ever now, he clung to his anger. He knew where the enemy soldiers were. The word among the prisoners was that they had taken over a group of houses near Basra Palace, and that the palace itself was their headquarters. He could not get into the marble palace, and shrank from the very idea: superstitious dread gripped him at the thought, until he hardly knew whether his fear was of Saddam Hussein's enduring power or the foreign soldiers. But he would find the houses the soldiers had taken, and see that the men in them burned as his mother and family had burned.

There were some empty bottles, lined up miraculously unbroken outside a deserted shop. Atif took three, filled them with the stinking petrol and ripped his T-shirt into three pieces, stuffing each into the neck of a bottle. Tears blinded his eyes, and for a moment he thought of the ripped flesh of his family and shrank from inflicting more filthy pain and death on the world. But he was a man, a man of seventeen, and he had his duty. Ten minutes later he slipped down an alleyway behind the houses they said the soldiers had taken, and climbed a fence into an unguarded garden plot – the fools, not even to set a sentry! He lit one of his bombs and threw it in at a window where a flickering light suggested that someone sat by a lantern. Fools again, not even to have got the electricity working, after all these days!

Then, under cover of the small blast, he lit and threw the second bottle into the window alongside. The boy was muttering hysterically now, and became slow and fumbling with the third: it exploded as he bent over it, slicing his face open with exploding glass and throwing him to the ground on a wave of agony.

He lived for a few days longer in pain, spat his story at his captors, but never understood enough of what they said to know that it was the wrong house. The rumour among the prisoners-of-war had been entirely unfounded; the British were billeted in Basra Palace itself. Inside this particular house a pregnant woman and her two children sat by their lantern, having a bedtime story about imaginary lands and adventures far from the miseries of Iraq. The first bomb set fire to the room where they were sitting, and the mother, Salima, managed to hustle them clear of it; the second missile landed flukishly on a rubber pipe which led from a half-full canister of gas. It blew the youngest child clear through the flimsy plywood wall.

Captain Callum MacAllister was out with the night patrol. His vehicle had coughed to a halt two minutes earlier, for it had been having sporadic trouble with grit in the fuel feed. Both his soldiers were bent under the open bonnet as he leaned on the side, looking warily around him into the unquiet night. So it was the Captain who saw the first blast and sprinted towards it, not stopping to gather his men. Then he saw Salima, her scarf on fire, bursting out with the elder child in her arms and collapsing in the street. He ran towards them, threw his tunic over the woman's burning head then turned towards the house, which was well alight.

'Baby – baby—' said the woman hoarsely, scrabbling free from his coat and pointing towards the house. Callum ran in through the doorway, pulling his T-shirt over his nose and mouth, and in his last clear moment he saw through the smoke the body of the dead child, face crushed to an unrecognizable mess, one pale chubby leg bare to the thigh sticking out at a grotesque angle beneath her dress. Then the ceiling collapsed, and he clearly heard his own leg crack. A wave of pain overwhelmed him and carried Callum MacAllister out of the war.

5

Francis woke, dry-mouthed and unhappy, in his narrow room over the railway line. It was a curious apartment, which explained the relative cheapness of the rent. Apart from its unpreposessing view of the Waterloo sidings, it was not unlike a section of railway tunnel itself: five times longer than its width, and that width barely able to accommodate Francis' bed. A window at the far end formed the light at the end of the tunnel, and the last few feet before it served as a kitchenette. The room was at the top of the house, so one wall sloped quite severely inwards, and an incautious cook, straightening up, could bang his head on it and come away with flaking plaster in his hair and in his soup.

There was a small sink in the kitchen area but the bathroom, which Francis shared with a solemn Sikh bus driver, was down three steps on a half-landing. The rest of the house was occupied by a fringe religious organization whose morose chanting filled the grubby staircase at odd hours of day and night.

For all this, Francis loved his lodging, and decorated it with an extravagance of theatre posters, coloured lamps and trailing scarves, which disguised his businesslike racks of working clothes. A wicker log-basket filched from home held his wigs, in net bags, and a couple of flamenco skirts which were too flouncy to hang without taking up half the width of the room. Awkwardness, and a crablike sideways gait, became a way of life for the denizen of this room: in order to open the door wide it was necessary to shift the wig-basket and move the electronic keyboard under the clothes-rack. But it was his own, it was cheap, it was handy for all the best London venues that hosted such acts as his. The Sikh didn't seem to mind him practising his songs at any hour, and when he was out of work he could walk up to the South Bank in ten minutes and loiter by the Globe Theatre and Tate Modern, collecting jokes and observations, watching the crowds, meeting acquaintances from Guildhall or the clubs. It was a place where a young man on his own could feel comforted by the buzz of new London culture.

On this morning, however, even the gaudy spectacle of his nest failed to cheer him. Turning over, he reached for a letter which had lain by his bed all night. It was on headed notepaper from the television production company, thanking him for all his 'fantastic input' but regretting that because of 'costing problems' the projected programme on Channel 5 would not, after all, be commissioned for this season.

He stared at it for a while, then crumpled it into a ball and threw it as far down the long room as he could. Rolling on to his back, he looked up at the cracked ceiling and blinked: real tears rolled down from the corners of his eyes and trembled, warm and viscid, in his ears. He had wanted that job, really wanted it. Much as he liked live work with a small and mainly young audience, the evanescence of it was beginning to weigh on him. He was nearly twenty-eight, would soon be thirty, and it would have been nice to have solid evidence of what he could create. Videotapes, CDs, whatever. To have laughter, real laughter from helpless audiences, echoingly replayable down the years, would have been a comfort. It would be nice to have the perfection of a costume, a song or a joke preserved as testimony to his craft.

He would also, he admitted to himself, have liked the extraordinary instant respectability that could only be conferred by television or film. From Danny la Rue to Julian Clary, Kenneth Williams to Lily Savage, his kind had flowered in the age of the screen. Over the years Francis' sharp eyes had observed that those who might shun a camp pub entertainer or comedy-club caricature, and regarded drag queens as next-door to male prostitutes were always sufficiently impressed by TV fame to giggle and nod approval at the rise of far ruder talents than his own. His parents' friend, for example – that cow in Salisbury – she would not have embarrassed Marion and Susie at Sandhurst if he had been on the telly. Probably would have asked him to open her next bloody fête.

Francis sat bolt upright, reproving himself. Yeah, he had wanted to be on television. It would have been good. It would have eased things with his parents' circle. He could have used the money, too; though in truth, it had not been impressive, and the proposed contract devoid of repeat fees would leave him little better off than if he had worked cash-in-hand down in Clapham. But nobody ever got anywhere by lying on a bed crying into their earholes.

He uttered a bracing obscenity, swung his legs off the bed, and reached for shorts and a singlet. After a series of careful stretches, he pulled on a pair of grubby training shoes and bounded down the stairs for his morning run: up the choking main road, on to the southern Thames embankment, and along past the great concrete theatres and concert halls towards the romantic castellations of Tower Bridge.

He was near the midpoint of his journey, running on the spot and looking down with laughter in his eyes at a pair of energetic mudlarks with metal-detectors, when the mobile phone in his shorts pocket rang.

'Ma?' he said. 'Hi. Sorry, bit out of breath. I'm running.'

'Francis, it's news from Iraq.'

He stopped jigging, glanced around, and sat down rather suddenly on an iron bollard. His breath was shorter than before, his heart pounding in his thin chest. 'Oh, Ma. Susie?'

'No. Callum. He's going to be all right, basically – thank God!'

Marion, standing in her hallway nervously pulling petals off a half-dead hyacinth, heard a gusty sigh down the line from her distant son.

'He's alive, then?'

'Yes. But he's got some burns, and his leg's very badly broken. He might lose it, even. They're flying him home. Pat rang.'

'Was he shot?'

'No. One thing that's holding her together is that he was a bit of a hero. He did it trying to rescue an Iraqi child from a petrol-bombed house. The other thing, obviously, is that he *is* coming home.'

'Did he get the kid out OK?'

Marion stared at the hyacinth. She had not asked, nor had Pat, or Richard.

'I'm – not sure . . .' she said.

'Only that'd make a difference to how he felt about the leg, wouldn't it?' Francis sounded anxious. 'I mean, if there was some point . . . if the kid was all right . . .'

'I'll find out. It's all been very sudden. Anyway, I thought you should know. You might be able to visit Callum in hospital, perhaps. He'll end up in one of the big London ones, apparently.'

'And Susie?' asked Francis. 'Does she get whatsit – compassionate leave?'

'Apparently,' said his mother a little bleakly, 'it was suggested that she could apply for it, and she refused. Didn't want to take advantage when all her men were staying out there.'

Francis looked around him at the sunny river, the oblivious group running their metal detectors over the mud, and the solid insouciance of London in general. Wartime! It couldn't be. It was too surreal to be believed. A couple of girls tripped past him on their high-heeled sandals, chattering; for a moment, thinking of Susie in her foxhole or whatever it was, Francis really hated them, and himself.

'Well,' he said carefully, 'it's their world. Callum probably wouldn't want her to bale out early either. He's a soldier as well. You know how *keen* they both are.' The edge of camp mockery was coming back into his voice. It was the only way he could defend himself against the horror.

'Yes,' said Marion. She looked down at the wrecked hyacinth and pushed the pot away from her. 'Daddy says much the same thing.'

'Where's he going to be in hospital?' asked Francis after another moment of silence.

Marion told him the name of the specialist unit at a London hospital which Pat had been told was going to pin together Callum's difficult leg once he could leave the military infirmary. Francis repeated it twice to fix it in his mind, and, suddenly intensely aware of his own taut strong limbs, ran slowly homeward to polish up his lyrics for the evening performance at the Vauxhall Tavern.

★   ★   ★

The weeks went by. It was the bedpan, thought Callum with loathing, that was the worst part. He could bear the peeling-off of burn dressings, the traction, the manipulation, the sense of his bones grinding, the long ache in the night when he would not call for painkillers. The hard part was when he had to ring the bell for a brisk young nurse with functional legs, and ask her for a bedpan or a bottle. In the first days, the drugs they gave him had a loosening, diuretic effect and he sometimes had to invoke this humiliation once an hour or more. Sometimes the pain tired him so much that he could not even wake from the recurrent churning nightmare of black petrol-smoke and smashed babies, and he soiled himself. The nurses were understanding and matter-of-fact about it, but Callum could not be. He was, even the most tolerant of the medical staff admitted to one another, a very bad patient. Handsome, though; he must have thrown his arms over his face, as he was trained to do, for the worst of the upper-body burns were on his forearms and the backs of his hands.

'And his fiancée is still out there, he must be worried!' said the most knowledgeable, who had seen a summary pinned to his psych file. 'He doesn't talk about her, though, does he?'

'Never,' said her colleague with a sigh. 'Denial, I suppose. It's happened to him, so he must live in fear that it'll happen to her. I hope she gets home soon, or he really will start worrying.'

But when Callum thought about Susie, it was not with fear on her behalf – for his imagination was numb now – but with a toxic mixture of longing and bitterness. Above all, as the long mists of the anaesthetics cleared after each bout of surgery, he found it hard to accept that she was a serving officer still and that he was not.

'But you are,' said the psychiatrist who came every few days to see him. 'The Army's still where you belong. Look at the messages.' For the room was littered with blueys and letters and scribbled messages passed on from the regiment.

'The doctor said I'll be lame,' said Callum sullenly. 'Lame. Unfit.'

'They've confirmed they can save your leg. It's been a difficult one, and you'll have a lot of pins and an artificial kneecap, but they can do it. It'll still be a leg.'

'Not much of a leg.'

'Better than nothing. And the burn grafts are coming on well, and there are jobs for an officer of your experience—'

'Behind a desk.'

'Well, perhaps.'

Callum, in traction, could not turn his back; he turned his head as far as it would go towards the wall, and became silent. When the man was gone he switched on the radio, and listened stony-eyed and tearless to the news. The war was technically over. Baghdad had fallen but was in no good order: museums and hospitals had been looted. The British Prime Minister gave a gushing interview to the press about how hard the war had been for him, how his eldest son, 'bless him', had rung home every night to support him, and how he had been cheered up because his youngest had not understood what war was since he was only two.

'Bloody well would have understood, if he'd been an Iraqi two year old,' said Callum aloud, and again before his inner eye rose the sight of the little girl's bare tiny leg and her smashed, smoke-blackened, gaping horror of a face. The news from the former battlefields went on: crimes and shootings and ambushes, power and water shortages. At home, day after day, the news relayed political attacks on the war and its aftermath.

The pain of a hundred thousand distant people distilled itself in Callum's sleepless, angry heart and became, as spring wore into early-summer, an extension of his own pain.

After a while, the television figures of servicemen and women became pointless little khaki puppets, Canutes waving their stupid guns at an ocean of misery. Suffering was Callum's theme, his core, the ocean that he swam in. When the fever came and he cried aloud in the night, he hardly knew whether he cried for his own hot pain or for the world's. When it cooled, and the ward and its doctors swam back into clearer focus, Callum MacAllister knew he was changed. His roots were torn up and had nothing new to grip. He was politer to the nurses, though, and told his visitors nothing of the dark inward changes in his heart.

'It's gone terribly well,' Marion said to Richard. 'Pat's thrilled. The doctors say he'll be able to walk, with a stick for a month or so, and maybe even without one by August or September.'

'What does Callum say about it all?' asked the General cautiously.

'Well, Pat says he's very quiet,' replied Marion. 'Sad, was the word she used. I'm sure he'll perk up.'

'Hmm.' Her husband would say no more. Marion, for a fleeting moment, thought she saw herself and Pat as the old soldier saw them: fussing mothers, caring for nothing as long as their chick was safe back in their sight, helpless and biddable in a warm bed. She flushed, and took herself off to make a pot of tea.

Susie's military euphoria gradually wore off. After the heat of the active war, her relay station's importance was downgraded and she was seconded to a unit full of strangers at

Basra Palace. Here, to her considerable dismay, her work became clerical and routine. She found herself, when she was alone, defiantly humming Staff-Sergeant Miller's 'Groundhog Day' ditty, as each tedious unrewarding day followed the one before. Gone were the rough nights under the stars with her lorries and aerials and little cadre of comrades; communications were better now, Signals officers buzzed around the southern desert freely and Sergeant Miller was left in charge of the remnants of the job. Very soon, Susie became stingingly aware that her new posting was given to her partly because of her gender. She shared an alcove containing two camp beds in the Palace HQ with another woman officer, and spent her days supervising the frustrating business of distributing food and medical supplies to angry, confused, frightened Iraqi civilians.

She knew that she was put there because it was thought easier for the men who collected the aid to ask for food and take their many complaints about it to a woman. She was, of course, glad that something was being done for the thin, big-eyed children who wandered the streets, school-less and unfed and often carrying cans and plastic bottles in the increasingly desperate search for clean water. As a human being Susie felt sorry for the suffering families of Basra, and a little disgusted at herself for hating the work so much. Her new room-mate, a forthright and stocky redhead from the Royal Engineers, was less troubled by such scruples.

'I didn't sign on to be a frigging aid worker,' she said. 'It's not as if they're even grateful.'

'You can't expect—' began Susie, but the woman cut her off.

'They ought to have aid agencies doing this. We're frigging military, not Social Services.'

As she went through her day, whenever she was in contact with the local population Susie tried to smile and express kindness, in particular towards the thin, impassive Iraqi women and their children, but few of them smiled back. One particular little boy haunted her: with his pale gingery hair and blue eyes, legacy of some Silk Road trader, he had an unnerving look of Callum about him. He became a symbol, a thin, ghostly, undersized, hopeless Callum, who entered her nightmares more than she liked to admit to herself. Sometimes the children's wounds, or their mothers', made her look away; she knew that they saw that and despised her, even as they took the packets of food to their battered homes.

The story of Callum's injury had been told her many times, with embellishments, since it had become generally known around the Basra military community that she was engaged to the gallant Captain MacAllister. A decoration was spoken of.

'He didn't manage to save the kid, though, did he?' said Susie with sad pride. Like Francis, she saw straight to the heart of the matter. 'He'll really be minding about that.'

'He pulled the woman and the other kid clear,' said her informant, inaccurately. 'Ought to get a medal for that. Any idea when you're seeing him? Are they sending you home?'

'I don't know,' said Susie. A burden of guilt lay on her. She had, with exceptional compassion in wartime, been offered the chance of leave as soon as the fog of war dispersed enough for someone to realize that she was engaged to the wounded Captain. She had turned the offer down when the message came through, for she was still too deeply immersed in her work to accept. She was unable to conceive of anybody else running her little signal station. With savage military irony, two days later she was posted away from it and put on to this welfare job; since then, the subject had not come up and she was too proud to raise it.

'I'll be home soon enough,' she said evasively when sympathetic fellows asked about Callum and her delayed leave. 'We all will, at this rate.'

'You wish,' said more experienced soldiers with a shake of their heads. 'It's still bloody chaos up in Baghdad, and there was a guy shot here yesterday. You don't think the Yanks are going to do all the mopping-up, do you? Could be here till Christmas.'

Susie went on with her daily lists and distributions and remonstrances about food and medicines that went missing. She sent Callum letters about her work and tender hopes for his recovery, and received deceptively cheerful bulletins from her mother and from Pat. Callum wrote once, an electronic bluey sent from the hospital's internet point; his tone was oddly formal, congratulating her on her work so far and hoping the weather was not too hot.

The weather was indeed growing hotter, unbearably hot at noon; the concrete buildings of Basra threw dazzling sheets of heat at her as she walked between two soldiers to the school building where she supervised the aid distribution. Only in the deepest marble coolness of the Palace HQ could she breathe easily. Callum and his shattered leg seemed a long distance away, a problem tucked far in the interstices of an uncertain future. For now, one must live day by day and do the job without complaint.

Sometimes, though, in her hot fitful hours of sleep next to the angry Royal Engineer, she dreamed she was with Callum on a boat. They were on the Clyde, sailing towards green and blue and infinitely cool islands. When she woke, slick with sweat and the sour smell of her own body, there were tears in her eyes.

Francis was, surprisingly, the hospital visitor that Callum minded least. Pat fussed and clucked, and Marion exuded a reserved, sweet, middle-class English kindliness which made him feel awkward and rumpled and sordid. General Anderson visited once, and sat at the end of his bed looking at him keenly. Too keenly for comfort.

Callum suspected that Richard guessed the level of rage in his heart, particularly against the Army. But the old soldier said nothing about this, and nothing about the fire and the rescue. He only asked brisk questions about the leg's progress, and left after a bare fifteen minutes. As for visitors from the regiment, they were almost unbearable to Callum: through the haze of his pain and the image of the dead child, the young officers he had happily messed with for years seemed bluff, crass and stupid, not to mention insufferably fit and nimble. He was beginning to move around the ward on crutches under close supervision, and this feeble degree of mobility filled him with a worse dismay than his previous bedridden state. His closest friend, Harry Devine, was back on leave and brought him news of the heroic reputation he was acquiring in the military community of Basra: Callum was cold and gruff and would not meet his eye. Harry, a simple-hearted and jolly young man, was hurt by his friend's coldness and at a loss over how to handle him. He, too, left as soon as he could.

Francis, however, was a visitant from another world altogether; fey, small, dark-eyed, flitting and perching and chattering like a good-natured monkey. He never spoke about the injury, or about Susie or his parents or the war. He merely passed on jokes and incidents from his own work. He came ten or eleven times to the London hospital, and always raised Callum's spirits a little. Once or twice, when Francis told a particularly outrageous tale from the dressing-room ('. . . *then* he tells him he's pissed on his wig!'), Callum even laughed. When Francis flitted past the desk after his fourth visit, the young nurse outside looked up and said, 'Oooh, I'm glad it's you, you're a real tonic to him.'

'Am I?' said Francis, surprised. 'He seems to me to be in a terrible moody. Poor sod. That leg's never going to be quite right, is it?'

'I can't discuss patients' prospects unless you're close family,' said the nurse primly.

''Course not. Nurses! So *professional*, I love it! 'Byee!' He blew her a kiss and clattered off down the corridor. Once he reached the empty stairway, though, he muttered under his breath, 'It's not going to be right, though. He knows it. Poor bastard.'

6

Weeks later, Susie stepped from the plane into a dream of an English summer. A cool northerly breeze lifted her hair, which had grown into a shaggy dark mane during the time of relative comfort in Basra HQ; it was early, and a heavy dew set the cow-parsley on the verges shimmering in the low morning sun. Cattle grazed the quiet fields of Oxfordshire as she was driven from the airfield, fat lambs wandered by the ditches and in the distance a church clock tolled.

'I don't quite believe it,' she confided to the middle-aged reservist driver who was throwing the vehicle exuberantly round the corners of the lanes. 'It's so green!'

'They all say that,' the driver agreed. 'You got much leave, ma'am?'

'Yes,' said Susie. 'I had special leave anyway for my wedding, which I put off, so now I've got nearly two months. Right through to September.'

'With a bit of luck,' said the reservist, jinking past an elderly cyclist, 'the Army'll be out of Iraq by that time and none of us'll have to go back.'

'You wish,' said Susie, for the prevailing cynicism of her peers had now become her own. 'Years, more like.' She immediately cursed herself inwardly for being over-familiar with this private; it was his age, and the holiday mood of homecoming, which had broken down her professional manner.

'You having the wedding soon, then?'

'I should say so,' said Susie, for it was too late now to become formal with him. 'My fiancé got injured, though. He's on crutches. Might not want to walk up the aisle on crutches.'

'I would,' said the driver stoutly. 'Nice girl like you, pin you down quick before some naughty Brigadier carries you off.'

Susie laughed politely, but bit her lip as she stared out of the window. Callum was home in Scotland, and she had spoken to him on the phone several times. On no occasion had he mentioned the wedding. He sounded flat, uninterested in anything, non-committal. She had modified her own excitement to match his manner. Now, with a long leave in prospect and green England all around her, her career and vocation receded and she was filled mainly with dismay at her own failure to move heaven and earth to rush home to a burned and broken lover. No wonder he was sore. What had she been thinking of? Even the Army couldn't ask so much, surely?

He was coming south, though, to stay for a while with the Andersons. Pat was coming with him on the train, but with luck would see the advisability of removing herself and not staying to fuss. Her own parents would stand well back, Susie knew, and she and Callum could grow close again in the peace of the old house. Then there would be time enough to talk of weddings.

'They need a holiday,' said Marion, four days later. The young couple's politeness and distance unnerved her. 'It's because we're here. They need time alone together.'

Richard agreed. He had his own views about Callum's state of mind, but would not express them to his wife. He had seen broken soldiers before, and knew that by this stage most of them were looking towards the future, whether in or out of the Service, and actively discussing what part they might play if they stayed in. He had known men burned in the Falklands, shelled in the Balkans and bombed in Northern Ireland who had carried on to do useful desk jobs, and others who had accepted the end of their military career, taken their gratuity and built themselves new lives.

Only once had he known a man like Callum who made no plans at all, changed the subject when the future was mentioned, and actively shunned contact with his brother officers and his regiment. That man had died a few months later at his own hand. Richard watched Callum unobtrusively but with hawk-eyed vigilance. He alone noticed the young man's flinching distaste for the militaria in the sitting-room, and on the second day quietly removed the silver tray, lighter and decanter-collar to the scullery for cleaning, put the bust of Colonel Gerald on the windowsill so that it was mostly hidden by the curtain, and wandered around the house looking for pictures which might fit the unfaded square of wallpaper if he were to move the portrait of the first General Richard. He found an inspid watercolour of the Thames at Marlow and brought it down, but it looked so ridiculous in that sombre room that he took it away again, and compromised by moving the furniture so that the sofa where Callum stretched out his stiff, atrophied leg faced the french window instead.

Callum noticed none of this tactful care. He seemed to be in a dream, or perhaps – Susie fancied – he was inwardly confronting some difficult but not insoluble riddle. When they first met again she had embraced him with all her pent-up warmth and tears, and he had duly put his arms round her; but his embrace lacked conviction. She had tried to talk to him about her experiences and to draw out his, but he would say little. 'Went in, not much resistance, a bit of routine gunnery to soften things up, smashed up the Saddam portraits, worked out who was who in the Ba'athist hierarchy, started to get the place in order. That's it, really. I was out of the game at an early stage.'

Susie wanted very much to tell him about her war, particularly the heady interlude running her signal station under the desert stars. She wanted to tell him how profoundly satisfying it had been for her to do a vital job; how in those hard hot days she had felt herself at last a part of the tradition, accepted, a soldier among soldiers. Once, when they were first courting, he had understood her longing for this trade and responded to it with understanding and empathy. Once this couple would, only half-mockingly, quote Kipling and Buchan to one another, and hold hands raptly on the sofa as they watched stiff upper-lipped wartime films. Both were moderns and not politically naive, yet a certain unspoken sentimentality about their trade had always linked them. When their two hearts quickened to the beat of a military band, no words needed to be said.

This should, thought Susie dismally on the third day, have been a time of talk and reconciliation, a period when quietly and without heroics the two of them could lay their wars to rest. It should have been the period when they helped one another to find their balance again in the supine, sybaritic culture of their civilian homeland. She had seen her father and mother reaching for, and finding, just such a balance when Richard came back from Gulf One, and had thought then how much better and easier it would be if the wife were a servicewoman and *really* understood.

She tried to express her understanding, tactfully and lightly, to the silent, grim new Callum. What troubled her was that this was not even his first war: he had been in Kosovo, and stood by during the opening of mass graves and torture chambers. He had talked to her then – though her own Army life was barely begun – and she believed that she had helped. Now, she was helpless. If she suggested a walk out of doors he would come, hobbling on his two sticks; if she praised his progress he merely gave her a dirty look. Marion had made him a bedroom out of an unused study on the ground floor, and lit a fire in the grate each day for his comfort; on the first night Susie came to this room to wish him good night, hoping to be invited to stay. But Callum said a polite good-night, sheets hauled up to his chin, with such an expression in his hard blue eyes that she knew herself to be unwelcome. Once, sitting on the sunlit bench on the lawn, she put a hand over his and said: 'Cal, do you want to tell me about the night of the fire?'

'Not really. You know what happened. Kid with a petrol bomb set the leaky gas-stove off, and the woman only got one of the two kids out. I was only in there a few seconds before the roof came down.'

'They thought a lot of you at Basra HQ, you know. Bit of a hero.'

'Bollocks. The kid inside was dead, and the others were already out, poor bastards.'

'You tried. You did what had to be done.'

The expression was a common one between them once, half a joke and half a serious statement of duty. 'Doing what had to be done' had held a meaning, clipped yet intimate. It covered all sorts of duties: telling someone an unpalatable truth, cleaning a filthy pair of boots, going out in the rain for the Sunday papers, reefing the headsail on a little bucking yacht on a Clyde holiday. Not a flicker of friendship, however, was discernible in Callum's reply.

'I was a fool. As for the woman, she's got nothing to thank the British for, or the Americans. The other kid's probably dead of starvation and dirty drinking water by now.'

'You shouldn't think of it that way. The job's only half-done, yeah, but we're still in there.'

'Huh.'

There was a moment's silence, and Susie pleated the soft cotton of her skirt between her fingers for a moment before answering. 'Cal,' she said earnestly at last, 'can I ask you something?'

'Yeah?'

'Have you changed your mind about the war? Do you think the peaceniks were right and we shouldn't have gone in when we did? Have you stopped believing in it?'

'What do you think?' He had developed a way of throwing her questions back at her like this. He stretched his bad leg and winced.

'Another question, then,' said Susie, and now her lip was trembling. 'Do you still want us to get married?'

Callum turned, wincing again, and looked at her with a stranger's eye.

'I see. It's a condition, is it? If I say it was a just war, you'll marry me, otherwise it's off?'

'I didn't mean—' Susie was overcome with tears, and leaving him and his sticks to their fate, she fled precipitately up the lawn towards the house. When he had hobbled back – it was, triumphantly, his first unescorted journey since he ran through the Basra night towards the burning house – she was gone, locked in her bedroom for the rest of the afternoon. The elder Andersons had gone out shopping in a kindly attempt to give the young people privacy. Callum, miserable as rarely before, poured himself a large whisky and sat until sunset staring out of the window.

That evening, though, after Marion and Richard had got back and begun making the supper together, he hauled himself upstairs and tapped on Susie's door. When she opened it he flung wide his arms, almost overbalancing, said, 'I'm sorry I'm a pig to you,' and accepted her tearful hug. Susie snuggled into his chest, thankful for deliverance from doubt and misery. Over her shoulder, though, even as his hand mechanically patted her back, Callum's eyes were distant. He had done what he had to do for poor Susie, and it was not enough.

Eventually, on the morning after this scene, Marion and Richard squared up to the children – as they still at times referred to them – and made their offer.

'You need a holiday, you two. Right away from it all. Your mother and I thought Portugal.'

'Why Portugal, 'specially?' Susie's eyes were bright.

'Robert's uncle's villa,' said Marion. 'Remember, we told you? We went there. Right on the Atlantic, gorgeous flowers, ten minutes' stroll to the village, and a warm swimming pool for Callum's physio exercises. It's free.'

'At this time of year? Really?' Susie was excited now, and

in her excitement failed to look at Callum. 'I thought it was
always bagged? You said it was such a bargain even with the
rent.'

'This is just a piece of luck,' said Marion. 'Robert and
Madeleine were going to go out there on Thursday for
three weeks. Now Maddy's got a part in some play, and
Robert says if he stays on at work he'll get brownie-
points and swing himself a good break in August. So they
were going to write off their three weeks. Basically, you
can have it.'

Robert's uncle's villa was a relatively new excitement in
local life. Two years earlier on a diving holiday, a friend who
worked in the City and lived in their village had met, for the
first time, an elderly and infirm uncle who had long since
retired to Portugal. Uncle and nephew had struck up an
unlikely but warm friendship, and when the old man
announced his intention of coming back to end his days in
a British nursing home, Robert and his wife had bustled
around to find him a comfortable and dignified one within
easy reach of their house.

They had assumed that he would sell the Villa do Beco
to fund his final retirement, but when Robert offered to
oversee the sale he was met with indignation. There was
plenty of money without that. Uncle Alfred insisted that
he might want to revisit his old home from time to time.
Since Robert was so kind, perhaps he would undertake to
find holiday lets to suitable people who would respect
the uncle's effects? And, of course, added the old man,
his nephew might care to use it himself. Keep it aired.
The swimming pool set into the rocks was shared with
the much larger next-door villa and maintained by the
gardener employed by his neighbour, a wealthy industri-

alist from Lagos. Everything must remain as it was. The rent was immaterial, only the house's welfare was to be considered.

The old man became quite querulous when this profligate line of action was challenged, and eventually Robert agreed to supervise the property from a distance and let it from time to time. In the two years since, the elder Andersons had had two holidays there, and returned each time dazed by its charm.

'Sea, and quiet, and wine and sardines!' said Susie. 'That is such a brilliant idea! Fancy it being free at this time of year, it must be perfect for Portugal!'

'You see, it's meant to be,' said Marion. 'I know you two despise villas and pools as a rule, with all your adventurous sailing and rafting and diving and all that, but just this once it might be a perfect place to get Callum's leg right. You don't have to report back to the regiment for a while, do you, dear?'

'No,' said Callum. 'Mid-August, I report back and the doc signs me off.' It was the first remark he had contributed to the conversation.

'Well, there you are!' said Marion. 'What do you think?'

'Susie?' said Callum, inclining his head towards her with cool politeness.

'Let's do it!' she said, and offered him a loving smile. His lips twitched briefly, but all he said was: 'Fine by me.'

Immediately, with joyful energy, Susie took charge of the arrangements and flights and packing and passports for both of them. Her efficiency was pure Sandhurst, thought Callum, as he watched her neatly rolling and tucking T-shirts into the grip. A part of his trouble with his fiancée at this time was that although Susie was neither bossy nor commanding, every day there came a moment when her energy and effectiveness and clipped tidy ways – indeed her very stride – reminded him of the Army.

7

<hr>

The bed was the only part of Uncle Alfred's life at the Villa do Boco which his nephew had presumed to replace. It was wide, new, and beautifully sprung, and only the heavy black carved bedhead fixed by ancient rivets to the stone wall related its appearance to the sagging horsehair mattress of days gone by.

'We burned it' Robert would assure his tenants. 'If the old man does ever come back, he probably won't notice a thing. Just assume he's sleeping better than usual.'

The room was dark, thick-walled, with a patterned net curtain over the deep window. Ornate black carved furniture and heavy chests added to its sombre dignity, which was leavened only slightly by the clean white cloths laid on every available surface, the pale linen of the bed itself, and a vase of vivid, unfamiliar red flowers on the dark chest of drawers. Maria had put them there. Maria, according to Robert's e-mailed page of instructions, was a marvel who could be summoned up by telephoning her home in the village at a day's notice. She would clean and produce breakfast and, for a consideration, dinner. 'But the local restaurants are good and cheap. I wouldn't bother her.'

Callum and Susie had arrived so late in the day that Susie thought they would get no supper; the invisible Maria, however, clearly knew the times of cheap UK flights to

Lisbon. She had left them, beneath yet another clean white cloth, some bread and sausage and cold sardines, with six large beef tomatoes ranged round the dish like sentries and a jug of red wine alongside under a beaded doily. Susie, only a week away from ration-packs, carried the tray into the villa's main sitting-room, laid out the food on two side tables and ate with gusto. 'Oh, wow!' she said. 'I can't believe this!' She looked around curiously at the heavy furniture and cool white walls. 'Isn't it fabulous?' she said. 'You can see it's been a home for years, not a holiday rental. I like that.'

Callum, whose poor appetite had been worrying his mother and Marion for some time, ate a slice of smoked sausage and bit into a tomato without pleasure.

'You should eat more,' said Susie, swallowing a lump of bread and wiping her mouth. 'My CO always says that convalescence is actually a job in itself. The body's got a lot of rebuilding to do. He was three months in hospital after a Humvee crew accidentally shot up his lot in Gulf One.'

If this was intended to raise Callum's morale, it did not succeed. He too was looking around the room, but instead of picturesque Iberian character he saw only traces of an old, old man: the shelf of much-thumbed books, the pipe rack, the antique brass umbrella-stand in the corner with two spare sticks in it, their handles worn. His own hurt limbs ached from the constriction of the flight, so that he felt like an old man himself as he noted the scuffed and sweated leather on the arms of the favourite chair, marks of Uncle Alfred's years of pulling himself unsteadily to his feet. It was, he thought, a house that had seen a lot of doddering. Now, with his crippled self, it would see a bit more.

Laying aside his uneaten tomato he stood up with difficulty and reached for his sticks. His right leg without its plaster still felt thin and light and weak, and the knee in particular gave him constant dull pain and occasional excruciating twinges. Putting his weight on the bad leg now, he felt the usual secret terror that it would collapse beneath him. His strong arms took his weight on the sticks, the good leg replaced the bad, and the pain receded. But as he moved across the room towards the view which had captivated him briefly when they arrived, it seemed to him that at every step a gremlin of pain and treachery and fear limped companionably alongside. A hateful, despicable, sapping feebleness invaded and inhabited him. It was, he thought, as if there were always a third person in the room, some crummy stranger lumbering between him and his fiancée, creaking and farting and stealing their oxygen.

'You're moving better every day,' said Susie happily. 'Gosh, I am looking forward to this. Mum is brilliant, isn't she?'

'Brilliant,' said Callum from the window, and the pain shot through him again, poisoning the wide moonlit ocean and extinguishing the stars.

Susie cleared up, then went to soak herself dreamily in Uncle Alfred's great claw-footed bath. Baths, as she had told her mother, had been one of the staple fantasies of the troops in the Iraqi desert; even the men would sometimes indulge in wallowing, girly fantasies of bubble-baths and deep hot water. There was a running joke with one particularly trusted companion: Staff Sergeant Miller would greet Susie, on her return from the screened privacy of her exiguous toilet, with a wink and a murmur of, 'Wanna talk clean, ma'am? Go on, say it . . . Badedas!' It was not a liberty she could possibly have allowed any less trusted soldier under her command, but somehow he always got away with it.

Here there were towels, stiff and rather small but plentiful and clean, thanks to Maria; there was hot water, and from her own luxurious store there were scented bubbles. Climbing out at last, Susie smoothed cream into her brown arms and legs, massaging the scented stuff into the dryness of knee and elbow. She combed her damp dark hair around her face and looked in the mirror, glowing. The thin hardness of her face was softened a little now by days of proper food and cooler air; she was beautiful again.

Three weeks here, three weeks with Callum. He could not walk far yet but they might hire a boat, perhaps, and sail from the little harbour. There must be boat hirers just up the coast in Setubal. There were a few modern guidebooks on the table, left presumably by Robert. Old Uncle Alfred would hardly have needed them after so many years. Yes, she thought: they would find things to see, and do, things which would ease her lover out of the shock and depression of his injuries. They would talk about the future. A man like Callum, even at less than a hundred per cent military fitness, had the world before him. Besides, the leg might mend better than the doctors said it would. And meanwhile there were three blessed weeks: time out of time, peacetime, with no more orders, responsibilities, threats or strain. It would be a true holiday. A honeymoon, almost.

She shucked on a long, cool white broderie nightdress which in her view nicely complemented the Hispanic decorum of the place, and marched towards the bedroom. Callum lay beneath the white sheet, a dim bedside light on the table beside him and his book lying open on the floor. His hands were behind his head, and he was looking up at the shadow of the black curled iron chandelier which hung in proud hideousness from the ceiling rose. Climbing in beside him, she followed his gaze and said, 'Spooky!'

'Yes.'

'Give us a cuddle, then.' She moved closer to his warmth and felt a faint, almost imperceptible flinch. He had, she noticed, changed from his usual side of the bed so as to present the uninjured leg towards her; a rush of love and pity overcame her and she threw her arm across his chest, pressing her breast to his.

'Sweetheart, do the burns still hurt?'

'Nope. Only the leg.'

'It'll get better. The doctor said the nerves have to settle down, and the pins and stuff they put in your knee—'

'Please,' said Callum as gently as he could. 'Please, no hospital talk.'

'Suits me,' she said. Then, quietly, 'You're all the world to me, Cal, you know that?'

Callum did not answer, but put his arm beneath her head and let her rest in the crook of his shoulder. It was the first time they had shared a bed since their winter farewell.

'It's all right, isn't it? I mean, everything?' said Susie, her cheek warm and soft against him. 'Cal, you'll be OK. We'll be OK.'

His eyes were closed, as if in sleep. After a while, Susie rolled gently away from him, laid his limp arm between them and tried to sleep herself. He turned his head away after a moment, although a patch of new skin on his burnt neck pulled with a needle-sharp pain. When his face was angled away from her and she could not see his eyes, he opened

them again and stared for some time at a heavy framed
tapestry picture of a Portuguese knight on horseback.

Back in England, Francis had dropped in for Sunday lunch
as he occasionally did, accompanied by a large floppy woman
comedian with a mass of dyed red hair and a raucous laugh.
'Zadie Zee,' he said, indicating her with a flourish. 'She was
on before me at Jongleurs and warmed the cruel bastards
up and frankly saved my bacon. I hate that audience. Too
cool by half. Where's Susie? I thought she was home nursing Callum.'

'They've gone to Portugal for a few weeks' holiday,' said
Marion. She was looking at Zadie with all the fascinated
horror of a prospective mother-in-law. Richard, who knew
better, played his part as a host with courtly brevity, before
retiring to his study to be out of sight and sound of her.

'Jesus!' said Francis. 'Portugal? You've never sent the happy
couple to Villa Creepi?' He knew the place: he had spent a
long weekend there during his parents' last holiday, thanks
to a short-lived £11 bargain fare to Lisbon.

'It's lovely!' protested his mother, half amused and half
irritated. 'Just what they need!'

'If you think they need to spend time in a fifteenth-century
Spanish loonybin! Ah, well, horses for courses. Yum, I smell
beef. You smell beef, Zade? Real Sunday food, provender to
build empires on.' He sidled round the room, missing nothing, noticing the absence of the silver tray and the half-hidden
bronze bust. If his mother had been watching she would have
noticed a faint lifting of his dark, neatly plucked eyebrows.
'Callum any better?'

'He's fine,' said Marion defensively. 'The leg's coming on
wonderfully.'

'I didn't mean the leg,' said Francis. 'I meant the mood.'

'Ohhhh! Is this your brother-in-law in hospital?' cried Zadie Zee, widening her kohled eyes. 'The one you said was doing the Big Sulk?'

'Oh, really!' muttered Marion, looking furiously at her son, who in turn threw a warning glance at the grinning girl. Later, when Zadie had gone to wander round the garden after lunch, his mother said to Francis: 'If you *did* say to your friends that Callum was in a sulk, I think that's terribly unfair.'

Francis grimaced and put his hands up in a gesture of surrender.

'Yeah, OK. I'm sorry. Only said it once, when Zadie gave me a lift from the hospital to my dance class. I'd just had an hour trying to cheer him up.'

'He's a hero. He went to war, and he got badly hurt trying to help civilians. You ought to show some respect.'

'I know,' said Francis. 'I honour the guy, I really do. I do know that I'm a mincing frivolous theatrical pantywaist, and he's a gallant soldier of the Queen. I submit. Maybe "sulk" isn't the right word, but—'

'It certainly isn't,' Marion broke in, her tone acid. 'He's got a lot of character. He's adapting very well.'

'Good,' said Francis without expression. 'Oh, God, I think Zadie's wanting to nick some cuttings. Is that all right? She's the window-box Queen of Battersea Mansions.'

For Susie Anderson the long white strands of Arrabida, the twisted pillars of the Igreja de Jesus and the sweet cold taste of Moscatel were to be, forever afterwards, connected with a sense of cold dismay. Callum went through the days at her side, obediently sightseeing, doggedly testing and exercising his leg, without complaint. He ate a little more, agreed with any observation she might make about the landscape and the local history, and took off his shirt to catch the gentle heat of the sun in the villa garden. Yet every day, she thought with a kind of panic, he drifted further away from her. Her mind, scrabbling anxiously for clues, went back to the time before the war and their year of happy betrothal. What had they talked about, then? What, apart from desire, connected them?

She knew the answer. They had talked about work: about their regiments, their army friends, the courses and exercises each was sent on. They had shared jokes – more often than not the in-jokes of their trade. They had talked about the likelihood of a second Iraq War, for its shadow had lain over the world through all the time of their acquaintance. They had planned their wedding and their future, and decided that a cottage between Salisbury and the sea would probably be their home base as soon as they could afford one. They had even discussed children, agreed that Susie would leave the Army in her mid-thirties to get pregnant unless she could join the General Staff and stay close to home, and with a sense of virtuous responsibility vowed that they would never, despite Susie's martial genealogy, pressure any child of theirs into a Service life.

'I mean, look at Francis,' Susie would say. 'If he'd been the only child, the Anderson fighting line would have stopped dead. But *imagine* how awful if they'd shoved him into the Army.'

They had talked of their childhoods, too, as lovers do: Callum spoke of his sketchy memories of his father, and of his bewilderment over the double loss by abandonment and death. They had talked about holidays and planned every

minute of their overlapping leaves, flying off to scuba-dive
in warm waters or heading north to sail the chilly Clyde
estuary. Looking back, with this new silent Callum next to
her gazing absently at the sea, it seemed to Susie that before
the war they had chattered incessantly for eighteen months,
face-to-face or over the phone.

Or maybe, she thought, she had chattered and Callum had
merely answered? No, that could not be it: how else did she
know so much about his life and tastes and feelings? She
knew why he joined a Scottish regiment, how Pat felt about
it, how irritated he got with the fluting, arrogant Englishness
of certain Sandhurst tutors, how equivocal he felt about
policing Londonderry, how he used to put a single flower
annually on his dead father's grave. She knew the names of
and many anecdotes about his brother officers and friends
like Harry Devine. No: her memory must be right. Callum
must have been a talker too. But now he had withdrawn. He
hardly seemed to know her.

All her old knowledge of him, all her old gambits
of conversation, were suddenly useless. She could not make
conversation about army matters or about his regiment
because this met no response or provoked a look so cold
she could not bear it. Nor could she fulfil her own need to
talk out the past war: the fears, the frustrations, the
professional satisfactions, and the continuing difficulty of
reconciling her memories of Iraq with the angry political
chatter of the news. She got the London papers every day,
a day late, though Callum would not even look at them.
Alone, she read in dismay how the war's aftermath was
unfolding in a series of ragged scandals and angry
allegations. Once or twice it was too much for her and she
raised the subject with him simply because he was her only

companion. But whenever she tried to talk Iraq, Callum fell silent.

As for the other old connection between them, their mutual desire, the memory of that was nothing but a torment. On this holiday, which was turning out to be nothing like a honeymoon, he had turned away from her every night. When she moved close to him in the sleepy dawn he would wake, yawn, push himself up to look around in a startled way, and swing his legs out of bed. Once he had reached the bathroom he would not return to bed. By day, when she put out an arm to help him climb down into the deep warm swimming-pool among the flame-red flowers, his flesh shrank from hers.

Susie shivered suddenly. It was late-morning, and they were sitting on a rough bench side by side at Cabo Espichel, gazing at the long rocks sheering into the blue Atlantic. A hundred metres away the hire car, which only Susie could drive, stood waiting for their return in the tourist car park. A year ago, she thought sadly, they would have hiked up to a headland like this without a second thought. Now Callum hobbled on his stick, uncomplaining but desperate, and sank gratefully on to a bench. He was looking out to sea, and with a brave impulse Susie said to him: 'What are you thinking, Cal? Right now?'

He did not turn to her, but raised an arm and pointed.

'I was looking at that boat.' She followed his direction, and saw a distant set of brown sails, squared off at the top by tall gaffs, moving southward along the wrinkled sea below the cliffs.

'Mmm, I was thinking we might do some sailing,' she said lightly. 'We could go down to the harbour at Sesimbra or along to Setubal and see if there's a charter company. I can't imagine that there wouldn't be.'

Callum was still looking at the boat. 'Looks like a Brixham trawler,' he said. 'Something like that anyway.'

'Shall we go and see?' said Susie suddenly. 'I think it's going into the harbour. It's quite close in.'

'OK,' said Callum, and stood up, using the bench to push himself upright and only then reaching for his stick. She followed him towards the car, telling herself that his limp was less pronounced than it had been, and that it was a good sign that he had noticed the boat.

Callum walked ahead, hating the stick and his wobbling leg and the sharp pain that marked every step; hating the very ground, foul springing turf with treacherous rabbit-holes. The earth itself had become his enemy of late. Ground which would once have sent him running and rebounding turned into a slippery enemy, hostile and mocking. The gravel in front of the villa would slide beneath his stick and jerk his knee into twisting agony; the sand of the long beaches betrayed his faltering steps, and once or twice made him fall heavily on his hip. The cool high grass of the headlands where children ran and cried for joy reminded him with an ache of warm boyhood days in Scotland, and then tormented him with its unevenness as it racked his leg again.

It would pass, he knew it would pass; the leg would strengthen, and even if it was never again to be an athlete's limb, he would walk without a stick. The doctors had promised. Yet still the blackness of his mood and his memories could not be lifted. He had been a soldier long enough to know, at second hand, the mental strategies for dealing with a hostile event like his own. You allowed yourself to think through it step by step until the memory anaesthetized itself; you talked if you needed to, joked bravely, cursed privately, and made the best of it. Above all you never, ever allowed the word 'unfair' to cross your mind, and if it did you swatted it aside and thanked God that you were even alive.

Nothing, however, had prepared him for the real thing, and certainly not for the loathsome corrosion of pity and self-disgust. The smooth surface of life was peeled away and the rest was mess and ugliness. What had happened, in fact, on that night in Basra? Some angry boy – hardly more than a child, they told him – had lost his whole world to an act of filthy war. In stupid revenge the boy collected his petrol, hit the wrong target and broke another family into bloody pieces. Now the petrol-bomber himself was dead. Callum could not hate or resent the dead Atif, but nor did he pity him. Because of the vicious dirty hatred that was the first law of the world, a baby girl had lain smashed and burning before his eyes. In the painful wakeful nights, her tiny bare useless leg often became confused with his own.

And what had he done, great beef-fed British soldier in his tidy uniform? What was his contribution to the mess? He had travelled to a land whose affairs were not much business of his. He had stepped into an Iraqi house where he could do no good, stared at a dead Iraqi baby, and been duly squashed by a crumbling Iraqi roof-beam.

In this mood – and it was an almost constant mood during his time in Portugal – poor Callum forgot all the rest of it. He forgot the obedience and discipline which had taken him to the war, the gentleness and tolerance of his unit in Basra, the little boys who hung around them and blagged chocolate which he and Harry sneaked out of the ration packs. He forgot the day the Saddam portraits came down in the school and he sang 'Ally Bally Bee' to the giggling schoolchildren.

He forgot the weeks when he and his companions had cheerfully endured bad food and gritty sand and the omnipresent shadow of death, in the understated belief that there had to be armies, and that theirs was at least an honest army which would free a poor benighted land from its murderous tyrant.

He knew quite clearly that he ought to discuss the war with somebody. It would have made good sense to discuss it with Susie, who had been there and seen a few bad things herself. But Susie was so positive, so hearty, so bloody military in her every move and word, that he could not bear to share his black doubts. The thought of a political argument with her filled him with a deep, bored weariness. As to his injury and his future, she insisted every day that he was much better, and the more cheerful she sounded the less possible it was for Callum to snarl out the pain and blank fury of crippledom.

On top of all this, he desired her. More than anything, he longed to make violent love to his woman, to lose himself in the moment, tangle himself in her limbs and hair and breasts and warm dark places. This tension between them might be dispelled, the soldier in him thought glumly, by one damn' good tumble.

But for some reason this was impossible. The dark carved bedhead, the spooky chandelier, the white expectant acres of the bed, made it impossible. The sudden ambushes of pain from his knee, and the knowledge that inside his human leg lay artificial pins and brackets, made spontaneity impossible. Most of all Susie herself, a benign jailer with her anxious watchful briskness, made it impossible. Thrice impossible, thrice doomed, his lust curled within him to become yet another snake in the heart, envenoming everything.

Hot and unhappy, the lovers drove down the hill towards the little harbour and together watched the Brixham sailing trawler *Miranda* drop her brown sails, slip round the pierhead and – after a brief shouted altercation with the harbour-master – find a mooring alongside a rusty fishing-boat.

8

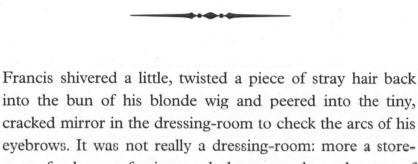

Francis shivered a little, twisted a piece of stray hair back into the bun of his blonde wig and peered into the tiny, cracked mirror in the dressing-room to check the arcs of his eyebrows. It was not really a dressing-room: more a store-room for boxes of crisps and cheesy snacks and crates of mixers which the landlord did not intend to hump up and down the stairs to the cellar. But since it had changed its name from the Duke of Wellington and managed to get itself listed as a live comedy venue in *Time Out*, the Frog In Waders was a pub with a mission.

It wanted to give the more famous comedy pubs a run for their money. The landlord, Jay Witham, known almost universally as Witless, was a middle-aged American who had fallen in love with the vivid, untidy British comedy scene. He had grown a long, greasy ponytail of greying hair and affected tight black T-shirts and tattered jeans; he dreamed of being featured in weekend magazines as one of the happening new impresarios for cutting-edge talent.

This ambition was some distance away from being fulfilled. Most of his acts until now had been recommended by customers or by the previous landlord; they were uniformly laddish in tone, tits, bums, shags and buggery being the staple of their jokes. Witless was aware that this would not get him far in the *bien-pensant* circles he admired. He very much wanted to get a name for presenting acts with a political, surreal, anarchic edge.

The problem he faced had a chicken-and-egg quality about it. His clientèle were of a type that intelligent comedians preferred to avoid; yet without a better class of comedy he could not lure in a new sort of audience. Witless did not much like his regulars, inherited when he bought the pub, and greatly resented their insistence on referring to it always by its old name. However, they brought in copious amounts of money and seemed very reluctant to go anywhere else. They were the major stumbling-block to his aspirations for a change of style.

The two rising Asian comedians he first approached took the precaution of coming round incognito on a Friday night to have a look at the customers. Having been roundly insulted and tripped up by laughing hooligans, they rang on the Saturday morning and politely declined to appear, even at double the usual money. He had better luck with one bespectacled and painfully liberal young man who agreed to do a twenty-minute set; he was a comedian of the type who did not believe in jokes that demeaned women, even Conservative women. This artiste lasted only five minutes before being hounded off the stage by a hail of ring-pulls and bottletops; secreted for just this eventuality by his prescient clientèle.

So Witless consulted the *cognoscenti* at the West End club he frequented in the afternoons, and was advised to seek another route to social acceptability by exploring the camp, or frankly gay, comedy scene. Although the Millwall FC supporters who regarded the Frog in Waders as home from home were not natural supporters of gay men, the latest generation of camp acts had a reputation for fearlessness, even aggression. Witless' advisers had personally seen a drag queen at the Giggle Club in Soho stepping off the stage and half-strangling a heckler with his spangled scarf; and Chiffon Elvis, the quiffed male rock stripper from West Mersea, was reputed to bring his own peacekeeping force of tattooed Essex men to every gig.

Witless therefore, on advice from a contact at the Vauxhall Tavern, booked Francis Anderson as Fanny Fantoni for this particular early-summer Friday. 'He's real class,' said the source admiringly. 'Witty, musical, works the crowd – I reckon he'll be the next Tina C.'

Francis had been nervously accepting all and any offers of work since the collapse of his television hopes, and although it would be the sixth show in four days, he immediately agreed. A little wary of the pub's reputation, he managed to cover himself by persuading Witless to book Zadie Zee as an opener. 'If we start with a real woman,' he said to her hopefully, 'it might soften the lads up a bit for Fanny.'

'I'd only do it for you,' said Zadie. 'It's a seriously rough pub.'

'You always say you like a bit of rough.'

'There's rough,' said Zadie darkly, 'and there's r-r-rough.'

Alone in the grimy stockroom, Francis had grave doubts. He knew, with precision, how and why his act worked. He was a character comedian, not a stand-up: the personality of Fanny Fantoni was a delicate creation. She depended on the audience grasping the back-story, her history, which he told in the first few minutes. She purported to be an Edwardian music-hall soubrette who had stumbled by accident into an experimental time machine being built by H. G. Wells in his back garden. She had been escaping from a lecherous admirer, had slipped into the box, caught a lever with a dislodged whalebone from her corset, and been transported a century onward, to turn up game but baffled in the world of AD 2003.

Her observations on modern life usually caused a ripple of warm, laughing recognition; her songs, delivered in Francis' high sweet sexless tenor, alternately moved and amused the listener. Her costumes and dancing merely astonished. Between these three solid peaks of technical achievement the act stretched out like a glistening cobweb, only just strong enough to suspend the audience's disbelief. The applause Francis won at the end of a successful gig was as much for his effrontery in keeping this farrago in the air as for the jokes themselves. And at one stage in every performance, fulfilling a quiet bet he made with himself, Francis always sang one song absolutely straight, quite beautifully, without trickery or coarsely knowing lyrics. His purpose was to demonstrate to the audience and to himself that he was an artist who could have moved their hearts to something deeper than jokes, if he wished. He needed them to know that if he chose to make them laugh it was as the result of a deliberate decision. He was no buffoon. Thus, stretched between laughter and sentiment, they were required to glimpse and share something of his own passion for life and for art.

The cracked mirror in the Frog in Waders reflected a pale strained face that told him he was in the wrong place, on the wrong night. Francis shuddered and put a damp forefinger to his right eyebrow. Poor Zadie was on her way to the stage. He had taken the booking, pushed her out there first, and now must take the consequences. Witless' offer of two hundred pounds was the least of it. Francis had to go over the top now, in every sense of the words.

'"Onward Christian soldiers",' he said aloud, and began

to take the deep, practised, settling breaths without which he could not perform. From along the narrow dirty corridor lined with empty barrels he heard a roar, a thumping and a chorus of wolf-whistles. Zadie was out, then.

Ten minutes later she was back beside him, sweating beneath her make-up.

'Bloody hell!' she said. 'Bloody zoo!'

Francis looked at her with consternation. There was a thin streak of red down her right temple, and he put out a finger to touch it. Zadie winced.

'Yeah, bottletop,' she said. 'Witless doesn't even sell bottles with the tops on. They actually bring them in, and bagfuls of ripped-off ring pulls. These are professionals.'

'How did it go otherwise?' asked Francis faintly.

'You've got to be dirty,' said Zadie judiciously. 'Very dirty. I used up all the dirty stuff right at the start, all the stuff I usually work up to. Tampons, blow-jobs, the Ann Summers sequence. Used it all up in ten minutes, which is why I'm back. I told Witless he could bloody well pay me for the full twenty, though. Years off my life.'

'What's he doing now?'

'Bar break. He said to tell you, five minutes.'

'I'm half inclined to do a runner.'

Zadie looked at him affectionately, her wild ginger hair framing a sharp, homely face. She hitched up a bra strap so that one heavy breast hung lopsidedly higher than the other, and said: 'I wouldn't think the worse of you if you did. They're not Fanny's people out there. Couldn't you leave out the H. G. Wells stuff? This lot probably think H. G. Wells is a furniture shop.'

'No,' said Francis. 'Fanny isn't anything without the back-story.' He stirred uneasily, tapping his shoes on the sticky plastic flooring, drawing circles with his toes. 'I knew I should have sold him something noisier. Kelly Kinko might've been all right. Got them stamping.'

'You don't still do her, do you?'

'I could. Only stopped because I hated the music. Still got the boots and the karaoke machine.'

'Anyway, it's too late now.' His friend in adversity looked with loving pity at the kohl around the young man's eyes and the purple satin flounces of his red dress.

'Yeah. Too late. *Alea jacta est.* Isn't that what Caesar said before they topped him?'

'Francis, don't—' But he was gone, sashaying down the narrow corridor, chin high, whisking his skirts away from the grimy barrels, singing under his breath, '"*Who-oo so beset him round, with dismal stories . . .*"'

In moments of stress he often resorted to hymns from his old school chapel.

Zadie sat down in the stockroom while Francis went out, heard Witless' extravagant announcement, and waited for the silence and the rising tide of giggles which usually met Francis' mock-bewildered entrance on to the stage, plumping down from the time machine in a flurry of ruffles. She heard his music, heard the running footsteps and the sliding thud of his entrance, and then the wrong sound altogether: a low male growling of disapproval and a cry of 'Pooftah!'

She jumped up, slipped along the corridor and looked out into the pub from the shadow of the doorway. Francis, strong-voiced, was beginning his introductory patter. She hoped he would cut it short and go quickly to the first song: music might soothe these savage beasts. He had in his hand a tiny remote control which would start his recorded accompaniment from the machine at the side of the stage, and Zadie knew that if he flicked it twice he could avoid the first song altogether and move to the grand introduction to his show-stopper – 'Only a Poor Little Country Girl'.

Francis, however, carried on with the routine and paused after a few dance steps, picking chewing-gum off his spangled shoe with a look of disbelieving disgust, uttering as he did so a gag never known to fail. But the pause gave the audience its chance, and the cry of 'Pooftah!' became, within seconds, a chant.

'Poof-tah! Poof-tah! Off! Off! Off! Poof-tah . . .'

Francis fought them for a while, challenged them, picked out the ringleader for contempt, raised his voice high and commanding, did all the right things. Louder and louder they chanted; bottle-tops and ring-pulls began to fly towards him like shrapnel. He had met coolness, apathy and indifference in his time but had never been hounded off a stage yet: Zadie, watching, could feel his determination not to be seen off this one. He flicked his control and began to sing; the audience seemed to pause, like a maddened animal briefly distracted. The watcher's heart lifted: bloody good trouper! He'd get them yet.

Then suddenly, to her horror, shapes began to rise in the dimness of the pub, big men lumbering up from their chairs to move towards him. 'Poof-tah!' One was picking up his plastic chair from the sticky floor: he threw it, narrowly missing Francis as he moved nimbly sideways.

'Get off!' she hissed in terror from the doorway. 'They're not fucking worth it! Where's Witless?'

Jay Witham was at the back, helpless. Francis lasted another minute, then gathered up his flounced and ribboned skirts, gave a brief bow and ran off the stage, his make-up streaked with sweat and, Zadie thought for a horrid moment, tears.

In the storeroom he scrubbed at his face with a flannel and said, 'You were right. Still, he's got to pay me now. Do you think I can claim compensation for trauma?'

His hands were trembling.

'We all die sometime,' said Zadie comfortingly.

She had a later booking to run on to. When she had gone, and Francis had finished changing, Witless came through with his money to find the young man sitting head in hands, shoulders shaking.

Susie rang her mother from Portugal, and Marion thought that her voice had markedly lightened with relief.

'Cal's walking better now,' she said, nurse-like. 'He's walked down to the harbour three mornings running, which is nearly two hours, though I do generally pick him up in the car at lunchtime. He tires himself out nicely for an afternoon sleep, he says.'

'He walks down on his own?' said Marion, and across six hundred miles the daughter could all but hear the expression on the mother's face.

'Yes,' she said with a touch of defensiveness. 'Because he needs the car to pick him up, see? If I walked as well—'

'Yes, of course,' said Marion hurriedly. She wished she could say what was in her heart: *take it easy. They come back with all sorts of problems a woman has to steer carefully round, especially if they've been wounded. It all comes right in the end when you love each other.* But she could not. For one thing, they had never talked about emotions. For another, was not Susie herself a war veteran now? Marion felt doubly helpless, faced with this troubled man and with the unknown quantity of a military daughter. Perhaps there was nothing wrong. Perhaps it was, as Susie insisted, a good thing that her fiancé took care to spend the mornings alone and the afternoons asleep.

'But you're enjoying the villa?' she said non-committally. Then on the next breath, 'By the way, you might be getting visitors!'

'Who?' Susie was startled. She looked out of the window at the blue sea beyond the stunted olive-trees, twisting the old cloth-covered flex of Uncle Alfred's telephone between her fingers.

'Harry Devine got leave – that nice friend of Callum's from the regiment. Quite suddenly. He had to swop with somebody in his unit. He and Rachel are driving down to the Algarve – apparently he loves these epic drives, frankly I can't think of anything worse. He lost his mobile in Kuwait with all your numbers, so he rang Pat and she gave him our number and I told him where you were, and, well . . .'

'It's right out of their way,' said Susie. 'They probably won't make the detour.'

'Not too bad, with the new bridge,' said Marion brightly. 'And I daresay Cal would love to see Harry!'

Susie asked after her father and Francis, and rang off. She glanced at the clock: there was still an hour before she need set off to the harbour to pick up Callum after his solitary hike. The previous day he had been utterly exhausted, done in, stiff and in obvious pain. She had begged him to take a day off.

'No,' he said. 'I need it. But it'd probably be better if you came around one o'clock, rather than twelve. Then I can cool down with a bit of sauntering round the quays.'

'We could have sardines in the café down there,' suggested Susie. 'That'd be nice.'

He nodded, and continued massaging his weak leg.

Conversation between them was still stilted, but Susie felt that it had improved a little since the arrival of the *Miranda*. On the first day, she and Callum had sat together on fish-crates on the harbour wall, eyeing the handsome old boat with its brown sails and heavy gaffs as thick as a man's waist. A motley collection of passengers – or were they crew? – had disembarked with heavy nylon sailing-bags, clambering over the rusty trawler inside of them, and been collected by two taxis.

The few remaining crew, whose leader had a long fair ponytail and the face of a hawk, busied themselves with mending and scrubbing; on the second day, when Susie found Callum sitting on the same box watching, the modern trawler had gone about its business and *Miranda* had moved into position alongside the quay itself. The skipper was stand-ing on the stern-deck, leaning on the flaking varnish of the mizzen-boom and scowling absentmindedly at the other four, one of whom was a solid-looking girl with short fuzzy hair. She was doing something to a bundle of sail on the foredeck; the three crewmen were variously occupied, one wandering aft with a pot of varnish, another tapping at a hinge on the forehatch.

Callum sat silent on his box, but Susie had a strong fleet-ing impression that a few moments before he had been in some kind of conversation with this crew.

'Did you find out anything about the *Miranda?*' she asked, as casually as she could. She was driving Callum home, and he sat next to her, his seat tilted back a little and his eyes almost closed.

'Yup. A bit. She's come from São Miguel. In the Azores.'

'Oh. Is she doing charter work round here? Might we . . . ?'

'No. Delivery trip to the UK. Her owner fixes the charters

and they're waiting to know where to head for. She had a
load of French punters on board, but they left early.
Seasickness, by the sound of it.'

'What a shame. Can't they do some charter work here? I
wouldn't mind a few days—'

'Nope,' he said shortly. 'Local laws. No licence. Got to
head back for the UK, the guy says.'

He closed his eyes completely and yawned with deliberate
intent to end the conversation. Susie drove on, glancing at
him from time to time with helpless solicitude.

'Your leg all right?'

'Still attached.'

'Do you fancy going to eat in Setubal tonight?'

'Dunno. See later.'

Then he had slept from two o'clock until six, done a series
of stretching and bending exercises in the swimming-pool,
and yawned his way through dinner. At least, though Susie,
the exercise seemed to be making him more relaxed. She
tried to move close to him that night, but he rolled aside
with the words 'Stiff leg' and lay there, inviolate and in-
accessible on the moral high ground of his injury.

While she settled down he lay awake, eyes closed, turning
over in his head the conversation he had had with Stefan,
the scowling, thickset captain of the *Miranda*. He had needed
to sit on the box near the rail for a long while before any
communication was struck up; something told Callum he
should not speak first like some curious tourist. Finally,
noticing his admiration, the skipper had nodded, and
indicated the broad deck as if to invite him aboard.

'Thanks,' said Callum, standing up. Then, mistrusting his
tired leg, he reached for his stick and eyed the gap and the
high rail with misgiving. 'But I won't get in your way right

now, while you're washing down.' For indeed the frizzy-haired girl crew had provided a face-saving excuse at that very moment by appearing through the hatchway with a hose and long-handled scrubbing-brush.

'She's a nice boat,' he continued, over the rail. 'How old is she?'

'Sixty-seven,' said Stefan. 'Not as old as *Leader* or *Provident*, but she was still fishing till the early-sixties. Vas on the mud for a while, then got sold to the Danes and converted as a school ship.'

'Is she yours?'

'*Nein*. Belongs to a businessman in Scotland who says there is money in chartering and tall-ships races and so on.'

Callum was trying to place the man's accent, and decided it was Scandinavian or rough North German 'And is there?'

'*Nein*', said the man again. 'I am paid less than I vould get for a straightforward yacht delivery, but I haf also to put up with holidaymakers to trip over.'

'How many do you need to work the ship?'

'Eight to sail fast. Ten is better. We got –' he indicated the figures on deck '– four. We can do most things, but slow.'

'I thought they used to run these things with a man and a boy,' said Callum idly. 'When they were fishing, I mean.'

'I told you,' said Stefan irritably, rolling his eyes to heaven, 'she vos a school ship. Everything takes a gang of people, she's rigged that way.'

He turned away and Callum sat back, quiet on his fish-box. After a while Stefan roamed back, and they exchanged more desultory conversation about the voyage from São Miguel and the defecting charterers. Callum formed a private impression that it might not be entirely seasickness which had made them take taxis to the first available airport; Stefan did not strike him as a man who cared much about the quality of people's holidays.

Lying in bed now, he thought about *Miranda* and for the first time since the accident in Iraq felt a warm curiosity and admiration flow through him. She might have a surly captain but she was a lovely little ship, workmanlike and tidily kept. The scruffiness of her crew was soothingly unmilitary, the rough practicality of her decks and the loose shaggy bundles of faded brown sails infinitely unlike a hospital. Thinking of her, imagining the high pale clouds blowing behind her tall masts, he drifted into sleep.

9

In the morning, Callum could barely walk. Susie was shocked, as she woke, to see him standing in the bathroom doorway, leaning on the frame with his injured leg twisting inwards in uncontrollable twitching spasms of cramp. The pain on his face made her instantly alert: she rolled from the high bed and ran to support him.

'I'm all *right*,' he said, several times, through his teeth. 'The doctor warned me that if it got tired the muscles might do this. Just needs a warm bath and a rub.'

Susie helped him back to the bed, and went to run a bath. When he had been helped into and out of it and was huddled angrily in his striped towelling dressing-gown, she said, 'You obviously can't walk down to the harbour today. Shall we drive? If you want to go down?'

Callum shook his head briefly. 'No. Save it for when I can walk.'

'I'd quite like to look at the *Miranda*,' said Susie, 'if she's still there.'

Callum realized that he really did not want her near the ship he had befriended when he was alone and free on the water-front. He demurred, hating himself for the tumult of pointless hostility in his heart. Why take it out on Susie, who did no harm? Even as he felt the stab of shame, though, he was saying ungraciously: 'Go if you like. I'm going to stay in bed for a couple of hours and then try to swim.' He knew that she would not go to the harbour and leave him alone if he mentioned that he might swim. She always hovered over him when he lowered himself into the pool. He hated himself even more for his guile.

But Susie said with every appearance of happy eagerness: 'You're right. I'll stay here and do some reading and tidy things up a bit. We'll have lunch on the terrace.'

Callum lay back on the bed, and watched her swiftly, efficiently, tidying round the room.

'Curtains open or shut?'

'Shut.'

Later, waking from a light doze, he heard the telephone ring and moments later Susie tiptoed into the bedroom.

'I'm awake,' he said, to prevent her from leaning over him. 'Who was that?'

'Harry Devine,' she said with a kind of hurried brightness. 'You know I told you that he and Rachel are driving to the Algarve? He got three weeks' leave.'

'He's hardly been back in Iraq a month since his last leave,' said Callum. 'I don't know what he's doing off again. And I don't think you did tell me, actually.'

'No, he hasn't been back long,' said Susie carefully. 'But he had to swop leaves with someone, and after this he's probably going to be back on duty for the whole summer, he reckons. I suppose I will, too, once August is over.'

It was the first time in their days together she had mentioned the fact that she had a job to go back to, and that this interlude of affectionate nursing was only a holiday. As she said it Susie felt a flow of relief, as if a taboo had been breached or a step taken towards freedom. She was not a nurse or nanny or even, God damn it, a wife. She was still a British Army officer with a job to do in the outer world, beyond this claustrophobic circle of anxiety and compassion and daily snubs. Looking at him, she felt a sudden un-expected stab of lust: oh, if only they could just make love, violently and abandonedly, and crash across the sour distance between them!

Callum found himself equally shaken by the reminder that Susie was due back on duty before long. Aloud he merely said, 'Well, good luck to them. Algarve, you say? I suppose he's windsurfing.'

'Well, they're dropping by,' said Susie. 'Tonight, he said. I'm sure I told you.'

'Jesus,' said Callum with feeling, closing his eyes again. 'Do we have to take them out?'

'We can't ask Maria to cook at this sort of notice,' said Susie. 'I was just going to do salad for us. Let's take them to Pesco.'

'OK.'

Later, he did his exercises in the warm pool and then sat in Uncle Alfred's sagging canvas chair, looking out to sea. In the bedroom Susie hesitated over what to wear for the evening out, and eventually chose a pink cotton sundress with a big skirt, plunging front and spaghetti straps, with a dark red fringed pashmina to wrap around her shoulders when the evening cooled. When she came into the garden, bare-legged and glowing, her shaggy black hair just touch-ing her golden shoulders, Callum in turn felt a stirring of desire. She had knotted the shawl around her waist, gipsy-style, and its fringes blew softly in the evening breeze. For once, he thought, she was all girl and no soldier. There was a softness in her manner, too, as she leaned over him and dropped a kiss on his head.

'Cal,' she said, almost apologetically, 'I do love you.'

As he was twisting his neck round to look up at her, long-delayed words forming in his heart, the roar and crunch of a car on the drive startled them both. Harry Devine always drove fast and braked with a flourish, sending gravel flying. The two in the garden froze for a moment, listening, then there was a slamming of doors and high, joyful young voices were heard beyond the corner of the villa.

'Isn't it gorgeous!'

'Mrs Anderson said it was pretty special. Some rich old boy lived here for yonks. Wonder if they're indoors or round the back?'

'Oh, look, a lizard! Swee-eet!'

Susie, reluctantly, took her hands off Callum's shoulders and set off round the corner of the house to greet the visitors. In a moment he heard her voice say brightly: 'You're lovely and early! Do you want a swim before we go out?'

'Hey, brilliant! Cozzies are deep in the packing, though – Rache, where did you put them?'

'Oh, deep, deep in the big bag. Under the even bigger bag. P'raps we could skinnydip?'

'Minx! What about poor Cal and Susie's neighbours?'

'They're away.' This in Susie's voice. 'Skinnydip if you must, but I can probably rustle up something to wear.'

Rachel, however, was a buxom girl and most unlikely to fit into anything of Susie's. After a rumbustious greeting to Callum, she stripped to pants and flopping breasts, and jumped in the deep end. Harry was wearing boxer shorts, and after a moment's consideration, winked at Susie and took them off before plunging in after his girlfriend and making her shriek with amusement as he dived between her legs and chased her round in a splashy, showy crawl.

'Orgies!' said Susie, amused. 'Thank God the neighbours

aren't there. I bet there was none of this in Uncle Alfred's day.'

'Bet there was,' said Harry, spluttering to the surface and shaking his dark hair like a dog. 'Probably had the pool full of Portuguese trollops every night.' Rachel shrieked again as he plunged towards her. Soon the splashing from the pool had darkened and puddled the pink tiles around it, which shone with a deep beautiful crimson. Susie realized with a curious sense of inferiority that in all the days she and Callum had lived in the villa, they had never larked and splashed, never seen this curious pretty darkening of the marble. She would swim up and down, while he did his physiotherapy stretches and bends, then they got out quietly and padded back to the house to change.

'Whoof! That was good!' said Harry, scorning the ladder and pulling himself out over the side with another vigorous splashing kick. Susie threw him a towel, which he knotted round his trim waist.

'God, you're brown,' she said, for want of anything else to say to him.

'The one good thing about Iraq,' he said. 'No need for sun lamps. You're much missed, Callum,' he continued. 'CO was asking if I'd had any informal-type reports on how you're getting on.'

'He looks *wonderful*,' said Rachel, saving the patient the trouble of answering for himself. 'Your face has really filled out since we saw you in the hospital.'

'Leg all right?' continued Harry. 'Your ma-in-law, well, immiment ma-in-law I mean, told me you were walking miles every day.'

Chattering, joshing, giggling, the visitors trailed off into the villa to change into their dry clothes and left Callum and

Susie in an uneasy silence. The grey, muted, conventual tone of their lives over the past week had become habitual. After the long strange weeks of Susie's army life and Callum's hospitalization, it had not seemed as odd or strained as it clearly was. The blitheness of Harry and Rachel, fizzing with frivolity and youth, threw their own suffering darkness into sharp contrast. Susie spoke first, as lightly as she could.

'Noisy bugger, isn't he?'

Callum was silent. He and Harry had been friends since their first day at Sandhurst, when Harry – an officer's son – had taught him all the tricks. It was Harry who tipped him off to keep one T-shirt and set of underwear permanently unworn, for inspection purposes only, and to sleep on the floor rather than make the bed with ruler-sharp folds every morning. They had joked together, drunk together, and told one another about each glorious new girlfriend. They had been alike. Now, they were not alike at all. A great gulf of suffering and doubt had opened between them; whatever Harry had seen and done in Iraq had not touched him one-tenth as deeply as the fire and the pain and the dead child had irrevocably altered Callum. In hospital his plasters and traction had made a visible difference between them, and furnished an excuse. Now, only the stick by his side signalled the unbridgeable gulf.

'Yes,' he said at last. 'Very noisy bugger. One forgets.'

At dinner Harry wanted to talk about Iraq, to tell his comrade about the news and the jokes and the daily irritations and perils of policing an unquiet city in the aftermath of war. Callum stonewalled every comment, seeming almost bored; Susie signalled frantically to Rachel to help break the mood. So then the women talked with forced brightness about Portugal, praising the food and the ragged coast and the cool elegance of the black-and-white patterned churches fading into the dusk around them. Harry, faltering slightly when it was clear that he could not talk military shop even to Susie (who, in truth, would have liked it), decided to lighten the atmosphere by flirting with her. She was looking very pretty, and Rachel was amiably tolerant of Harry's devilment.

'You look gorgeous, may I say,' he began. 'I would have said that earlier, but I didn't trust myself not to lose all control and fall on you like a ravening lustful beast.'

'Licentious soldiery,' said Rachel to nobody in particular. 'They *are* beasts, face it.'

'I bet you never had any bloody trouble getting your men to obey orders, flashing those eyes at them,' he continued, rather less felicitously.

'I don't bat my eyelids at my soldiers,' said Susie flatly. 'I look like a boot on duty, and a boot camp is what I run.'

'I bet you don't fool them.'

'I tell you, I do. One night, when we were coming up to the GOSP on the road towards Umm Qasr . . .' She stopped, glancing at Callum, suddenly afraid to talk soldiering. But he was absent, his eyes blank, looking down towards the harbour road and the darkening sea. Lamely, she finished her anecdote and steered Harry on to the subject of windsurfing; Callum said nothing for most of the evening. When the bill was paid Harry, apparently on an impulse, announced at eleven o'clock that he was not a bit tired, and thought that instead of staying in the guest room he and Rachel would press on southward towards their own holiday.

'Then I can windsurf first thing. Every day counts, with these short leaves. Was brilliant to see you both. See you soon anyway, Cal?'

'They didn't want to stay,' said Callum later, limping around the bedroom. 'Couldn't get away fast enough.'

'I think it really was the windsurfing—' began Susie, but he cut across her protest.

'I'm not complaining,' he said. 'I couldn't have stood the racket at breakfast time anyway. Good riddance.'

Susie lay awake for a long time. When she politely walked him out to his car, a few paces behind the oblivious Rachel, Harry had turned to her and said in a low angry voice, one soldier to another, 'He's acting up a bit, isn't he?'

'He's been badly hurt,' said Susie.

'Yeah, but some guys we knew,' said Harry flatly, 'are dead.'

She had no words to answer him.

Aboard *Miranda* that night the meal was frugal and tempers short. The young woman with the frizzy hair, Jez, had made a fish stew out of some pollack and mackerel which had been in the freezer since Ponta Delgada, and sought to improve their inspid frozen staleness with a great deal of equally antique garlic and some chilli powder which was the only condiment left in any quantity in the bare galley. They drank some wine bought as they left the Azores.

'How much did you pay for this?' said Maarten, the Dutchman, grimacing over his plastic tumbler. He shook his head like a dog shaking off water, and in the lamplight his long pale dreadlocks shimmered fuzzily against the dark greasy bulkhead.

'Thirty-five Euro cents,' said Erik the Dane. 'Local stuff. It's not so bad.'

'You can't taste it because you smoke tobacco,' said Teddy, who was American and, despite his wild dark fuzz of hair, perceptibly older and tidier than his companions. 'Jeez, thirty-five cents!'

'That's less than thirty p in English money,' said Jez, tasting hers with caution. 'You was robbed. It's pure antifreeze.'

'Antifreeze is expensive,' said Stefan. He had drunk a full glass and was embarking on another. 'It's not so bad.'

'When are we leaving, Stef?' asked the girl.

'Soon as we damn' can. We haf to get back to take any charterers. I don't know whether Mackenzie's got any but if we get them it will be in Britain. He thought perhaps Scotland.'

'Well, I ought to provision. We've done the water, but we've only got two days' food even just for crew.'

'So, do it.' He finished his second glass.

'I've got no money left.'

'Erik? Maarten?'

'You know we haven't.'

'Come on, Teddy!'

'Oh, no, man!' cried the American. 'I've got enough for a flight home when this circus folds up, and that's it. I'm not subsidizing Mackenzie. The deal was bunk and board in return for work. We work. He's getting a bargain. He's got to feed us.'

'Vell,' said Stefan, his accent thickening, 've can't starve. OK, Jez: one hundred Euros, and buy cheap.'

'I don't know anything other than cheap,' said Jez resignedly. 'Anyone want more stew?'

Four cracked plates were thrust towards her, and she ladled the meagre remains of the scarlet fish on to them with maternal fairness.

10

On the morning after Harry and Rachel's visit Callum was up first, looser of limb than the day before, and eager for his walk to the harbour.

'Shall I pick you up at about one?' asked Susie. She seemed subdued; Callum registered this fleetingly but did not allow it far into his consciousness. Something was growing in his mind, an excitement he could not put a name to. If he allowed Susie's quiet distress to pierce it, it would be gone for ever.

'Two o'clock would be fine,' he said. 'Then I can take it slowly on the way down.'

'What about lunch? Do you want to get something in town?'

'Ate too much last night,' he said briefly.

Rather than taking the walk slowly, he took it fast. For some reason the idea had gripped him that the *Miranda* would have sailed during his enforced day off, leaving the harbour wall bare. In his haste he stumbled several times, each time enduring a violent stab of pain from his fragile knee. It was, he thought again with bitterness, as if the ground itself hated him. The planet which used to roll steady beneath his glad youthful tread had turned traitor, and twisted viciously beneath his feet. The world whose hard brave surfaces once gave energy to his rebounding heels now sneered at his frailness, and waited its chance to rise up and smash its hardness against his suffering body. He fought it, stabbing the earth with his stick, slipping dangerously on the loose stones as the wooded track sloped finally downwards to the little town.

Coming round the end of the black-and-white church, he saw immediately that the brown masts and topped-up booms of the little sailing ship were there, tranquil against the sky. He gave a great shuddering breath, almost a sob of gratitude. As he slowed to a more decorous limping walk on the final approach to the harbour, the world seemed to steady beneath him.

There was activity on board. The man with the dreadlocks and the frizzy-haired dark one with the American accent were passing boxes over the rail to the young woman. Captain Stefan was nowhere to be seen. Approaching, Callum sat as usual on his fish-box. After a few moments there was a cry of irritation from on board. It was the woman, who had bent over a box and vanished behind the rail. Straightening, popping up like a puppet in a Punch-and-Judy show, she said loudly: 'Bloody cockroaches! Maarten, I do *not* want any cardboard boxes on board. They're infested. Take the tins and stuff out on the quay and pass them over in the bread-trays.' She indicated a dozen plastic bread trays, each bearing in large clear stencilled type the words PROPERTY OF SUNSHINE BAKERIES DO NOT REMOVE.

'It'll take hours,' grumbled the Dutchman. 'I've got to go back for the other boxes.'

'If you like,' said Callum politely, 'I could transfer the tins for you. I'm just sitting here, after all.'

Jez straightened up and looked at him as if for the first time. The crippled guy – so she thought of him – had been talking to the captain and was presumably English, by his accent. Not a nutter, then. You always had to watch out for nutters who got too interested in boats.

'Thanks,' she said after a moment's consideration. 'It would help.' Callum heaved himself up and moved across to the boxes; he could kneel, although he winced at the touch of the hard stone quay on his rebuilt knee, and began to sort the tins out and stack them neatly in the plastic trays. After fifteen minutes of silent industry it seemed that he had earned his place in the girl's esteem. Jez paused in her own occupation and said conversationally: 'That's really kind. Are you on holiday?'

'Sort of. Been here nearly a week.'

'I'm Jez,' she said.

'Short for Jezebel,' said the American crewman, emerging from the hatch. 'You watch out for her, buddy, she's a man-eater.'

Jez curled her lip in disdain, jerked two fingers at her shipmate and said, 'In your dreams, Mr Ugly.' Turning back to Callum she said, 'And you are?'

'Callum MacAllister,' he said, amused at the young woman's irritation. It seemed years since he had had a casual, joshing conversation with people who had no especial interest in him. It was balm to his spirit to be among strangers to whom he owed nothing, and who saw him as neither a hero nor a victim, neither a failed soldier nor a fragile patient. 'So what *is* it short for?'

Beneath the mop of brown frizzy hair the girl blushed scarlet; he noticed the swell of her breasts and her strong broad shoulders beneath the shabby T-shirt. 'It's Jessica, actually,' she said. 'Ghastly name. Have to shorten it to bear it.'

'Not a bad name,' said Callum. 'Mine gets shortened to Cal.'

'Hi, Cal.'

'Is there anything else I can do? I am quite seriously bored.'

Jez considered him again, and decided that perhaps he could be admitted a step further into her domain.

'Can you get over the rail and down a couple of ladders OK?' she asked. 'If you seriously want to help, I've got a dry-goods store in a state of total chaos, and Stefan keeps saying we could sail any minute.'

'Sure.' This time, Callum was determined not to be afraid of the gap between ship and shore; resting his weight on his good leg he took hold of the rail, swung the weakened one over, and as it gave slightly under him he flopped forward to clutch the rail with both arms, threw the other leg over and slid into an undignified crouch on the planked deck. As he stood up, a passing fishing-boat made it rock very slightly, and he felt a rush of pleasure at the sense of watery life beneath him. 'No problem,' he said, half to himself.

'Was your leg broken?' asked Jez, having satisfied herself at close quarters that his clumsiness and the normal angle of the limb did not suggest a lifelong lameness.

'Yes. In a lot of places,' said Callum briefly. 'Pins and brackets and stuff in there. I'd better not go near the compass.' She laughed, and he followed her down the companionway and then down a further short ladder, to a cramped compartment lined with shelves whose high fiddle-bars showed their serious maritime nature. On the floor of this irregularly shaped cupboard the bread-trays were stacked, full of tins and bottles and jars and packets. Somebody had long ago written in felt pen on the peeling paint of the shelves, indicating where the categories of food were to go. He glanced around and said briefly, 'Fine. Do you want the flour decanting into those bins?' There were large metal hoppers against the wall, labelled BROWN AND WHITE.

'If you don't mind. I hate getting all floury. It puffs right up at you however careful you are.'

'Whoops, cockroach!' said Callum, glancing at the nearest shelf, and squashed it firmly with a quick thumb.

'You're *good*,' said Jez with a gurgle of laughter. 'I waste that vital half-second by wincing, and the bastards run into the cracks. I shouldn't have bought that cardboard box below, I wasn't thinking. It's not as if it was Africa or somewhere.'

'Do you spray for them?' He was already unstacking the boxes with quick neat movements.

'Not near the flour-bins. They're not airtight. Should be, but nothing on this boat is A1 at Lloyds. Anyway, Stefan's very anti-chemicals.'

She left him to work, and with a contentment he had not felt for months Callum organized the dry-store, breathing in the faint smells of flour and old potatoes and the stronger, more romantic smells of the old wooden boat. After half an hour he had nearly finished, and his leg hurt horribly. He began to massage it and shake the muscles loose, noting with some pleasure that they were beginning to fill out to a more normal shape after their earlier atrophy. As he dispersed the last of his cramp, the pink round face of Jessica reappeared in the square hatch above his head.

'Cup of tea?' she asked. 'The guys all drink coffee, being Europeans, but I make myself proper English tea.'

'Love one.' He climbed up and joined her in what he saw to be a large saloon, taking up most of the after end of the accommodation. Looking towards the boat's bow he glimpsed stacks of bunks, three deep, behind faded and frayed curtains, and a further compartment opposite the cavernous chain-locker, marked 'WC'.

'She's nice,' he said.

'Could be nicer if she wasn't always so broke,' said Jez. 'The owner rather overstretched himself on the last refit, not that you'd notice from the accommodation, but there was a lot to do on the hull. He got this really lucrative charter party for the Azores and the Mediterranean, which would have paid off the bills and a bit over for a refurb, but then they all said it was too uncomfortable and walked out. No fans in the heat, no shower, and the mattresses are a bit crap, too. The trouble is that *apparently* they hadn't paid the full whack up front. Stefan's not saying much, but I think we're seriously skint.'

'Where next, then?' asked Callum, cradling his mug of tea.

'UK,' said Jez. 'And I suspect that if Mackenzie can't start paying the crew, we'll all have to leave her. Even Teddy the American guy has run out of money, so he says.'

'Are you – er – professional yacht crew?' asked Callum. 'I mean, is it your fulltime job?'

Jez laughed again, a raucous, mannish sound, and looked at him beneath surprisingly long lashes.

'Nah,' she said. 'Stefan's got all his tickets, and he's technically the paid skipper. Erik got his mate's ticket from some maritime academy in Holland – though he's actually Danish – and he's going to take up a job with a shipping company this autumn, so he says this is his gap year. Maarten's just a perpetual student doing it for the fun and the food. He's got a catering qualification and he's actually supposed to be the cook, only he gets fed up when there aren't good ingredients. Then I have to do it. Teddy's basically a preppy bum who wishes Woodstock wasn't over.

I guess he'll go home to Daddy and turn into a real-estate shark any minute.'

'And you? What are you?'

'I did a lot of tall ships races when I was at school and college,' said Jez. 'I just like sailing so I sign on as a volunteer. If you look at the ship's articles, Maarten and I are "apprentice deckhands".'

'What do you do normally?' Callum found himself enjoying the novel sensation of enquiring into someone else's life instead of contemplating the ruin of his own.

'I left university and worked for a charity. They had this yacht to take deprived kids to sea. It folded. I suppose I'll get another job on a boat somewhere when this one folds. Not,' she added, sipping her tea, 'that the *Miranda* has the slightest thing in common with a charity. To be honest, I reckon the charterers *were* ripped off, the price they were paying.'

'You're not a career girl, then?'

Her fuzzy, amiable manner cooled and hardened abruptly. Suddenly he saw her not as the bohemian scruff Jez, but as the upper-crust Jessica she was raised to be.

'When,' she asked with hauteur, 'did anybody last use that expression? Career girl? Jesus. I earn my living, or I would if any bugger ever paid me, I don't take money from my parents, and I'm not a ship's tart or a trust fund brat. If that's what you're thinking.'

'Sorry,' said Callum meekly. 'I didn't mean it to come out like that. I just wondered if you were following a plan? I mean, do you get some kind of qualification from working on all these boats? The – er – mate's ticket, or something?'

'No,' said Jez. 'More's the pity'.

She stood up, and waited for him to do the same. Callum

hauled himself to his feet and began to thank her, but she cut him off brusquely. 'Should thank *you*. Very useful. Anyway, enjoy your holiday.'

He climbed back over the rail with some difficulty, as the wind by now was blowing the boat away from the stone quay. Her mooring lines hung taut, thrumming over the two-foot gap and the water below. Jez watched him, standing close enough to grab him if he slipped; gritting his teeth, demanding obedience from his weak leg, Callum did not slip. Glancing at his watch when he had regained his balance on the quay, he saw that it was a quarter to two. Susie would be here; the morning's escape would be over. As he stood there, tasting Jez's oversweet milky tea in the back of his mouth, he was distracted by the arrival of Stefan. The captain was arguing furiously with a uniformed policeman who walked alongside him with an air of menacing authority. Behind them trailed the harbourmaster, the patent rim of his peaked cap glistening in the sun.

'Jez! Erik! Here!' shouted Stefan, skipping a step ahead of the Portuguese officer, who immediately sharpened his stride to come abreast of him again. Callum made as if to sit on his fish-box but then stayed upright, so he would be able to move a step closer in a casual manner and follow the conversation if the group moved along the quay. He was pleased and intrigued to watch someone else's drama.

'Our owner will pay by bank transfer, OK?' Stefan was saying in slow exasperated English to the Portuguese. 'You – give – us – bank – details.'

'Cash,' said the policeman. 'Only cash. I have this paper—' He was stepping over the rail with long-legged confidence. Stefan reached out a hand to try and restrain him and then pulled it back inches from the man's leather gun-belt, as if he realized that more trouble would result if he got physical. Callum had only seen Stefan before in his slightly arrogant, short-tempered role as skipper. This impotent and anxious figure was new to him. In a moment he understood why the situation was grave. The crew gathered round the German and heard him say exasperatedly, in English: 'It is for harbour charges. They vant three hundred Euros, including double penalty, or he put the paper on the mast and we cannot sail.'

Callum was intrigued by the idea that 'nailing a writ to the mast' still applied in the world of small-time shipping. But Stefan's furious distress affected him more, and he listened closely as the crew exploded into questions.

'But we paid!' said the American. 'You paid five days, we've still got one night to go!'

'Not here. Charges from Ponta Delgada,' said the skipper morosely. 'Azores is Portuguese territory. Same police.'

'I thought we paid up at the harbour office before we left? I remember you doing it,' said Jez.

'They say we gave the wrong ship's-length and only two nights,' said Stefan.

'Did we?' This was from Maarten, one hand twisting in his wild pale locks.

'That is not important,' said the skipper, struggling to look aloof behind a faint blush. 'But we must pay three hundred Euros now. I cannot go to the bank. There is no money. Teddy? You can lend this?'

'Oh, no. I said, no!' exploded the dark American. 'I need my fare home! How many friggin' *times* do I have to tell you? I've friggin' had it anyway. Stefan, I'm taking my kit ashore and heading home.'

Stefan shrugged at Teddy, and spread his hands in a disdainful gesture as the American hopped over the rail and vanished into the cabin. He did not ask the others for money but paced away along the quay, then looked back at the policeman who had come ashore again and stood with arms folded next to the tubby harbourmaster. Their dark Latin faces were impassive now: the ball was in Stefan's court.

'You pay. Then you can sail,' said the officer loudly, after a long moment's silence from the skipper.

'*Si,*' said the harbourmaster, nodding.

Stefan roamed up and down, furious. Callum leaned on his stick for a moment irresolute, then limped forward and put a hand on the skipper's arm.

'When did you plan to sail?' he asked in a low voice. 'Before this – ah – misunderstanding?'

'Tomorrow. Eight o'clock,' said Stefan, still wrapped in thought. 'Not much tide, but what there is will take us round the headland.'

'Right. I'll pay your three hundred Euros,' said Callum, and pulled out his wallet. 'I'll get it out of that cash machine over there,' pointing with his stick. 'Give me five minutes.'

Stefan pulled his arm away, turned, and stared at him in astonishment.

'It is not your business,' he said rudely.

'It means you can sail,' said Callum.

'Don't spit on it, man,' said Teddy, astonished but pragmatic, returning with a loaded kit-bag. 'If he wants to!'

'In return,' said Callum in a low voice, unheard by the policeman and the harbourmaster, 'I'll take a passage north with you.'

Stefan was still regarding him with unflattering suspicion. 'You got European passport?' he said sharply.

'Of course I have. I'm British. You're going to Britain, right?'

'No drugs,' said Stefan. 'Not for any money.' He lowered his voice further. 'Only for onboard smoking, at sea. No importation.'

'I am *not* a drug dealer,' said Callum. The Portuguese policeman was regarding him, eyebrows satirically raised, half-understanding the situation. Callum, taking Stefan's fresh silence for assent, limped off towards the cash machine and returned five minutes later; the little group was in almost the same position as when he left, not speaking. Jez sat astride the rail as if it were a horse, one long leg in frayed denim dangling, her foot in its shabby training shoe occasionally kicking against the stone quay.

'Here,' he said. 'Three hundred.' He counted the notes out in front of the policeman without flourishes, handed them over and said, 'Receipt?'

The officer wrote out a receipt, then climbed back on board the *Miranda* and removed his other paper from the mast.

'You are free to go, Captain,' he said blandly. 'Tomorrow. Otherwise there will be more charge. I must remind you it is not permitted to take paying passengers for charter business.' He winked at Callum, who returned a bland and stony stare.

Stefan watched him walk away, then turned to his prospective passenger, still unsmiling.

'I don't know why you suddenly vant to sail to England,' he said gruffly. 'But we will be five, six, seven days at sea. Maybe more if the vind is bad. Passengers is seventy Euros a day, minimum. Three hundred is not enough.'

'I'll settle the rest when we get there,' said Callum, who was disliking his captain-elect more every minute. 'Meanwhile, it wouldn't actually hurt you to say thanks.'

'You don't know Stefan very well, do you?' said Jez from the rail. 'It would hurt him *very* much. He never says thanks. We'll say it, right, boys?'

A murmur of slightly resentful gratitude rose from the two remaining crewmen. Callum limped quickly away, for he had seen Susie climbing out of the hire car up on the road and did not want her near the ship. Exhilaration fought with bewilderment and guilt.

But there was, he told himself, really no need for the guilt. He wouldn't go. He had spoken only on impulse, to feed the morning's rising sense of possibility and escape, and to test his ability to step outside his invalidish world. The *Miranda*, he strongly suspected, would be gone long before morning anyway. Moonlight flits with unpaid debts seemed to be a firm part of the little ship's culture. He had paid three hundred Euros to enhance his mood, and it had worked. A lightness stole over him, and he smiled at Susie without really seeing her.

'Hi-yee!' said his fiancée with forced jollity. 'Did you have lunch in the end, or do you fancy some tapas?'

II

'He did what?' said Francis, big eyes wide with astonishment. 'Ran away to sea? What is this, Gilbert and Sullivan?'

He was sitting at the kitchen table opposite his mother. Marion twisted a tea-towel between her fingers, struggling to keep her rattling emotions under control. Her son's wisecrack, designed to defuse the tension that tormented her, signally failed. It was typical of Francis to have turned up at home unexpectedly on a weekday with a dreadful strawberry-blond cowlick dyed into his dark hair, just at the very moment she was taking that terrible call from poor Susie.

Moments before, Francis had swept into the hallway, dropped a scruffy leather holdall and hugged her shoulders from behind, impervious to the crisis. He had felt the stiff horror in his mother's body and backed off, moving in dismay to the kitchen while Marion listened to the cheeping sadness of her distant daughter down the crackling line from Villa do Boco. When with a damp and trembling hand she put the receiver down, heart racked with empathy for her younger child, she walked back into the kitchen almost in a daze and found Francis making tea. The sight of him did not immediately gladden her heart: flaunting his pinkish-orange stripe like an effete badger, he was a jaunty figure of harlequinade wholly unsuitable for the receipt of serious news. He gave her tea and sat down; Marion collected herself in silence for a moment before telling him what Susie had said. At his Gilbert-and-Sullivan joke she gave an inarticulate little groan, scowled at her son and sank her face into her hands.

'Sorr-ee,' said Francis. If she had looked at him she would have seen that he too was pale, and had a slight pink scar down the side of his face from one of the bottletops hurled at him two nights earlier. If she had been in any state to study him closely she might also have guessed that he had not kept any food down since that night. Ever since he was a little boy, Francis' emotional difficulties had always gone straight to his stomach. But his troubles were nothing, nothing at all, next to Susie's, and his mother could not see them.

Francis, genuinely sorry now because her face was so bleak, promptly abandoned his camp manner to say again, more gently: 'Sorry, Ma. It was the shock. Callum, of all people.'

Marion accepted his apology and his new tone. Glancing across now she did, without registering it too strongly, see his pallor; her heart, still wrung over Susie, was too over-whelmed to consider it. It took a moment for her to reply.

'Well, he's been under a lot of strain. It's probably not quite as it seems.'

'You say he's got on a boat, and just gone?'

'Susie was hysterical. Not at all like herself. I think some-thing else might have happened first. I didn't get all the details, she says she'll ring back. She wanted to go down to the harbour and see if he really has gone. But she rang me first. And you know Susie . . .'

'Yes,' said Francis. 'Susie wouldn't have rung first usually, would she? She'd be down at that harbour, order-ing out a gunboat or a flotilla of Royal Marine Commandos or something.'

Marion ignored the levity, and frowned into her tea. 'Something's gone badly wrong,' she said. 'Susie did say that Harry had been there a couple of nights ago. I wonder if that's part of it.'

'Oh, that great jock friend of his? Yeah,' said Francis. 'Might have said something tactless. *What* a surprise that would be.' His sharp delicate features lost their habitual piquant lightness and became stony. Susie had brought Callum and Harry and Rachel to his one-night show at the Soho theatre studio, and supper afterwards had been distinctly strained. Harry's guffaws had been gratifyingly audible during the show, especially at the more risqué jokes, but he seemed to find it difficult sharing a table with a man who had been wearing skirts an hour earlier.

'Susie sounded awful,' said Marion. 'Awful.'

'Awful, how?'

'Sort of – winded,' said his mother slowly. 'All the stuffing knocked out of her. Look, someone's got to do something!'

'What?'

'I don't know. All she said was that there was this rather scruffy hippy-looking sailing boat in the harbour. Germans or something. And that when she woke up this morning Callum had gone. He took the little wheelie-bag with him – you know, the soft one she borrowed so she could carry his heavy stuff as well as hers – not the big blue one.'

'Mum,' said Francis gently, 'perhaps his actual *luggage* isn't the most important thing.'

'Oh, but it is. You see, he used to walk down to the harbour by a woodland track, but he must either have got a lift really early in the morning, or else walked all the way by road, which is a mile more, because the bag's got such little wheels and he couldn't possibly lift it, with his leg and his stick.'

A figure flashed into both their minds: a tall, limping man on a dusty Portuguese lane, trundling a wheeled bag behind him towards a harbour in the dawn. They sat silent, against the ticking of the kitchen clock.

'How on *earth*,' asked Francis, 'did he manage to pack without waking her up? I can't see him planning that sort of caper in advance. Not Callum.'

But, thinking back to the hospital visits, he had to admit to himself that it was quite possible that none of them actually knew Callum any more.

Susie stood by the quiet quay alone. The trawlers were at sea, and only one old man fiddled with some nets in the sunshine. Looking beyond the harbour wall she saw the flat innocent Atlantic, and a couple of dinghies criss-crossing one another's wakes, their sails bright circus splashes under an empty sky.

Her night's sleep had been long, heavy and unrefreshing. The night and day after Harry's departure had brought her little peace; once Callum had left on his harbour walk she had tried to read, tidied the villa and roamed from room to room, stiff with unfocused anxiety. She could not get Harry's scornful parting remark out of her head: 'Acting up a bit, isn't he?' After she had collected Callum, he went straight to bed pleading tiredness and slept until nearly six. He did not want to go out, so she gave him an omelette cooked by herself. But Callum ate almost nothing on that last night, and spoke barely at all. He seemed to be wrapped in thought. Finally, tired and near the end of her resources, Susie had gone to the lonely dark bed at nine while he sat near the window watching the fading of the light. She knew nothing until morning, when she woke under the carved headboard to find herself still alone. Pulling on a jacket, she ran out in her nightdress to the pool, dreading what she might find; back in the kitchen she found the letter.

With it were two fifty-Euro notes. She looked at them in disbelief for a moment and then read:

> *Dear Susie*
> *I think we both know it can't work. Not now. It's not*
> *your fault and I'm sorry. I've gone on the* Miranda, *so*
> *I'll be out of the way. You deserve better than me anyway.*
> *I had to take the wheelie-bag, sorry about that. There's a*
> *luggage shop in Setubal, better buy another.*
> *Sorry.*
> *Callum*

The silence of the villa bore in upon her; she wanted to scream and never stop. But screaming was not what she did; it was not what officers in the British Army did, however powerful the provocation. The call to her mother, garbled and disoriented, was the nearest that Susie could allow herself to such a scream.

Even so, by the time she reached the harbour she was sorry she had made that pathetic call. Iron restraint was clamping itself, cold and stiff, around her wounded heart. Just because Callum had bloody well lost it, that was no reason why she should do the same. She told herself through a veil of tears that she was well rid of him.

Then, with enough force to shake her physically, a choking fear possessed her. Lame, angry and hopeless, he was out on that unforgiving sea with only a low rail between him and oblivion. The wind was rising now as the sun climbed; a cold northerly breeze chilled her neck. Susie sat down on the same fish-box from which her lover had been spirited away, and wept.

Richard Anderson came home from his morning walk, dispatched his obedient old dog to its basket with a pat, and wandered through to the kitchen.

'Hello, Francis!' he said heartily. 'Got pink paint on your head? Been walking under ladders again?'

Francis smiled up warily at his father and said, 'Temporary. Washes out. Cheering myself up.'

'Things not so good in the old showbiz, then?'

'Had a bad night. Bit of a rout, actually. They threw things.'

'Oh, well, happens to us all. Onward and upward. I remember one ENSA show in Cyprus, rough lot of lads . . .' Richard poured himself some tea from the warm pot and came to the table, spreading his elbows luxuriously, forgetting his drift. 'Lovely day, out.'

'Darling, there's a crisis,' said Marion. 'Awful thing. Susie rang.'

He put his mug down and stared at her.

'Not an accident?'

'No. It's Callum. He's, well, left the villa . . .'

'On his own?' She nodded. 'Where's he gone?'

'Run away to sea,' said Francis, seeing that his mother was close to tears. 'Susie found a note when she got up in the morning. Some sort of sailing-boat. He'd made friends with the crew on his walks and – well, apparently the note just said goodbye and that he was getting out of the way.'

Richard looked down for a moment, then across at his wife.

'Oh, God,' he said. 'We did wonder, didn't we, darling?'

'He was so bottled-up,' said Marion. 'So furious. He didn't ever talk about the accident or the war at all.'

'Never thought he'd cut and run, though,' said Richard. He stood up and began to pace, his footfall heavy on the worn vinyl floor. 'I knew he was acting up a bit, but never thought he'd do a thing like that to Susie. I thought they were OK.' Anger shook him briefly. 'Poor sprat. Poor little Susie.'

'I know,' said Marion. 'She was off down to the harbour to check that the boat had really gone.'

Richard looked up, hope in his eyes.

'You mean, it mightn't have? Might just be a sort of cry for help thing?'

Francis got up.

'I'll leave you to it,' he said. 'If you want someone to go over there and bring Susie home, I will. There's nothing I can't cancel.'

Outside in the garden he leaned on the warm brick wall of the house and fumbled for a cigarette. He rarely smoked, not least because he couldn't afford to, but he always carried a packet with him; in case, as he put it to his friends, the need for something to suck became so overwhelming that it was either a fag or his thumb. He lit it, drew in the smoke, coughed violently, then stood holding the cigarette, watching the thin smokestream rising and spreading in the still summer air.

'Fuck you, Callum,' he said aloud. 'If you do bloody kill yourself, I'll bloody kill you.' Hearing himself utter this absurdity, he smiled without mirth, and then threw the cigarette down and ground it into the mossy interstices of the path.

In the kitchen his parents were cautiously circling around the same thought. They had been among servicemen, old and young, for all their adult lives. They had seen strength and the will to recover conquer greater injuries and disappointments than Callum's. They had also seen bold spirits overcome, and had stood dry-eyed at the suicides' funerals, supporting relatives whose grief was lethally mingled with shame.

'It seems impossible,' said Marion. 'I don't think for a minute . . .'

'I don't want to,' said her husband. 'I wish I could see the note.'

'His poor mother, too,' began Marion, then her eyes widened in dismay. 'Would he have told Pat – do you think I ought to?'

'She might know more than we do.'

'Do you think so?'

'No.' Richard stood up. 'I don't think anything. We'll have to wait till Susie rings back.'

It was Pat, however, who rang first. Susie, after walking the quays for a while, had ascertained from the old man with the nets that *si*, *si*, the English *senhor* with the lame leg had been seen on board the *Miranda* when she went out between the breakwaters in the dawn. The Americano had gone in a taxi yesterday, but the Englishman with the stick had certainly sailed. Calling in at the harbourmaster's office she discovered that the stated destination of the little ship was Scotland. Therefore, by this time outwardly quite self-possessed, she had telephoned Pat to inform her in bright antiseptic tones that Callum had taken a marvellous chance of a boat trip home all the way to Scotland, since his leg was so much stronger now. She, Susie, would be rejoining her regiment quite soon and so could not be with him, but not to worry.

'It's an odd carry-on,' said Pat's cheerful tones down the

line to Marion Anderson. 'But Susie seemed relaxed enough about it. The young are pretty unromantic these days.'

Marion exchanged a few light comments and put the telephone down.

'I'm not fooled,' she said to her husband. 'Susie's putting a good face on it. Who wouldn't, with Pat to deal with? The last thing she needed was her going off the deep end.'

'I suppose she'll come home anyway. Shall we ring?'

In the end, the parents kept an anguished silence. A few hours later Susie herself rang. She had closed up the villa, given the keys to Maria, and was about to head for the airport. Calling on her mobile she sounded cold, composed and unruffled.

'She's taken her engagement ring off,' said Marion, return ing white-faced to her husband and son in the living-room.

'Did she say so?'

'No,' said the mother. 'But I could tell she wasn't wearing it, just from her voice on the phone.'

Even Francis did not laugh.

12

———

Callum woke hot and breathless, and stared in momentary confusion at the planks a few inches from his face. The space around him was confined and dim, despite a violent streak of light from the sun framed in a porthole by his feet. The world lurched and rolled, slanting more to one side than another, so that his injured leg lay pinned uncomfortably against the upright wooden side of the bunk. There was not enough headroom to sit up, so he rolled on to his stomach and got on all fours – with a violent pang to his knee – before cautiously putting his feet down on to the cabin sole. Pulling himself upright, he banged his head on the edge of the bunk above his own, then stood, swaying slightly and holding on to the uppermost one.

'He's awake,' said a voice surprisingly close to his head. Turning, Callum saw that there was a square window cut into the bulkhead near his bunk, half-obscured by a tatty curtain and framing the face of Maarten, the big Dutchman, with his pale dreadlocks falling around it.

'You OK?' the face asked. 'You been asleep all day.'

'I was awake all night,' said Callum. 'Sorry. What time is it?'

''Bout three. You want some coffee?'

'Please.' He looked around, hoping to sit on the bunk, but there was too little overlap beyond the jutting side of the one above. Half of the tiny cabin's floor was obstructed by Susie's blue wheeled bag, and the sight of it afforded him such a surge of guilt that he looked away. He was wearing trousers and a T-shirt, and decided he could manage without any outer garment, so he pushed the bag under the berth with his toe, and made his way through the stacks of empty bunks to the central passageway that led back to the saloon.

Maarten was in the cramped galley that lay beyond, and Callum limped towards him, moving cautiously from hand-hold to handhold as the boat's motion allowed. He took the mug, and looked uncertainly upward at the ladder to the deck. Once, he thought sourly, he could have climbed that heeling, lurching ladder with a mug in his hand without the slightest hesitation. Now, with the boat leaning and sliding through the lively water, it loomed like an assault course. He sat at the table instead and drank the coffee as rapidly as he could. He was dizzy, on the verge of sickness, and a wave of self-pity came over him as he saw the young men, Maarten and Erik, scrambling carelessly up and down with various tools and objects in their hands, and heard the raucous laughter of Jez from the deck. Soon, though, her face in turn was framed against the bright sky, and she spoke to him with such unaffected cheerfulness that his sulk began to lift.

'Hi-yee, Cal! How're you doing?'

'Okay. Getting my sea-legs.'

'Brilliant strategy, going straight to sleep. I'm always sick until I've had the first sleep, and once you have, you sort of adapt to the motion unconsciously and you're never sick again.'

Callum closed his eyes, and the dizziness resolved itself

into a rising irresistible malaise. He should not have had the coffee. Leaving the mug, stumbling on to the deck, he was copiously and humiliatingly sick over the leeward rail. He was reminded horribly of the way he had vomited after each anaesthetic in his long hospital incarceration. Here he was, back where he started, a stumbling invalid. The vileness of it all overcame him; tears ran down his cheeks and mingled with the dribble of nausea.

'That'll sort you out,' said Jez, who was steering, one eye on the horizon and one hand on the wheel. 'Have some water. Erik!' she called to the mate in the cabin. 'Gi's some water for Cal.'

She left the wheel momentarily to lean down and pass it across to him, and through his sickness he admired the way that the heavy boat held its course, with only the slightest tremor of her three big jibs as Jez returned and swung the wheel to correct it.

'She's going well,' he said shakily, when the water had cleared away the taste of sickness from his mouth.

'Not bad. Wind's in the north, though. We're pointing at America right now. She's not that good to windward. But Stefan wants a long tack offshore to get out of the shipping lanes.'

'Where is Stefan?'

'Up in the fo'c'sle trying to fix the generator.'

Callum saw that there was a new place to sit; a low bench with a wooden grid for a seat, lashed expertly alongside the rail next to the helmsman. He sat down, leaned his back against the rail and stretched out his bad leg. Looking around, he saw no land in any direction. Looking up, a suit of great brown sails filled overhead, heeling the boat on to her port side a little, powering her through the water and throwing up a clean white sheet of foam which bubbled from her bow to her stern. There was such life in the ship, such ebullient joy, that his spirits rose a little more. Suddenly he was hungry.

'Is there any chance of a hunk of bread or something?' he asked. 'It might help stop that happening again.'

'Erik!' shouted the girl. But the mate had vanished and the saloon and galley were empty. 'Oh, bugger. Take the helm a minute and I'll get some – you can sail, can't you?'

'Y-yeah,' said Callum. He stood up, pulled himself across to the wheel, and noted the course on the compass at his feet. Seeing his downward glance, Jez said: 'Don't bother with that. We're only taking a long board offshore. Steer by the wind. We've been making 275, maybe 285 on a gust. Just keep the headsails pulling.'

After a moment the furthermost sails began to shake: Cal moved the wheel experimentally a spoke to the left, and almost immediately they settled, and pulled. As the boat gathered speed again, he eased the wheel back; within a few moments the outer jib shook, and again he corrected it. By the time Jez returned with a hunk of bread and honey, he was almost enjoying himself. As she handed him the bread he thought fleetingly of Susie, making his supper in silence the night before; but the thought hurt him, and he banished it sharply. Looking up at the brown sails, feeling their weight pulling the ship forward as she leant from the wind, he closed his mind to the past and to the future. For now, the journey was enough.

Seeing that he was comfortable and able to eat his bread and steer with the other hand, Jez sat down on the bench, arms spread along the rail, and watched him in silence.

'The course isn't too good,' she said. 'I suppose the wind

might go more north-westerly and give us a fetch on the other tack.'

Stefan appeared through the hatchway on the bows, pushing himself through at arms' length and swinging his bent knees on to the edge of the opening with an insouciance that made Callum wince with envy and remembered pain. The skipper stood up, and without touching a hand-hold strolled back along the bucking deck.

'It is not a good course,' he said to Jez after a glance at the compass. 'Vind is dying, too.' He ignored Callum.

'It's not, is it?' said Jez. 'We're still doing four knots.'

There were no instruments in sight except the compass; Callum assumed that she knew this at a glance.

'*Ja*. It is dying,' said Stefan with authority. 'By dark, it will be very slow.'

'Do you use the engine much?' asked Callum, nettled by the captain's continuing failure to address him.

'No,' said the German. 'Ve don't.' He turned away and clattered down the main companionway.

Jez said to Callum in a low voice, 'Don't worry about him. He's got a lot on his mind. To be honest, I don't think we've got much fuel left, so it's a sore point.'

The wind died, as predicted. By dusk the *Miranda* was barely moving. Forty miles out on the flat emptiness she rocked gently, as if at anchor; Stefan leaned on the wheel, yawning, and Maarten and Erik passed a joint from hand to hand on the side-deck in a blue cloud of cannabinoid fragrance.

'Smoke?' asked Erik of his new shipmate with punctilious politeness.

'I don't, thanks,' said Callum a little stiffly. And, in a faintly censorious tone, 'How do you work the watches? At night, I mean?'

'Six on, six off, day and night, unless someone thinks different,' said the Dane absently. 'But not Stefan. And when sail handling, everybody. And when no wind . . .' He giggled, a high-pitched sound that came oddly from the big man. His hair, Callum noticed, was breaking free from its rubber band and falling in elflocks round his face. He looked stoned already. 'When *no* wind, we sleep.'

'But you always have a watchkeeper?'

'Oh, yes, Mr Policeman,' giggled Erik. Maarten, who seemed less affected by the skunk than his friend, kicked him.

'*Ja*, we do,' he said shortly. 'Why do you ask? You don't think this is a safe ship?' He rose, obedient to a jerk of Stefan's head, and lumbered back to take the wheel from the skipper.

'Sorry,' said Callum humbly to Erik. 'I wasn't criticizing.' He heaved himself to his feet and glanced down into the cabin. 'Perhaps I should help Jez with the food.'

'You do that,' said Maarten from the helm. 'Get your feet under that table!' He made an obscene gesture, letting go the wheel to do so; it swung a little, idly, for there was no wind at all in the sails.

'Do you think Stefan *will* use the engine tonight?' asked Callum.

'Shit, no,' said Maarten. 'Price of fuel. Price of moorings. Slower we go, the cheaper life is. There is no timetable.'

'Nooooo timetable. No time. Just sea and sky and sea,' said Erik expansively, and fell backwards, his head making a hollow knock on the deck, to gaze up at the darkening sky.

In the galley, as he began chopping carrots under Jez's direction, Callum strained to listen to the increasingly rambling conversation from the deck, and the girl threw him an unfathomable glance.

'Not what you expected?' she asked.

'No. But it's fine.'

'Don't worry about the spliffs. If there's a crisis the guys always seem to be OK really. And Stefan doesn't touch it, and nor do I at sea.'

'Fine,' said Callum, a little embarrassed. 'I suppose it's just not what I'm used to.'

'What *do* you do?' asked Jez, as if the question had only just occurred to her. She had, in fact, been sizing him up all afternoon, trying to work out whether he was a wealthy dropout or some kind of academic on a summer break. She had almost decided that he was a teacher, at a private school probably.

'I – er—' Callum was thrown by the question. He did not want to tell her his story, or to think about it himself, yet the breezy openness of her manner made him dislike himself for the deception. 'I'm between jobs,' he said finally.

Jez gave him a long, level stare. Finally she shrugged and turned back to her stewpot.

'Aren't we all?' she said coolly. 'Pass the carrots over. Lovely. Thanks.'

Later that night, while *Miranda* wallowed aimlessly beneath the Iberian stars, Susie's flight touched down at Gatwick airport. She had phoned home as soon as she got a standby seat, and as she came through the barrier, pale and tired with her awkward new suitcase, she saw her brother. Francis was standing amid the relatives and the chauffeurs with their placards, a pink streak vivid across the darkness of his hair. He stepped forward, took her case and put an arm round her shoulders; Susie was as tall as he was.

'Come on,' he said. 'Let's go home.'

Tears sprang to her eyes, and she bowed her head and shook it with a gruff, 'Right.' When they were in Francis' little Renault, he looked at her in the dim light of the multistorey car park and said softly, 'You OK, Sooze?'

'Drive!' she said. 'Just drive. Thanks.' Then, when he had negotiated the roundabouts and got on the fast homeward road, she asked in a small voice: 'Are Mum and Dad home?'

''Fraid so,' said Francis. 'I told them not to wait up, though.'

'Thanks,' she said again. Then, explosively, 'Jesus, Francis! I feel a fool. A complete idiot. Is that wrong?'

'No,' said Francis. 'Inaccurate, but not wrong. Look, Callum's been weird for months. When I used to go and see him in the hospital, it was obvious he wasn't himself. It isn't anything to do with you. He just can't stand the idea of being lame.'

'Other people cope!' said Susie, and a little of her old briskness was creeping back into her tone. It was good to discuss this with Francis: possible, in a way she knew it would not be with her parents. 'Harry said so – he obviously thought Cal was out of order.'

'Oh, Harry!' Francis broke in with real anger, and his profile was pale and peaked against the sodium lights of the motorway. 'Harry has got as much imagination as a roll of khaki webbing!'

'We've all got imagination,' persisted Susie, who was trying hard not to cry again. 'But you just have to handle things. Get on with life, whatever life you've got left. I mean –' she struggled, almost choking, staring at the damp windscreen before her – I wasn't injured but I was *there*, I know what it was like, I saw people dead, I know how you sometimes felt it was pointless and cruel and—' She could not go on. A few moments later, into the comforting gentle silence her brother left her, she said: 'Francis, I really, really tried to make things easy for him – but he wouldn't even – he didn't touch me—'

Francis glanced at her. 'Poor Sooze. Don't tell me, don't tell me, you'll regret it.'

'Why did he run away? Why?' Her tears made her snort; she ran the sleeve of her crumpled cotton jacket across her face. 'Francis, he left me a hundred Euros to buy a new wheelie-bag. Can you imagine? As if I was someone he'd just been staying with for the weekend!'

'He wasn't thinking straight,' said Francis, but a pulse of anger beat in his pale temples. 'I like old Callum, but he isn't a great one for social graces. It's the Ulsterman in him. I suppose he just lost it.'

'Lost it!' said Susie angrily. 'Well, he has now.'

'It was nice of you to ring Pat,' said her brother. 'That was really – chivalrous.'

'Chivalry!' she said bitterly. 'We had a guest lecturer at Sandhurst once. We were all so tired we could hardly keep our eyes open in the evenings, but I liked this guy. He was a historian. He gave a definition of chivalry – "the courtesy of the strong towards the weak". I liked that.' She scowled, and the tears were really gone now. 'Not exactly Callum's strong point. A hundred Euros! I felt like a tart!'

'Poor old Callum,' said Francis, more to himself than to her. 'I suppose he couldn't do chivalry any more, once he stopped feeling like one of the strong. Hard to be a gentle-man when you don't feel like a man, even.'

'I don't want to talk about it,' said his sister, rather belatedly.

13

Two days later Francis found his sister alone in the garden, scuffing along the path by the rhododendrons, nudging at a huge snail with the tip of her shoe.

'Leave it alone,' he said, coming up behind her.

Susie did not start or turn, but merely said in a flat dry voice: 'I'm not hurting it.'

'How do you know how a snail feels? They have their dignity, you know. It's probably using its whole brain and heart and soul to slime along the path, it's probably *proud* of sliming to such a high professional standard, and now you're upsetting it and buggering up its karma.'

'What d'you want, Francis?' She turned, and in her thin drawn face her eyes were huge and hot. She had been crying, he saw, and his heart went out to her. He wanted to hug her as he had when she was a little girl, to make her laugh, to bring on that choking giggle of outraged mirth which he had always been able to command in his earnest strait-laced little sister. Instead, he merely said: 'Well, the thing is that I have to slime off along my own chosen path tomorrow. I've got a gig.'

'Oh, good!' She showed a little animation now, for it was an old instinct with her to worry about Francis' rickety career, and to want for him what he wanted for himself. She smiled a little. 'I was wondering why you were lurking around at home when I got back.'

'Sixty per cent brotherly devotion, forty per cent pure funk. Stage fright. I actually turned down two gigs last weekend.'

Shaken right out of her sorrow, Susie stared at him in amazement. 'Bloody hell! You *never* turn down work!' 'Bottled out,' he said with studied lightness. 'I had a bad time at a pub. Missiles, abuse, everything triple-strength. Really nasty. I should have gone out straight away next day – somewhere, anywhere, open-mic night, busking, anything at all. Get back on the horse after it's bolted.'

Susie nodded gravely, her eyes on his face.

'But I licked my wounds a bit too long, and when Jarvis rang wanting me to cover the surprise guest spot at the Gay Goat, I said I was busy, and came home to Mum.'

'But they *love* you at the Gay Goat!' she protested. 'You said last Christmas that it was your favourite audience.'

Francis turned his attention to the snail, which had withdrawn its head and horns and lay unmoving on the path.

'Get on, you stupid bugger!' he said. 'Someone'll tread on you there!' He picked it up with decision, and dropped it into a bush. 'I know,' he said. 'I told you, I bottled out. They might not have loved me this time, and if the Goat turns nasty on you, that's it.'

'Just after one bad night?' said Susie incredulously. 'And all the good ones you've had?'

'It was extra bad,' he said. 'Got to me. But thank God for Jarvis, bless his evil little heart, he rang again. I heard the welcome creaking of his leather jacket down the phone and took it as a Sign. They want me tomorrow, and then I'm doing the Comedy Store on Sunday, and then on Tuesday I'm going back to the *Frog in Waders*. The one I died at.'

'Why? If they're so horrible? They might freak you out again.'

'Different act. Arnie rang up pretending to be Jarvis, and sold it to the witless idiot who runs the pub under a false name, for cash. I'm going to do the Kelly Kinko, leathers and all, and drown the bastards in obscene gestures and glam-rock-crash-bitch anthems. I'm going to knock 'em dead and moonwalk on the grave.'

His sister looked at him with affection.

'Still got the boots, then?'

'Yup. And the backing-track. And, God willing, I can squeeze into the leathers.'

'Suppose they throw things at you again?'

'Bloody throw them back!'

'Attaboy! Knock 'em dead!'

Francis gave a little caper, bashed an imaginary guitar, and then said with careful lightness: 'What are *you* going to do, that's what I wondered? I mean, it's only a futon under the keyboard, but you could come up to London and stay at my pad for a couple of days – I'd even take you to the Frog as a sort of military escort – you could wear your uniform . . . think of yourself as my *equerry*. It'd do you good to see a real enemy mob after all those soft Iraqis.'

Susie shook her head. 'Nope,' she said. 'It's a nice thought, and it's sweet of you, but I rang up today and managed to speak to my CO. They're quite short of people, as I thought, and our regiment's got to provide someone to do recruiting in the North East. They wanted someone who'd been in Iraq, to answer up-to-date questions about war zones, and they wanted a woman. I can't be sent abroad again for a couple of months, so I volunteered.'

'I thought you still had quite a bit of leave left?'

'I do. Wedding leave. Don't need it now, do I?'

Francis twisted a fat head of flowers off the rhododendron

bush beside them, and began scattering its blood-red petals savagely around him on the path. As the discussion returned from his affairs to hers he seemed to lose all his lightness.

'I still think it's a bad idea,' he said baldly. 'Callum might reappear any day. It can't take all that long to sail from Portugal to Scotland. You'll both need to sort things out. He can find you really quickly in London, he's got my number, and you could talk things over without Mum and Dad being around, exuding sorrowful understanding.'

'You don't understand,' said Susie flatly. She took the remains of the rhododendron from him and threw it over the bushes. 'Stop torturing that thing. Francis, it's over. All bets are off. We are not engaged. We are not getting married. That's what he wants, that's what I want, end of story. And I'm not staying here as if I was bloody waiting for him like Mariana at the moated grange. I'm not. We made a mistake. I obviously wasn't someone he could talk to when he was in trouble, and he didn't care enough about me to . . . to . . .' Her voice faded, her big eyes glittered with tears, and she looked away.

After a moment her brother said: 'Will you be OK?'

'Once I'm back with the regiment. Back at work. Then I'll be OK.'

'I suppose he can e-mail you,' said Francis, riskily ignoring her previous statements. 'I'm sure it won't be long. They're probably halfway back by now.'

Susie squared her shoulders and did not answer.

By the flickering, grimy GPS unit over *Miranda*'s chart table, the ship was in fact only two miles closer to the English Channel waypoint than on the day when it had left harbour. Callum appeared to be the only person on board who ever looked at the instrument; Stefan, deprived of wind and surrounded by oily calm sea, seemed content to go through his day as if he were in harbour, working on pieces of broken gear, touching up the varnish here and there, and resting on his bunk for long hours with a dog-eared thriller in German, its cover bearing a brightly coloured picture of a young woman having her dress ripped by a masked Arab. He had been on the same book for three days and never seemed to turn a page, at least while Callum was watching.

The others similarly busied themselves, seeming to find nothing alarming or unusual in their lack of progress. Maarten sometimes tried to make conversation, asking Callum about where he lived and what he did; Erik talked more about women, with crude innuendo thrown constantly at Jez. She remained impervious to this, and went about her tasks with equable good humour. The four nationalities on board used English as a common language, but from time to time Erik and Stefan would talk earnestly in German, and Maarten could clearly follow everything they said and threw in occasional remarks in Dutch. At night, Callum lay in his bunk and heard the low buzz of incomprehensible conversation from the deck – for all the crew slept in cat-naps round the clock, and never settled for the night. He felt oddly soothed and lulled by the sound of humanity, so close and yet relaxingly unconcerned with him.

Jez was Callum's main companion and, as the days went by, his comfort. He was not physically attracted to her: her broad-shouldered sturdiness, solid features and frizz of hair made him forget, most of the time, that she was a girl at all. She seemed to divine that he was in some kind of trouble, and did not question him. As a result, from time to time he let slip more than he intended to.

She now knew, for example, that he had been in Basra. A contemptuous remark from Maarten about the war-mongering Coalition powers and the British Army had stung him into a muddled defence which, he thought later, he did not even particularly believe. Maarten had not completely understood what he said, shrugging and putting it down to mere general patriotism; but Jez was more attuned to English idioms. She put clues together, heard the way that he spoke of soldiers, saw his glance down at his injured leg, and realized the truth. It was twenty-four hours, though, before she asked casually: 'Was it in Iraq that you did your leg in?'

The two of them were scraping potatoes for another dull and meagre meal. Callum finished the one he was working on before replying with a gruff affirmative. Jez in turn scraped a large potato in silence before saying: 'Must be tough. Is it going to get properly better?'

'Never a hundred per cent. Knee's smashed. They've done a sort of replacement but my days of bunny-hops are over.'

They scraped on in companionable silence. Then Jez said: 'What happened?'

Callum hesitated, but she already knew more than he had wanted to tell. Eventually he offered a half-truth.

'House came down on some of us after a fire. Ceiling beam. RSJ sort of thing. It's mainly the knee that's in trouble now.'

'Was it a bombing?'

Callum threw his knife down petulantly on the scarred Formica surface of the galley shelf.

'Look, I don't fucking well want to talk about it. Tell me *your* life story if that's what you want.'

Jez absorbed this graceless verbal blow, and said even-temperedly: 'OK. Here's my life story. Home Counties family.

Dad was a doctor. Pony Club. Scholarship to a minor boarding school. Loved it till the sixth form, then hated it. Full of anorexic fashion victims and people banging on about Oxbridge. Got suspended for smoking. Ran away rather than tell my parents, got a job in a boatyard, got hauled back, pushed into university. Dropped out, spent the winters in another yard sleeping on whichever boat we were working on, and did crew jobs on tall ships in the summers. One year I managed to get to the Caribbean and work afloat all winter. In the end my parents washed their hands of me. I do boat jobs, at sea and ashore.'

'No ambitions?' He had not really been curious about her life, but there was a defiant pathos in her account of it which suited his present mood.

'When I'm twenty-five,' she said, 'which is next year, I get thirty thousand pounds from my grandparents' will. I'll buy a boat and do charter work in the Caribbean.'

'Can you get a boat for that much?'

'In the Caribbean, yeah. And I'm collecting the skills to maintain it. I'll do a skipper's ticket once I get the money. Part of the deal here is that Stefan's teaching me.'

Callum did not, privately, think that he had seen much sign of Stefan teaching anybody anything. But perhaps navigation was better taught while a boat was actually moving. He pulled himself halfway up the galley ladder, looked around at the bland coppery horizon and wondered whether a distant streak of cloud to the west of them boded well.

Dropping back to her level he said to Jez, kindly, 'You sound as if you've got it all worked out.'

'I have.' There was a faint defiance in her tone, as if she knew she lied. She looked at him and seemed to be coming to a decision. 'You sound as if you haven't. Are you going back to the Army?'

Callum was defeated by the frank innocence of her questioning, and did not slap her down again.

'I don't know,' he said. 'That's the honest truth. I don't know. I don't even want this ship to arrive. I want to stay in limbo.'

Jez looked at him with real affection, so real that it startled him and made him blush a little. She seemed to be on the point of saying something, but brushed her hand dismissively across her face instead, and grinned. After a moment's silence she said: 'Well, lucky for you. If you want to be on a boat that goes nowhere fast, you picked the right one.'

'How long do we have food for?' he asked, glancing at the sacks and nets in the galley.

'Three, four weeks. Sugar always gives out first, with Maarten and Erik chucking it in their tea. Erik eats it with a bloody spoon.'

'D'you think he'll use the engine soon?'

Jez hesitated, looking up through the companionway at Stefan's feet where he stood, idly leaning on the wheel, his eyes on the horizon. Then in a low voice she said: 'I told you. I know it's hard to believe, but I don't think we filled up the diesel on São Miguel, and I totally bloody know we didn't in Portugal. There's no money left. He got really stroppy with the charterers when they kept on at him to motor. Erik says he dipped the tank yesterday while Stefan was asleep—'

The skipper had heard his name, and stooped to peer down at his cooks. Jez broke off. When the German had lost interest, Callum muttered: 'I've got money, and I'm going to owe him the rest of my passage. I could pay—'

Jez shook her head. 'No, I mean we probably haven't even got more than a few gallons. Not enough to get back to Portugal. It's wind or nothing. Actually, I rather like it that way.'

For the first time since his precipitate flight from land, he felt a faint pricking of alarm as his sense of self-preservation cut through his nihilistic mood. So he was stuck on this boat, with these strangers, for weeks on end, out on the Atlantic, at the mercy of the wind?

'The wind always comes back,' said Jez comfortably. 'Just roll with it.'

'I wish I'd brought something to read' said Callum.

'I'm sure the boys will lend you some German porn,' said the girl comfortingly, and tipped the potato-water into the narrow sink.

———◆•◆———

14

Francis parked his car, as usual, in the driveway of a tall gloomy house in the outer suburbs. His old Guildhall teacher lived there and did not keep a car of her own. He rapped on the window, whose curtains were never closed, and saw her sitting bolt upright engrossed in a score, fingers beating time, her tea on a ringed and cluttered mahogany side-table and her crutches leaning at her side.

He received only an absent-minded nod. Miss Creadley sometimes wanted a few moments' company or an errand in return for this parking beneficence, but more often she preferred Francis to go away. He turned away from the window with a smile, for the scene was pure Dickens, even down to the long white dress hanging from the picture-rail. An opera costume, presumably: Miriam Creadley's other expertise was in theatrical clothing, and she had indeed made Fanny Fantoni's dress in return for having her kitchen and hallway painted.

Francis' life was a network of such small favours and inconsequential friendships; he was, he thought in his new mood of determined confidence, blessed. The collapse of a few days ago, the tears and clutching of bedclothes, were past. He had crossed the valley of humiliation and sauntered up the slope at the far side. He knew that when he got back to his room there would be the detritus of his misery to deal with: the broken mirror to throw away and the crumpled, ripped costume to mend and clean. He could face that. He had faced worse.

Whistling, skipping a little, he hurried up the road to the station with his overnight bag. The world was good. Life was fun. He remembered his father, when he was a child weeping over a grazed knee, saying, 'Come on, boy. It's a grand life if you don't weaken.' With a giggle he remembered quoting that one day to his friend Arnie, whose life was louche and disgraceful; he had been rewarded with much batting of eyelashes and a murmur of, 'Mmm, but trust me, it's even better if you *do* weaken.'

Susie, thought Francis as he swung himself on to the commuter train, seemed determined not to. He was genuinely dismayed by the setback to her life. It was not a life Francis himself would ever have wanted, indeed it seemed to represent the worst of all worlds: so tight, so responsible and disciplined – and yet so submissive to authority that you had to go off, on some idiot politician's say-so, to a distant and dubious war and never speak a word against it. But he was enough of a soldier's son to admire his sister, and enough of a perceptive brother to see that she would be happiest if she married someone like Callum, rather than anyone from his own world.

He liked Callum, too, in a warily admiring way. During the long weeks when he visited his future brother-in-law in hospital, friends would rib him about it, talking about 'Francis' bit of war work' in no respectful spirit. Francis, for whom the chattering, joking hospital visits were almost as much of a performance as any of his gigs, actually felt much the same about them. Callum had gone off to fight as a British soldier, Callum had been grievously injured trying –

even if vainly – to save a foreign child. He was owed a bit of entertainment. If Francis could function (he put it to himself) as a sort of one-man ENSA, keeping the hero's morale up, that was worth doing. He did it for Susie, but also, in a shy and inarticulate way which he would have denied if accused of it, he had done it for his country.

Now Callum was off his trolley, nuts, running away to sea, leaving mean messages for poor little Susie. Francis scowled furiously across the half-empty carriage as it jolted towards Waterloo, turning over the problem in his mind. Right out of his tree, bloody old Callum, way out of order! Just because he'd got a bad leg and a few burns, to duck out on Susie and leave her that money for the suitcase – ugh! He flushed with vicarious embarrassment. He tried to remember the wording of the note Susie had shown him. *I think we both know it can't work . . . I've gone on the* Miranda, *so I'll be out of the way. You deserve better than me anyway.* He hissed aloud, considerably alarming a neat, pinstriped business-woman who sat opposite. *Deserve better than me!* Lovers who ran away from people always said that. Creeps! It was the oldest, the cheesiest, the most cowardly naff let-down in the lexicon.

His thoughts wandered off then, into his own past; he recalled them with a snap, for there were sorrowful things and confused longings that it was best not to dwell on, lest mirrors get broken and costumes ripped. Callum! He must think about Callum, for Susie's sake. Seriously, why would a man do a thing like that?

'Desperation,' he said, aloud. The woman in the pinstripe suit gave him a startled glance. He grinned.

'Sorry,' he said. 'It's all right, I'm not a care-in-the-community day release. I was thinking really hard about something.'

The woman smiled; she was stoutish, and weary-looking, and had a Penguin Classic open on her lap.

'I hope there wasn't too much desperation in it,' she said.

'It's not my despair. It's another chap's. He's run out on my sister.'

'Oh, dear,' said the woman. The train slowed. 'Well, you get him back. Read him the riot act. Chaps like that have to be kept in line.' She wrenched the door open, grimacing at the stiff handle. Francis jumped up to help, but she was gone; he watched her down the platform, her wide bottom swinging, and felt as he quite often did a pang of pure affection for the human race.

At home, he climbed the stairs, gave a high-five salute to the mournful Sikh who was putting up some poster on the landing, and began to clean up the litter of his own night of despair. When the room was calm and tidy, and he had ascertained that Fanny's flounces needed only a few tacks to tidy them up, he went to a battered tin trunk covered in old rugs which stood against the end wall and which served as a windowseat.

Throwing the rugs aside, he pulled it open and fingered the bundles of clothes rolled in it. With a slight shudder of distaste he hauled out a leather catsuit with heavy industrial zips up the front, and Susie's old boots. Fossicking further into it, he pulled out a straight black wig, witchy in its dishevelment. He pulled it on over his pink-and-black hair and looked into the largest remaining fragment of the mirror, practising a twisted sneer. Picking up the electric guitar which leaned against the keyboard, he slung it over his shoulder and began to strut up and down the narrow patch of unimpeded floor, muttering, 'Thass neat, thass neat, wanna see your tiger feet.' Then he giggled, threw the guitar down, and fell backwards on the bed, arms spreadeagled, still smiling.

'"Ours not to reason why,"' he said aloud. '"Ours but to do or die!"' And then, more thoughtfully, 'It's a grand life if you don't weaken.'

The relief of being back in uniform was almost overwhelming. It was, thought Susie, as if the very clothes around her formed an exoskeleton, holding her upright, trim and decisive. She drove the truck northwards with real pleasure, enjoying the unemphatic gentle greenness of an English summer, forgetting Iraq and Portugal alike. Her colleague was a bright, keen young Geordie called Kevin, and as they drove they discussed the logistics of assembling and striking their new recruiting-stand at a series of schools, agricultural shows and county fairs across the North of England. They would have considerable help from Catterick and Preston barracks for the big shows, but for the first few days they were to visit schools to impress children fresh out of their summer exams.

'I loved the County show when I was a kid,' said Kevin. 'Used to love scratching the pigs' backs. I lived up the scabby end of Newcastle, and it was the only time we saw any animal that wasn't a dog or a cat.'

'I suppose I could let you have half an hour or so of pig-scratching, Corporal,' said Susie. 'But we're going to be quite busy on the stand. They're bringing a gun across from the Bellerby range, did you know? We'll have to stop kids climbing all over it.'

'What is it, an AS90?'

'Dunno. More likely a towed one, FH- whatsit?'

'I thought they scrapped the FH70. Just about the time I was training.'

'Well, they might have kept one just for agricultural shows!'

'Nah, they wouldn't, would they? Show off old kit, I mean? Those FAs are big boogers, though, ma'am. Think we'll need more netting? Are we supposed to camouflage it?'

'There's two more rolls in the back of the vehicle,' said Susie.

To talk harmless shop with this keen, uncomplicated boy was balm. Slowly, her assumed holiday identity as careful nurse and anxious helpmeet washed away from her, and she became a clean-cut energetic woman of action again. She stretched luxuriously in the driver's seat, and Kevin noticed and said: 'Shall I take the wheel again, ma'am?'

'After we stop for lunch,' she said. The boy looked around him.

'I know a good pub,' he said, 'if you turn off twenty miles or so north of Birmingham. I don't think we've passed it.'

'You know this bit of the country, then?'

He laughed.

'Last time I was up here I was setting fire to piles of dead cows in the foot-and-mouth. The macaroni cheese at the pub was the only good thing about it.'

'You're on.' The khaki vehicle rolled northward, its canvas sides fluttering gaily against their strapping, its crew in perfect, undemanding accord. After lunch, at the wheel, Kevin began to talk about his fiancée, and Susie felt herself in danger of thinking about Callum; but resolutely she closed her eyes and indicated that she meant to sleep.

Back at home, Marion and Richard walked together in the garden, Richard occasionally stooping to pick up a snail or large black slug from the path and throw it over into the field beyond the hedge. He did not like to kill anything; this gentleness had long been a source of ribald mockery from his troublesome son.

'There is nothing inconsistent,' Richard would say reprovingly, 'in being a soldier and not wanting to kill things. Soldiers don't want to kill people, they want to defend them.'

'But the snails are at war with your plants', Francis would tease. 'Surely a pre-emptive strike . . . ?' Yet he did not kill snails, either.

Now, Richard and his wife walked peacefully, inspecting their flower borders, desultorily discussing whether to replace the sagging garden bench with something new and expensive in green oak.

'It's not as if we sat on it often,' said the careful Marion.

'Susie did, when she was home,' said Richard. 'I saw her out here quite a lot, thinking.'

Marion frowned, and for a moment smoothed and patted the back of the old bench as if it were itself a troubled child.

'D'you think they've really broken up for good?'

Susie had told her, the night before she left, that the engagement was formally over. She had not shown them the note, as she had Francis: the shame of it was too much to share with a parent.

'I hope not,' said Richard heavily. 'I do like that young man. And Pat has no idea, she thinks he's just having a rest cure at sea because Susie had to report for duty.'

'Well, someone's going to have to tell her,' said Marion, perversely glad of the opportunity to be annoyed rather than merely sorrowful. 'Susie should have. But I suppose she thought it was Callum's business to tell his mother. Wherever he is.'

Gloomily the parents walked on, reflecting separately on the complication of sundering two families which had seemed to be on the verge of becoming intertwined for ever. Did they have a duty to Pat, who had become a species of friend, a future co-grandparent? Did Susie? Or did it all rest with the invisible, untraceable, seafaring Callum?

'I wish there was an *etiquette* manual about these things,' said Marion pettishly. Then, 'Oh, God, I sounded just like Francis when I said that.'

Richard smiled. 'He's back on form, anyway.'

'Do you think so? I thought he was absolutely sweet with Susie, but he didn't look right when he first came home.'

'Something'll have happened. But I reckon he got over it. He was very chirpy the other night.'

'Dear Frankie,' said his mother, who only rarely reverted to her son's nursery name. 'I do hope he settles down some-time. Finds a home.'

Richard said nothing for a moment. He read a great deal in the newspapers these days about the importance of 'coming out' and the acceptable normality of 'gay' relation-ships. He had long assumed that his son would never develop an interest in women, and wished that Marion – who probably suspected the same, in his view, unless she was stone blind – would come out with it and discuss the matter.

But she never had, and Francis had never done this 'coming out' business that the papers wrote about, or volunteered any information at all on the subject. Certainly he dressed up in flounces and bows and sang saucy songs falsetto, but that, Richard judged, was a purely theatrical matter. He had slipped into a performance once in Winchester, unnoticed in his dark parka at the back of the pub; he'd thought it highly polished and rather amusing, in a music-hall sort of way. Marion had never seen Francis perform, not that he knew of anyway.

'Frankie's all right,' said his father at last. 'Got a lot of grit.'

'They've got to find their own way,' said Marion mournfully. 'Same with Susie and Callum. Whatever's going to happen, will happen. Or not.'

Richard glanced at her with a flash of sly amusement. They had been married long enough for half their conversations to be unspoken.

'You're right,' he said. 'It's a bugger. It's much harder than when they were children and we called the shots.'

'Much harder,' agreed his wife. 'Oh, well. Anyway, the bench – ?'

15

North of the Azores the summer high-pressure system set up its habitual whirl of clockwise winds, nudging against the fringes of a deep depression which hung over Spain from the Picos Mountains to Andalucia. In that hot summer the Iberian low deepened, and the air between the two systems squeezed into a fast northerly airstream. Winds from north-east to north-west accelerated, whipping thousands of square miles of sea into white-streaked peaks and ridges. Rolling towards Europe, pressing into the stubborn grey low, the great wheel of air gained speed, humping salt water into waves which tipped over the edges of the Continental Shelf to break in troubled, roiling explosions of foam. As the fronts approached trouble lay written in the sky for sailors to read; it was at dawn that Stefan stood by the wheel of the *Miranda* and ordered the sails reefed hard down.

The little ship was not yet overpressed; she lumbered along at three or four knots on a north-westerly course in barely fifteen knots of wind, making slow progress through a threatening, disproportionately heavy swell. But Maarten and Erik had felt the unease of her movement during the few hours that they slept; on Stefan's shout they raised no questions but scrambled from their berths half-dressed, pulled on boots and began to haul down the outer jib while the skipper loosed its heavy sheets.

Jez, at the wheel, looked upward with pale pinched features; she had steered since just after midnight in a steady, depressing drizzle and a rising sea, and was feeling weary, sick and apprehensive. She had sailed for thousands of miles, and loved the sea more than anything in her life, yet still there would be in each voyage one night like this, when primitive fear and physical debility closed in on her. '"Thy sea so great, my boat so small,"' she muttered, for her upbringing had been religious. '"Have mercy on us."' Then a modern sense of shame made her flush briefly, and glance around to see if anybody had noticed. She wondered whether any of the others prayed; not Maarten and Erik, certainly, and it was hard to imagine the granite-faced Stefan murmuring a humble plea to any deity. Callum, perhaps . . .

He rose in front of her from the companionway, wearing a ripped old black oilskin jacket over his jeans and sweater; it had belonged to some former crewman, and he must have found it thrown into the bottom of the wet-locker.

'OK?' he said. 'I heard Stefan call all hands.'

'You don't have to come up,' she said.

'I could take a spell on the wheel,' said Callum, nettled.

'Well – in a minute perhaps.' She was looking forward now, watching the men fight to pull down the big mainsail to its smallest size and bundle in the fat brown reefs; she steered carefully to keep the ship steady as the sail reduced, working to minimize the risk of the boom jerking suddenly against its restraints as the three men leaned across it, tying their reef-knots. Callum stood beside her, steadying himself on the rail, looking around at the tossing sea and the angry orange dawn, glancing down at the compass, trying to get the picture. The wind was stiffening even as he watched, and under the small mainsail and jib the boat heeled suddenly and sharply to port then wallowed upright, though not before a large wave had slapped her side and sluiced across the deck, soaking Callum's and Jessica's trousers to the knee.

Stefan looked up from his task near the mast and shouted something to Jez. She raised an arm in assent and said to Callum: 'Yup, could you take her a minute? We've got to get the mizzen off, it's pulling us all over the place now we're off-balance.'

Callum came to the wheel; he could see the problem and immediately felt it through the kicking wheel. With the other sails reduced, the full mizzen was taking control of the ship. The wind hardened minute by minute; he could hardly hold the course. Jez was bending to loose off a halyard, and he felt a slight slackening of the pressure on the wheel as the mizzen-sail began to climb down its mast in fluttering brown wrinkles. Then the sail was down, the boat rocking more violently, and before he saw what was happening the girl had swarmed above his head like a monkey up a tree, and was balancing astride the bucking mizzen-boom, leaning over to gather up the sail and tie it to the boom. The steering would matter, in the next few minutes; he locked his knee straight, willing the leg to hold him against the movement of the boat.

The men were finishing the mainsail, and then Erik and Maarten went forward to roll up the discarded outer jib with some difficulty and stuff it down the forehatch. Callum kept glancing back; he wished that one of them would come and help Jez with her task, as she shuffled along the mizzen-boom, bundling and tying the sail. The steering was easier now, but what the girl was doing two feet beyond the stern of the rushing boat and out over the water did not look to him like a task for one person alone. He glanced down, and checked that the mizzen-boom was properly restrained, if a little loosely, and could not swing far either way. He tried to work out how to tighten it, but even as he did so a particularly violent jerking wave put a bight of slack into one of the restraining preventer-lines, and then tugged it sharply out again as the ship came upright. The line did not break; but the heavy teak cleat to which it was attached pulled clean away from the deck and whizzed past Callum's startled face, to clack and rattle against the mast.

Freed, the mizzen-boom began to jerk and swing wildly; the girl slipped and fell forwards, her arms wrapped desperately round the boom as she began to slither sideways with the bundle of sail. Callum could see that the only way to calm the mizzen was to tighten its sheet, but he could not reach the line without letting go the wheel, and did not trust his leg to support him in any hurry. There was one other way to do it: instinctively he twisted the helm hard to port, so that the wind still bearing on the boom pulled it hard out against the sheet, the broken cleat dangling over the rail. This stilled its jerking; against the sound of the sea he heard a faint 'Shi-it!' from Jez, and turned to see that she was hanging under the boom, half over the rounded sternrail and half over the water. *If she went in now*, he thought, *there'd be no chance at all.* There was a life-ring next to him; he decided that if she fell he would throw it, let go the helm, and dive to push the man-overboard button on the GPS. If it worked.

Nausea swept over him; but in the same moment Jez wriggled violently back along the mizzen-boom and unclasped her legs, dropping them just inboard with a clatter. Now he turned from the wheel, trusting the ship for a moment, and threw his arms round her waist as she hung there; staggering backwards as she let go her grip on the boom, Callum pulled her inboard.

They sat together, panting, on the deck; it was Jez who first reached for the spokes of the wheel and corrected the galumphing, violent course of the little ship through the waves. She pulled herself up, and put out a hand to haul him to his feet as she steered with the other.

'That came up quickly,' she said in an unsteady voice.

'The cleat pulled off,' said Callum, hardly calmer than her. 'It carried away when she rolled.'

'I bet there isn't a backing-plate.' Jez masked her slowly ebbing terror in irritation. 'Everything done on the cheap.'

The men were returning from the main deck now, Stefan glancing up at his reduced sails, eyes darting everywhere, checking for sources of trouble. The orange gleam of sunrise had vanished behind slate-grey cloud, but it was light enough for Callum to see the fatigue in the captain's seamed face.

'Is going to blow,' he said, though he rarely volunteered any remark to his paying passenger.

'Yes.'

'You know sea weather, *ja*?'

'Quite well. I've done more coastal sailing than open ocean, but the seas look as if there's something quite big out to the west.'

'*Ja*. We haf sea-room. It is not a problem.'

Stefan vanished below, followed by Maarten, and Erik the big Dane came over to the wheel and took it from Jez. The boat was moving faster now, climbing each wave and sliding rapidly down the far side under her small sails; the wind rose higher every minute, screaming in the rig.

'Thanks, Erik. I'll make some breakfast,' shouted Jez, and moved stiffly towards the companionway. Callum followed her, and when they were in the comparative quiet of the big saloon, he asked: 'Did you hurt yourself when you came off the boom?'

'Bruises,' said Jez shortly. 'Porridge?' She limped across the saloon, holding on to the big table, and strapped herself into the webbing belt in the galley, before starting to clatter the pots and pans and the big grey tin of porridge oats which was lashed to the bulkhead by a piece of fraying shock-cord. Clinging to the bucking boom, she had looked down at the waves, felt and tasted them as the foam flicked upward round her face and hair. She had gazed at death. Her arms ached from the sudden convulsive grasp which had saved her; a cold and deadly and wholly inappropriate sense of shame paralyzed her more rational feelings.

She knew, from past experience, that the shaming fear would pass away and leave her calm again. Terror was an old seafaring acquaintance, as old as exhilaration and exaltation. For the moment, though, she did not want her private weakness exposed to this near-stranger.

Callum failed to understand any of this, and continued with solicitude: 'Seriously, I could make the porridge. You ought to rest for a moment, you were steering for hours and cold muscles damage easily.'

'Oh, piss off!' cried Jez in helpless rage. For a moment, across the heaving galley shelf, they glared at one another and despite the grime and weariness on their faces, each saw something new and felt a treacherous, faint squeak of attraction. Both flushed a little; Callum backed away, confused and horrified, and sat on the saloon bench listening to the ship's strained creaking and looking in any direction but hers. Eventually he said as lightly as he could: 'Sorry. It's the first-aid training. Can't shake it off.'

Jez, glad to sweep the moment away, laughed at him with forced ease and busied herself with the porridge. Outside, beyond hundreds of miles of heaving sea, the lines of pressure squeezed closer, and between the depression and the nudging anticyclone, a stream of cold air accelerated from the north.

Francis sat on the edge of his bed, rolling tights carefully over his toes and up his elegant legs. A friend of his, known generally as Arnie but christened Eric Jolyon Pratt by long-ago suburban parents, lounged on a denim beanbag, watching.

'People *think*,' said Francis petulantly, 'that men in drag enjoy putting on tights. If they but knew.'

'Some of them do,' said Arnie judiciously. 'It's the tightness, see. Chiffon Elvis—'

'Yeah, but he's a recreational trannie,' said Francis. 'I mean, doing Elvis with floaty bits is the nearest he gets to dressing as a bloke, ever. With me it's strictly business. I wouldn't wear tights for anything if I didn't have to.'

'Why *do* you have to wear tights, for Kelly the Kink?' asked Arnie. 'She wears biker leathers, doesn't she?'

'Can't get the bloody trousers on unless I put on something slippery,' said Francis. 'It's like when you're putting on wetsuit trousers for scuba. You put your foot in a plastic bag and they slide on lovely. With leathers you can either wear proper slithery silk-mix tights – which, let me tell you, these *are*, and they cost twenty quid – or else you have to slather yourself in so much bloody talc that when you take them off it's like a sweaty greasy white snowstorm . . .'

'Ugh, ugh! Stop!' said Arnie. 'Too much information, dear. But, yuck. I mean, do girls have to do that?'

'They've got less hairy legs.'

'Usually, anyway. You've got very choice legs, if I might say so.' He blew a kiss.

'Wasted on an unappreciative world. They only ever get an airing when I do South Seas Sadie.' Francis shimmied his tights into a more comfortable conformation, and reached for the leathers.

The two young men had been friends for three years. Arnie was extravagantly, cheerfully, promiscuously gay, and worked more or less menially in a theatrical management agency. This organization, Gigz, had briefly signed Francis after a successful show in Soho and had promised him great things before a change of policy saw him dropped from their list without warning. Arnie, who thought Francis' act was much more promising than his bosses could see, came round the same day that the agency rang him, banged on the door and handed him a bottle of champagne.

'Because you're worth it,' he had cooed, and Francis' stiff disappointed face had relaxed into giggles. Since then Arnie had made a point of cultivating Francis' friendship, attending his gigs and passing on to him various highly useful pieces of inside information on which of the comedy and variety venues were scratching around for new musical acts. It was Arnie who had introduced him to the pub booker, Jarvis. There had been the inevitable pass, as automatic to Arnie as a handshake; it had been rejected with graceful politeness, and now the pair of them co-existed in an amicable, squabbling, jokey and wholly celibate friendship.

Francis pulled on the leather trousers, wriggled his bare chest into a cotton T-shirt and added the jacket, buttoning and zipping it down to create a catsuit. Then he crouched, jumped, lunged like a fencer and wriggled his hips, testing the resilience and fit of the material.

'Thank Christ, that fits,' he said. 'Now, boots!'

He stamped up and down the room, testing the heels, winced a little at the narrowness of the toes and picked up an electric guitar on whose stem was perched the dishevelled black wig. Rounding on Arnie he snarled, banged the guitar to the floor, stamped and shouted: 'Yayeeee! Are ya readyeee?'

'*Terrifying*, darling,' said his friend languidly. 'And you're really going to do that to the poor morons at the Frog in Waders?'

'I am. I have scores to settle,' said Francis. 'Come on, let's get there.'

'Put your wig and make-up on here,' said Arnie. 'Or he'll recognize you.'

'Witless? Never!' But Francis hastily made up his face, pale base setting off blood-red lipstick and heavy black false lashes. 'Oh, God, I hate going out in the street in slap. I feel like a bloody rent boy. But I suppose you're right.'

'You can get straight into the car. It's almost opposite. Bring your proper clothes, it docsn't matter if he recognizes you afterwards.'

'Thanks.'

In the car Arnie turned to Francis, who was squinting into the sunvisor's mirror with some distaste, and said: 'You really don't like Kelly, do you? Not your sort of girl any more?'

'I like doing Fanny,' said Francis mournfully. 'And South Seas Sadie. Sweet stuff. I suppose I like fantasy and musicals and romance more than crude rock.'

'You can't sell fantasy and romance to the Frog's clientele.'

'Nope. You have to be cruder than crude to penetrate their sensibilities.' Francis flipped the mirror away from him, out of temptation's reach. 'Arn, I haven't said thanks properly.

It's sweet of you to do the driving and the music and pretend to be my roadie.'

'I wouldn't,' said Arnie, 'miss this for worlds. And if ever a man needed a getaway car with the engine running, it's you. I think you're bloody mad. You don't *have* to go back to a bad audience. Screw them, I say.'

Arnie's battered little car threaded its way through South London towards the pub, and Francis put a damp hand to his leather bosom, to see whether the hammering of his heart could be felt from outside.

16

It was on the second day of the gale that the *Miranda* began to take in water. She was, of course, an elderly boat and always took in a little; as a rule the electric bilge pump hummed decorously for a quarter of an hour every five or six hours, in obedience to its sensor deep in the bilge. It ran for even less time in calm weather, unless heavy rain found its way below. In the two years that Stefan had commanded her he had never had to ask a crew member to pump by hand; during this storm his mind was far more preoccupied with weaknesses in the rig above his head than with potential swamping from below.

But after a wild wet night labouring to windward against a northerly gale, the twisting and pounding of *Miranda*'s progress began to force the Edwardian planks of her hull apart and ajar. The electric pump's motor lay close behind the bulkhead of Callum's bunk; resting below in the second wild dawn, he became aware that the high-pitched whine of the machine had been on for longer than usual. He snapped awake. Hauling himself out of the berth, he made his way cautiously round to the saloon where Jez sat with her hands round a mug of tea. Her hair was straightened into an unfamiliar thatch by repeated soakings of salt water, and her grimy woollen hat lay on the table in front of her dribbling moisture from its saturated fibres.

'Had a couple of big ones over,' she said briefly, indicating the hat. 'It's really sloppy up there.' As if to confirm this, an explosive Danish oath floated down to them from Erik, who had tied himself on to the binnacle with a rope round his waist.

'The bilge pump's running,' said Callum. She cocked her head and listened, trying to discern the familiar whine amid the confusion of creaking, rattling, howling and whistling from the boat and the wind.

'So it is,' she said. 'Been going long?'

'It was running when I came below at four,' said Callum. 'And I don't think it's actually stopped.'

Jez glanced at the battered brass clock. 'Nearly six,' she said. 'Better have a look.'

She pushed her mug into his hand for safekeeping, for the boat was heeling hard to port and jerking violently. Then she slid from the bench on to the floor, and crawling aft under the big table, found a floorboard into which was set a little folding brass ring. Flipping it up, she pulled sharply, and peered into the darkness. There was not enough light filtering down from the bleak dawn to illuminate the hole.

'Torch?' she said. 'It's in the clip by the galley hatch.'

Callum passed it to her, switching it on as he did so, and was distracted by a heave of the boat which threw his painful leg against the corner of the table. Recovering, rubbing the knee as he steadied himself on the bench, he heard a sharp banging noise and an exclamation of, 'Holy shit!' Looking down, he saw that the banging had been made by the girl's head hitting the underside of the table as she jerked upright; she was kneeling bent over now, rubbing it and cursing.

'What?'

'Look!' Jez shone the torch into the hole; even from where he stood he could see the dark, slopping water.

'Pump's not doing much good,' he said, keeping his voice level. 'Think it's blocked?'

'Nope. We'd hear if it was choked. I think it's just over-worked. Get Stefan, quick.'

The skipper rose from his bunk as fast and alert as if he had not been sleeping at all. A moment later he called harshly: 'Maarten, deck pomp! Jez and – er – you!' He never gave Callum his name. 'Cabin pomp! Now!'

Scrambling on deck, he bent to loosen the main and jib sheets and ordered Erik at the wheel: 'Run off!' Erik spun the wheel until *Miranda*'s bows lay at right angles to the wind and her boom slanted diagonally away from the direction of her travel. Palpably, her speed increased; glancing down, Erik saw that despite the tiny reefed sails they were moving at seven knots. The motion remained as violent, almost more so now that the heavy listing of the boat away from the wind had stopped. But there was something else, which filled her captain with alarm: she felt heavy despite her speed. She was low in the water and wallowing. Stefan scowled, and hit the cabin-top with the flat of his hand.

'Pomp!' he shouted to the pair in the cabin, where Jez had fitted a long iron handle into a socket beside the stove. 'Quick!' And to Maarten, who was struggling to assemble the deck pump alone while being jerked and thrown from side to side, 'Fast with the deck pomp!'

Maarten looked up, startled and frustrated, lost his footing as the deck beneath him lurched, and slid towards the rail. One hand was still clutching the handle for the pump, the other clawing at any handhold that slid past. With a sicken-ing thud he hit the raised bulwark, snatched at a heavy iron pin in the rail, and fell forwards, his torso half overboard. Erik left the helm and lunged towards him; for a second the Dutchman hung balanced over the spitting waves, then the boat rolled back, throwing him heavily on to the deck. Maarten lay there, sprawled and winded, while his crewmate bent over him and dragged him by his jacket to the comparative safety of the after deck. Sitting up, he groaned and clutched at his side before falling back with a grimace of agony.

The pump-handle was gone, and with it the fitting on the end which connected it to the assembly of the apparatus on deck. Without this smaller piece, it was impossible to press another spar or pipe into service as a handle. Stefan swore. The galley pump was the weaker of the two, and seconds earlier there had been a clanking, choking noise rising to a brief scream and cutting off abruptly to silence: the electric pump had jammed, blocked with some floating detritus from the swilling bowels of the boat. Giving the helm back to Erik with a curt instruction, and ignoring Maarten who lay pallid on the deck, he leapt to the companionway and bellowed down to Jez and Callum.

'Keep pumping! Don't stop! We haf lost the deck pump and the electric! You take watches, *ja*! No stopping!'

'*Ja*,' said Callum. Beside him, Jez was pumping fast and efficiently, taking long full strokes. The degree of emergency was plainer to him even than to the captain, for the galley floor was set slightly lower than the main cabin sole and was already awash: water bubbled up through the cracks and finger-holes in the floorboards and swilled idly around their feet.

'Can you carry on for ten minutes or so, then I'll take over?' he said to the girl, and without speaking she nodded.

Callum grabbed a medium-sized saucepan from the rack, knelt beside her, ripped up the nearest plank and plunged his utensil into the hole. Next to his left hand was the outlet pump for the galley sink; by throwing panfuls of water into the basin by his right shoulder and pumping it out intermittently with his other hand, he could dispose of at least some of the water. It seemed an absurdity, but he could think of no other way of assisting. His knee hurt horribly and cramps stole up his legs, but after a few minutes the galley floor was dry and the level beginning to drop below the floorboards. Running free, the boat was taking in far less water than in the night hours before.

'Old saying,' panted Jez, 'there's no better bilge pump than a frightened man and a bucket.'

'Swop?' he said when she briefly flagged; she nodded, and took his saucepan from him as he stood up with relief, wedged himself in the galley corner and began to pump.

He had time to notice that the violent, urgent activity had lifted the fear which had visibly haunted his companion. It had infected him too, more than he could have admitted at the time. But now she was calm, active, even cheerful. When Maarten crawled below and collapsed on to a bunk, Jez went briefly to attend to him while Callum pumped, and returned, saying, 'Cracked rib, I reckon. He'd better not move for a while.'

On deck, Erik steered on through the wild morning. Up forward, in a narrow damp compartment which jerked and crashed without respite, Stefan fiddled painstakingly with the wiring of the electric pump. After an hour he carefully put his tools aside, came aft to the galley and said curtly: 'You stop. I pomp one hour. You rest. Then Erik, one hour. This *arbeit* with the saucepan is not necessary now.' The water had stopped seeping across the galley floor, and it was clear that the single pump could hold it at bay for a while.

Callum moved away from the handle, thankfully, and sat massaging his leg on the bench. Immersion in icy water had stopped it hurting while he worked, but now the pain returned in full measure. Jez made hot drinks and sawed up a stale loaf, spreading a lump with thick black jam for each of them. Robotic, unemotional, Stefan pumped with long regular strokes, keeping the water level steady – and eventually falling – in the deep dark bilge. After an hour he sent Callum to the helm and Erik to the pump; the four uninjured members of the crew worked hour on hour as the little ship crashed westwards and the day wore on into evening.

Arnie slipped into the back of the crowd at the pub, and with practised ease shimmied towards the bar, sliding easily through the thick-necked, tipsy clientele. It was ten o'clock; a pretty but indifferent girl singer had just been trying to make herself heard over the roar and grunt of general conversation. Cries of 'Get'em off!' and 'Woof-woof' had been only sporadic; the natives, he reassured a shaking Francis in the back room, were clearly not particularly restless tonight.

All the same, Arnie's hands were damp as he took his half-pint from the barman, and he moved back to the far end of the room to be near the door. He could go round and comfort Francis quickly if it became necessary. Arnie grimaced; he was sweating with nerves. It was not like him, not like him at all. Arnie saw himself as a very cool customer. He had seen more pub acts and comedy shows than he could count, assessed them for his employers, given them the bad news and the good, and dashed his share of theatrical hopes. He had grown a thick skin and a keen, merciless judgement. He knew that for the hungry ones who lived on dreams and worked below the level of national fame, of newspaper profiles and TV chat shows, humiliation and poverty were daily companions. He kept his work and his private life as far apart as possible.

But this was different. He had been unprecedentedly touched by the lonely valour of Francis as he dressed in his ridiculous leathers and pulled on the rock-chick wig. The absurdity of the act, of their whole trade, sometimes struck home to the part of Arnie which was still sensible Eric Pratt from Willesden Green. It came to him, not for the first time, that while the comedians' and performers' characters were burlesque fantasies, the pain and rejection they courted were real. He had never seen Francis as shocked and broken as after his last appearance in this pub. He would not, himself, have counselled a return.

'Woof-woof!' shouted a shaven-headed youth in front of him. As Arnie watched appalled, the oaf picked up a half-empty plastic pint glass and hurled it, with drunken accuracy, at the makeshift stage. The girl faltered in her line as the thing hit the microphone stand, but sang on; she was, Arnie noticed, a good deal older than he had at first thought. There was a beaten sadness in her eyes; this, he thought, was not the first missile she had faced. Two of Witless' bouncers moved heavily forward and pulled the bald boy down on to a chair, and Arnie had to shrink back against the wall to avoid his flailing.

They did not, however, throw the drunk out. A moment later he was at the bar, shouting his order at the weary bartender. The woman's song was finished anyway; she left to a faint scatter of applause and rather more boos and raspberries. Arnie's stomach turned over.

Jay Witham was lumbering on to the stage, giving ill-judged high fives and air punches to the contemptuous audience.

'Annow!' he yelled, judging the microphone's direction less than well. 'Weegot – a famous and remarkable rocker, a girl you might say with real balls!' He snickered. 'Liddle Tiger Feet herself – Mizz Kelly Kinko!'

Behind him, a wisp of stage smoke crept along the stage and billowed upwards. The red and orange lights which Arnie had brought with him shone low from the side of the little stage, colouring the wafts of smoke from the machine also borrowed by Arnie. He sighed with relief; Francis had remembered to flip the switches. He would have preferred to do it himself, but his friend had begged him to be out front. 'One friendly face, just one!'

The bright smoke swirled, and the room fell momentarily silent, as they had hoped, while the audience peered with myopic drunken caution at these new phenomena. Then with a crashing chord on the overamplified electric guitar, a lithe black figure leaped sideways onto the stage and stood, legs apart, knees slightly bent, beneath its tousled black wig a pale face motionless but for a snarling lip drawn back in contempt for the world.

'Two, three!' it shouted, and with a disdainful right hand hauled a deafening, twanging wall of sound from the guitar. Smoke and noise shimmered around the singer, and the first high growl, quite unlike Francis' normal light tenor, took his friend aback. 'Yayyyyyy!' cried Kelly the leatherette rocker.

The patrons blinked, stupid with drink and smoke, and then the beat took them; Francis was using a boom-box but it was his hammering of the electric guitar which carried them along: that and his stamping, snarling, strutting, aggressive domination of the stage. He crossed the boundaries, moved too close to the audience; they shrank back from the noise and anger of him. Arnie relaxed little by little, and began to enjoy himself. After the first song the man-woman on the stage went into a riff of fast, angry, mainly sexual jokes, taunting the audience; it was a thousand miles, Arnie thought wonderingly, from Francis' usual whimsical gentleness, and farther still from the plaintive cockney humour of the Fanny Fantoni character. Well, he thought admiringly, the man's an actor. You do what the part requires.

The room was altogether on the singer's side now, stamping and rocking and swaying and laughing with pure appreciation when one of his sallies defeated a front-row drunk. There was no more fear, only an unexpected and incongrous sense of community that was, thought Arnie, something like love. At that moment he loved Francis quite a lot himself: loved the talent, the energy, the taunting courage of the performance. He had a sudden tender memory of the young man sitting on his bed in that narrow room, pulling up the despised silk tights with economical care not to snag them.

Witless was standing open-mouthed beside the stage, savouring his first ever real triumph as an impresario. 'I have the nose for a rising star,' he was saying to himself, practising for a bragging session later. 'You either got it or you ain't.'

When his half-hour was up and his last big number had stamped to a close, Francis raised two fingers to the house and swaggered off the stage with a loud, 'G'night!' The regulars did not like this at all. There was shouting, cries of 'More!' and a slow handclap when the hapless pudgy figure of Witham climbed on stage to read out his future attractions.

He could not be heard; the customers stamped their feet, rattled the tables and banged beer-cans together. 'Kel-ly! Kel-ly!' they cried. 'More!'

Arnie slipped out and down the alley to the back door. He found Francis sitting on a barrel, hot but composed.

'You were amazing,' he said. 'They want more.'

Francis shrugged. 'Done my set,' he said. 'Proved my point. God, these trousers are tight.'

Jay Witham appeared in the doorway.

'Encore!' he said. 'They want you back for another number.'

Francis did not reply. He was looking at his fingernails in a detached manner.

'Come on! Get out there, boy! They love ya!' said the American.

'Why should I?' said Francis. 'They're yobs.'

Witless gaped. Arnie stepped in with all the smoothness of the professional agent.

'Half an hour, you paid for. You had thirty-five minutes.'

'Yeah, but—'

'Hundred quid,' said Arnie. 'Hundred quid bonus for an encore.'

The landlord scowled. Francis turned quickly to his friend and said, 'Anyway, I don't want to—' but Arnie broke in, speaking to Witless slowly, as if to a small dim child.

'See? He doesn't need to. He's doing you a favour even coming here, this boy's a headliner. Hundred and fifty or we go straight home.'

The original fee had been a hundred and fifty pounds, negotiated with some difficulty by Arnie a few days earlier; he had taken over the management of this gig on discovering that Francis was only planning to ask thirty pounds for it, and assisted his case by showing Witless a set of convincing-looking UK and US press cuttings carefully forged on his office computer.

The noise from the bar was now rising, and there was a distinct sound of a chair being smashed against the wall.

'More! More!' shouted the clientele, and Witless nodded.

'Just get out there. Ten minutes or you don't get a cent.'

'Cash,' said Arnie. 'Upfront.' When the landlord had counted out eight twenty-pound notes from the roll in his pocket, Arnie nodded to Francis and said, 'Go get 'em, Tiger.'

'I need a tenner change,' said the American petulantly as the first chords silenced the bar.

'It's the insurance element,' said Arnie, pocketing the bundle of notes. 'I think if you look at the small print . . .'

There had never been any size of print involved in their negotiation. Defeated, the landlord retired. There was no sign of him when, fifteen minutes later, a sweating and exhausted Francis came back to the barrel-store, lugging the smoke-machine and the orange light.

'Get changed, I'll get the kit in the car. We're going up West,' said Arnie. 'To drink to Kelly and her brilliant future.'

'I am never, never doing that show again,' said Francis. 'So don't you dare!'

'Would I?' said Arnie meekly.

Much later, drunk and exuberant, the pair reeled through Leicester Square with arms around each other's shoulders, revelling in the lights and the crowds and the grubby fairground decadence of the summer night. Francis threw a handful of coins down for a young man who sat on the pavement singing scat jazz through a sawn-off traffic cone. Over the lad's meaningless, jovial, boomingly hollow vocalizations he raised his own voice in high counterpoint, and letting go of Arnie's shoulder gave a wild, Bacchante skip on the grimy pavement.

'Showbiz,' he said happily, returning to his friend's side. 'Nobiz like it.'

17

The gale's ending found the crew of *Miranda* exhausted and low in spirits. When the wind eased on the fourth morning Stefan ordered the ship to be hove-to for twelve hours in waves which still humped and swayed with the memory of their torment. The uneasy sea threw Maarten around in his bunk, and he moaned pitifully at every movement until Jez devised a way to lash him down with an old sail. After more pumping, the water-level sank in the bilges and Erik was able to clear the inlet of the electric pump while the skipper replaced the blown fuse. At last it was possible to put away the galley pump-handle; by the end of the day the ship was dry. Soon the wind died right away; the wheel was left lashed unattended, and *Miranda* became mere flotsam.

The skies stayed overcast, with flurries of rain. Callum slept through the morning, Jez through the afternoon; at sunset she made a stew out of tins, adding fresh onions for flavour and stirring in some powdered mashed potato at the end. It seemed to Callum that he had never tasted anything so good. Before eating her own, Jez went and sat on a box beside Maarten's bunk, propping his head and shoulders on a sailbag, carefully spooning the thick stew into his mouth and offering him sips of water; then she helped him carefully to the sea-toilet in the bows and escorted him back to lash him down again with the sail. Under this rough nursing his spirits rose sufficiently for him to make an indecent suggestion to her and have his face very gently, symbolically, slapped.

'He's gonna be OK,' she said, returning to the galley. 'I think he's cracked a rib, but his breathing looks fine. Won't be able to work much, though.'

'Should we get him ashore?' said Callum. 'In Portugal, perhaps?'

'We are closer to Africa,' said Stefan curtly. 'I do not think so. We can go north, soon. The wind will come souwest.'

'How many days to the Channel?' asked Jez, through a mouthful of lukewarm stew.

'Eight, nine, ten days, two weeks,' said Stefan contemptuously. 'It is no use asking me, ask the wind.'

'I'm asking,' said Jez, unruffled, when she had finished her mouthful, 'because of food. I need to check the store and work stuff out. So give me some idea, because I'm not wasting my breath asking the sodding wind.'

Callum hid a smile; he remembered reading somewhere that the only crew members on the old sailing ships who could regularly challenge the captains were the bo'sun and the cook, because they held undisputed sway over vital practical domains.

'OK,' said Stefan grudgingly. 'You make it so we haf food for two weeks and a half, and we go to Scotland without a stop.'

'See about that,' muttered Jez, and after scraping her bowl clean and passing it to Callum to wash, she took herself off to the deep store. Ten minutes later she returned to the swaying saloon where the men were sitting, smoking. Even Callum, who had given up his teenage tobacco habit when he joined the Army, accepted the simple comfort of a roll-up from Erik.

'It's not good news,' said Jez. 'The flour-bins flooded.'

'Rice? Pasta?'

'Not too bad,' she said. 'Tins are OK, obviously. The fruit and veg were high up, thank God, but the potatoes are a bit damp. They'll sprout.'

'We eat them first, then. Fresh water?'

'Fine.' Turning to Callum, she said in politely explanatory tones, 'We usually carry enough for charterers having showers all the time, so that won't be a problem. But no showers for us now.'

Stefan pulled himself up and peered out of the darkening companionway hatch.

'Wind,' he said. 'From sou-west. Make sail.'

Callum took the wheel and gradually, as dark figures moved around the boat's length and each of the five great sails climbed aloft, he felt the strength of the little ship returning. A great white moon rose, and the clouds cleared to a starry night. When Stefan and Erik had retired below for a few hours' nap, he and Jessica stood side by side, listening to the hiss and rush of the water past the hull and watching the swaying curve of the headsails against the glittering night.

For a long time they said nothing, each wrapped in private contentment. Then the girl said softly: 'Glad you came?'

'Yes,' said Callum. He turned to her, smiling in the darkness. Jez hesitated, then leaned across the edge of the wheel, put a hand on his shoulder and kissed him. Taken by surprise, touched at a deep animal level by the unexpected tenderness after heavy physical exertion, he leaned into the warmth of her breasts and kissed her back, briefly. As he did so a wave of something like horror overtook him: Susie's presence, Susie's body, Susie's fearless love, came back to him in their entirety. A turmoil of shame rose in him for the first time since he had left her. He drew back and looked away from the girl, forward into the night.

Jez did not move away, nor sense his trouble. She stood for a while peacefully at his side, then said in the same soft voice: 'Starry, starry night.'

Callum flinched inwardly, his dismay growing, the bright night ruined. The boat, unconscious, drove on northward.

Susie lay in her narrow bed in Catterick, staring at the circle of dim light the lamp cast on the ceiling, her book unread in her hand. She was physically weary, after two school visits on consecutive days and another afternoon spent haggling over the recruiting stand's position at a country fair. Her stomach had troubled her intermittently ever since Iraq, and reacted uneasily to almost every food, bringing on violent transient cramps which it took all her self-discipline to conceal. As a result she ate little, and the bones of her hips jutted alarmingly beneath her nightshirt; she did not like to feel the knife-edges of her skeleton, and rucked the thin army blankets double over them even in the hottest July nights.

Her heart ached, too. The proud and active anger of the first days after Callum's desertion had ebbed, leaving her with a flat grey sadness. She could no longer cheat her memories, and finally, one night in the darkness of the small hours, she admitted to herself without subterfuge that she had not been deceived from the beginning, and that she was not, as she had been trying to persuade herself, well rid of Callum. They had loved one another very much. It had been real.

Love had cast a golden glow of optimism over both their futures. They had shared an invincible hope; together they had been strong, able to face separation and the terrors of war with light and gallant hearts. The love they once had was a jewel.

But they had lost it. Love was not invincible after all, then; not strong, not proof against the misfortunes of war and the angry pain of convalescence. She had tried, really tried her best, to smooth his way to recovery. And he would have recovered, Susie told herself with a spurt of resentment: not perhaps to full military fitness but to far better condition than many, and he still had his life and brains. The way he carried on was bad form, unmilitary – what had Harry Devine said? – 'acting up'. Bad news came only sporadically in the television reports from Iraq now, but still it came. Every death or maiming made Susie sorrowful and angry in a way that her colleagues did not entirely understand. The reason was, of course, Callum. God damn him! Could he not have shown some courage after the event, as well as during it? Courage enough, at least, to stay with her? Shouldn't a soldier hold fast with every nerve and brain and sinew? Wasn't that the whole point of the life they had chosen?

And now he was at sea. She despised herself a little for doing it, but nonetheless each night on the Officers' Mess TV she watched the weather pattern off Portugal, and saw the Atlantic high moving in, squeezing the isobars off that ragged coast. The wind would be against them, for sure. It would be rough. She imagined the weather out there as a magnified version of the holiday gales they had endured together on smaller boats in the Minch; on nights when sleep evaded her entirely, she would close her eyes briefly only to jerk awake at a vision of Callum drowned, Callum's ship sinking, Callum stepping over the side deliberately, courting a dark sea-death. *Better off without me*. Francis read that line as a cowardly lover's excuse; Susie in her darkest moments understood it only as a suicide note.

On this night, though, the isobars on the weather bulletin had slackened, and she slept and had for once a peaceful dream. She had eaten nothing since breakfast, and pure weariness floated her away until she dreamed of a moon and stars and a silvered ocean, empty to the horizon.

In the morning, Corporal Kevin met her as usual with a broad smile and a salute, and the news that a team of PT instructors in training were joining them at the show: 'To do a demonstration, like.'

'Oh, hell,' said Susie wearily. 'Are they wanting to rig an assault-course? Because we sent the nets and poles and tyres on to Newcastle.'

'Nah, I told them that. They reckon just to do a log-run. They've got a four-man log they can bring on the truck.'

'Hot weather for that,' Susie grimaced, but the Corporal gave a foxy smile.

'Very fashionable, ma'am, is hot weather work. Blame Saddam.'

When they got to the showground the first members of the PTI team were already there, fixing ropes to a heavy log so that it could be carried between four running soldiers.

'It's a grand bit of ground,' said the instructor. He was a red-headed, thickset Scotsman of the indestructible type about whom people say 'not a nerve in his body' and 'built like a brick shithouse'. He was bouncing around, finding fault with the trainees and appreciating the terrain.

'A bit of rough, fight through those trees, and run up the hill tae the end. We'll make up two teams and have a time trial.'

'Mmm,' said Susie. 'How many've you got?'

'Eight. Four girls, four boys. Don't want straight competition, I dinna like that. Thought we'd pair them two and two. Show folk that fitness isn't aboot gender.'

Susie grimaced. 'If you think that's a good idea . . .' she began, but was interrupted by the newcomer's mobile phone.

'Ah, I see,' he said after a moment. 'Mmm. Can't be helped.' Then, to Susie, 'We've lost one. Atkins went to fetch the others but one's pulled a sickie.' He looked disgusted at the idea that any member of his team could show weakness.

'I could stand in,' said Kevin keenly.

'It's a girl we've lost.' The PE instructor looked severely put out. Then he and Kevin both glanced at Susie. She, who was after all the senior officer present, affected not to notice for a moment, but habit and dutifulness took over and she heard herself saying: 'No problem. I'll run a leg of it.'

'Grand! Good tae show that officers aren't just for decoration,' said the instructor approvingly. 'Two o'clock, then? I'll get them to announce it on the Tannoy. I'll be off now, we're doing some drill for the kiddies at twelve.'

Susie's head was thumping unpleasantly, and her stomach was in turmoil after the two pieces of dry toast she had eaten for breakfast. She looked with disfavour at the deadweight of the log and the hard ropes being fixed to it. But the young Corporal was gazing at her with relieved pride: his officer was not letting him or the regiment down.

'Two o'clock,' she said dismally.

★ ★ ★

Arnie and Francis sat on the riverbank together, enjoying the sun. The night of glam-rock delirium at the Frog In Waders had marked a turning-point in Francis' fortunes, and the management agency Gigz where Arnie worked, had made overtures to renew their relationship with him.

'Witless rang them, *raving* about you,' said Arnie smugly.

'What made him think of ringing Gigz? Why'd he think I had anything to do with them any more?'

'We-ell,' said Arnie, 'might have been something to do with me. Might have dropped a word in.'

'But they wouldn't sign me up just because of Witless!' protested Francis. 'You've been doing good by stealth again, haven't you?'

'I may have made a few calls,' admitted his friend, 'in a few different voices. Some of them were about Fanny, some Kelly. There may even have been e-mails. Anyway, you're flavour of the month. Three gigs . . .' he ticked them off on his fingers '. . . Haverhill with Fanny, the Birmingham summer school Uni ball – that's Kelly, obviously – and Fanny at the Sudbury Community Centre. And we might get your hula-girl an outing at the Aldeburgh Pumphouse.'

'I'd rather do Fanny. Aldeburgh would love her. Apparently they adore Madame Galina, and Tina C went there, and that's not a dumb act.'

'I sold them South Seas Sadie. She needs practice. The thing is, Francis, I had an idea.'

Francis stretched his long legs luxuriously in the warmth of the sun, and wriggled a little at the hardness of the stone bench.

'What?'

'A showcase. All three of them. Quick change. Call it *Take Three Girls*, like that old TV programme my mum used to go on about.'

'How do I do a quick change either way with those bloody leathers? And anyway I *hate* doing Kelly, the very smell of the costume makes me heave now.'

'New costume? Better-fitting. Could be stretchy vinyl stuff, even. Two minutes during the entr' acte. Or wear the trousers under Fanny's dress . . .'

'In this heat? I'd die!'

'. . . and you could have a straight man doing the introductions, building a plot, explaining how they fit together, all that. It could be about reincarnation – the time machine thing – we could have them talking to each other on tape offstage. Kelly could come on after the interval.'

'Arnie,' said Francis patiently, 'I can't afford a straight man, I can't afford any more clothes, and I've never, ever had a gig long enough to have an interval. Stop bloody fantasizing.'

Arnie's wild pale-blue eyes narrowed to mischievous slits. 'I am your fairy godmother,' he said. 'You *shall* go to the ball, Cinders.'

'Birmingham Uni ball,' said Francis. 'God help us.'

'No, after that. Edinburgh.'

'Now you bloody *are* dreaming,' said Francis crossly.

The febrile, crowded streets of August Edinburgh had been a memory and a dream for him ever since he had hitch-hiked to Scotland in his teens and wandered round the Fringe venues for three glorious days, sleeping rough, before he was caught gatecrashing one of the bigger shows and returned home by the police.

Arnie could no longer contain himself or extend his tease. He jumped from the bench and bounced on his toes in front of his friend, flapping his arms.

'I – got – you – a – BIG – gig!' he chanted. 'Biggie biggie big! Big big!'

'What?' Francis stared.

'You know the Ethnic Elvis Show?'

'The one with the three different Elvises, yeah? Chiff does it—'

'Chiffon Elvis, Bollywood Elvis, and the spinning guy in the wheelchair. You know—'

'What about them? I suppose *they're* doing Edinburgh again,' said Francis, a touch bitterly.

'Yeah, *but* only the first two weeks. They got an offer to do a Dutch comedy festival from the fifteenth to the thirty-first, two gigs a week, twice the money. So they're going. Maggie at Gigz is *furious.*'

'Bloody hell! Where were they going to be on?'

'Pleasance Oblique. It's on the courtyard . . . you remember the courtyard? A hundred seats, or it might be eighty, can't remember. But the thing is that either Gigz comes up with a show for the last two weeks, or we lose it. And if we lose the venue, the Elvises don't go up at all.'

'But they were on the Perrier shortlist last year!'

'Mmm. But apparently they don't care. The Dutch are paying them more, and the flat that Gigz rents is completely crap, bunk beds in two of the rooms and the wheelchair guy hates it because of the steps, they have to carry him up, so—'

Francis' eyes were shining.

'So?'

'So I told Maggie that you've got this amazing concept show, with all three girls, forty minutes first-half, twenty second-half, and that you did it in Hereford Town Hall and it was a total rave.'

'Why Hereford?' asked Francis, bewildered.

'Maggie's never been to Hereford.'

'Nor have you!'

'Yes, I have. School choir competition, nineteen ninety-one. We lost. Anyway, so *desperate* was Maggie to say something confident and arrogant-sounding to the Fringe people that she bought it. She's claiming she pulled you out of a Norwegian tour to do it.'

'But I haven't written a show!'

'So write it. You don't need any new songs, do you? You've got the songs, it's just the patter.'

'I haven't got a straight man to do links, either.'

'Look no further,' said Arnie smugly. 'I always wanted to be on the stage.'

'No, you didn't!'

'Well, I could force myself. It's only ten minutes or so you need for the first costume change and a couple of links.'

Francis jumped up now and began to pace the walkway, talking rapidly, gesticulating, joking, scribbling on the tiny pad he always carried in his pocket, imagining a show. Arnie followed him to and fro, listening, throwing in ideas, skipping with spurts of glee.

It was over an hour later that Francis slowed down, stowed the pad in his hip pocket and said seriously: 'Thanks, mate. I know you put yourself on the line for this one.'

'A pleasure,' said Arnie, and his eyes rested on Francis with a softness that passed entirely unnoticed by the rising star. For Francis was gazing out into the river, his own eyes misted. Edinburgh, he thought, was the fine line that divided riff-raff like him from the rising, Perrier Award professionals. And Pleasance Oblique was not some dingy lecture-room, but a hundred-seat showcase off the main courtyard. His parents would even quite enjoy saying that he had his own show at Edinburgh. A thought struck him and he whirled round in dismay.

'The programme'll have been printed weeks ago!' he mourned. 'I won't be on it!'

'Flyers,' said Arnie calmly. 'Bloody thousands of bloody flyers. And the radio. And we'll get you on Nicholas Parsons or the other guy. Buzz, that's the thing. Create a buzz. Is it OK to say your dad's a General, by the way? We can sell the story of you leaping into the breeches of Chiffon Elvis like the Relief of Mafeking. Nulla problema.'

'I love you!' cried Francis, leaping on to the bench and beginning an approximation of a tap-dance. This time it was Arnie who looked at the river in silence.

Later that evening, Marion Anderson put down the phone and turned, smiling, to her husband as he drowsed over his book.

'Francis sounds terribly excited,' she said. 'He's going to do a one-man show at Edinburgh in a few weeks' time. Apparently that's quite something.'

'Mmm – ah – good,' said Richard, waking up with a start. 'Edinburgh Festival? Er, short notice, isn't it?'

'Yes, he says he's filling in for a cancellation. Apparently these three Elvis Presley impersonators got a sudden job in Amsterdam.' A faint note of defensiveness crept into the mother's voice. 'He was very proud . . .'

The senior Andersons looked into one another's eyes for a moment, attempting solemnity, then fell into long, gasping whoops of laughter.

The rope cut into Susie's shoulder, and her whole body was slick with sweat. An unfamiliar tremor ran through her legs as she lifted the log's weight, and the voice of the

Scottish PTI drilled into her head. 'Want to see ye spark-
ing! Now! Switch on!' The sun that day was merciless, not
a cloud to cool it. She glanced along the length of the
treetrunk at two big Pioneer Corps soldiers and a tough-
looking young woman with hair even redder than the PT
sergeant's.

'I'm not fast,' she mouthed at the nearest, and made a
slowing gesture with her hand. 'Take it steady.'

He smirked, and nodded with an air of patronising male
understanding. Susie was immediately angry with herself;
for all the slight grace of her bearing, at Sandhurst she had
been physically one of the strongest girls and known for
endurance. She had kept up her runs and her weight
training.

Well, usually. She had not done much in these past
weeks, what with having to drive the hire car on holiday
and slow down for Callum, and then these stomach gripes
. . . another spasm of pain went through the centre of her
body, and her legs shook. When the whistle blew, she
lurched forward with determination, nearly lost her footing, but then found enough strength to catch her stride
and begin running at the slow, laborious pace of a log-
run. She turned her head, shaking the sweat out of her
eyes; the knot of curious onlookers, sucking at their drinks
and shading their eyes against the fierce sun, blurred into
a multicoloured blob. Halfway to the trees now, still going.
Soon it would be over. She would not give up, not weaken.
Nerve and brain and sinew. Don't give up. Drop dead in
your tracks first.

She dropped. Pitching forwards, catching her leg on the
log with a hard thwack which she did not even feel, she fell
on the rough grass and lay motionless. After a stunned

moment, the PTI and her corporal ran up to lean over her. The instructor jerked his head up and shouted: 'Medics!' and across the grass the volunteer first-aiders ran, excitedly, with their clean new stretcher.

18

The hospital ward was light and bright with primary colours and a bustle of nurses and ever-swinging doors. In Susie's floating weariness it swam in and out of focus, not unpleasantly. Later, the army medical centre room was small, silent, with walls of a pale despondent cream and paintwork the colour of goose-turds. Here she was alone, and among the hard dull surfaces she longed for the drugged sleep which now eluded her. For most of the day she lay in a narrow bed, reaching from time to time for the glass of water on the locker, occasionally reading a few lines in her paperback novel, keeping her mind blank.

'Exhaustion, chiefly,' the Newcastle Infirmary doctor had said briskly. 'And I'd say there was a touch of dysentery. Can't imagine how she was allowed to get into this state.' The senior woman officer at her side had glared: Susie was well aware why. It was an officer's duty to stay healthy, abhor personal weakness, and to report promptly and appropriately any falling-off from optimal health. By drifting irresponsibly into debility, she had let the company down. She had collapsed on a routine PT exercise, in front of two of her own soldiers. Worse, she had done it in front of an NCO instructor from another regiment.

'But I *was* in bloody Iraq,' she said aloud now, addressing the cracked green paintwork of the windowframe. 'Which is more than that hearty little Jock, or Captain snotty Conway.' Then immediately she sighed. The brief moment of revolt had worn her out. She wanted to be back in the loop, respected and competent, not lying here feeling her horrible hip-bones jutting under the thin grey army blanket. Two more days, the doctor had said. Total rest. 'Why not go home?' he had added. 'They say there isn't a problem with sick-leave.'

Susie did not want to go home. She did not want her parents' anxious pity, any more than she wanted the Army's disapproving solicitude. With an effort she wrenched her weary mind into considering the question of what, or whom, she *did* want. After a few moments she rolled over, reached into the shabby locker for her mobile phone, and began to tap the buttons.

Moments later, Francis heard his mobile bleep. TXT MSSG, it said. READ NOW? He was on a bus on the A1 motorway, watching the tarmac flow by and repeating the words of his new opening song to himself, lips moving silently to the discomfiture of nearby passengers who suspected him of praying. He finished a verse before bothering to stab the YES button. It would be Arnie, probably, with some note about the gig he was heading for, or another change to his itinerary. The last one had said FIRM BKG NCASTLE FEST – 15 MINS KELLY – GOON DRCT TO EDBRO, BED FXD. After some consideration he had worked out that Goon meant Go On, and texted back OK BUT NEED BIGBLUE BAG FROM DIGS B4 EDSHOW STARTS – KEY WITH GURBUK ON 1FLOOR. He felt a pleasant sense that his career was spinning out of control, going faster than he had ever dreamed, but somehow safely because Arnie was at the wheel. The last two shows had been a knockout:

intelligent, provincial community-centre audiences of an age to understand the subtleties of Fanny Fantoni. Under the sweet rainfall of their laughter the character had grown, developing sly new lines, making sharp observations about her hearers. The songs were a revelation: he had never been in better voice. He had written a new song which was very good indeed.

Now he had another paid engagement, conveniently on the way to Edinburgh, and so he need not come back to London to sit and worry about the triple show. He would have several days up there before he began (BED FXD) so he could live in the sort of unhomelike, exciting creative limbo where he worked best. It all fitted splendidly. Dear Arnie.

Finishing the verse, he pushed the YES button and saw to his surprise that the message was from his sister. He leaned forward, squinting carefully at the tiny green display.

IN CAMP SICKBAY NOT SERIOUS. DNT TELL PARENTS BUT FR GODSAKE SEND JOKE, GDNEWS, NYTHING TO DISTRACT. OR RING WHENCHEAP. SUSE.

He was touched that she had used text rather than phoning him; she was always financially tactful, and knew how problematic it sometimes was for him to top up his mobile account. He was about to text back when it occurred to him that he was already past Sheffield. Her last message had suggested that she was on her recruiting tour up north; perhaps, he thought, it was the same sort of north as he was heading for? In any case, England got a lot narrower near the top, didn't it? It couldn't be far. Instead of texting he rang her.

'Susie? Francis. Hi. Where the hell are you?'

'Where are you? Sounds like a bus.'

'It *is* a bus. Can't take the car to Edinburgh, wouldn't make it past Milton Keynes, no parking up there anyway, Arnie says. Going to Newcastle on the way.'

'Why?'

'Got a gig. The Kelly glam-rock bit at some sort of festival. Moneymoney! And a lovely outing for your old boots, dear.'

The cheeping voice on the other end of the line became excited.

'Francis, I'm only fifteen miles from Newcastle! I was in the infirmary there! Now I'm back at camp and it's dire! Could we meet up?'

'What's wrong with you? Are you allowed out?'

'Got to stay on bed-rest for a couple of days. Not much wrong. Stomach thing, left over from living on American ration-packs or something. I could see if they'll let me go into Newcastle, if you're still there when they let me up.'

'Shall I come to you? I haven't got the car, but I could get a bus?'

'No, I'll get up and come to your gig. God, Francis, I need a night out!'

'Fab!'

But when the army doctor looked in, he banned any movement.

'You're badly run down. I don't like your breathing and your blood pressure's up. I think you ought to go on leave. Total rest.'

'Nowhere to go,' protested Susie. 'Really, I'm fine – I'd be better for some company.'

'If you want visitors,' said the MO austerely, 'they can come here. You can sit up for a couple of hours, though, and do some stretches and walk up and down the corridor.'

'Super,' said Susie grumpily, and when he had gone she wept, but not before texting another plea to her brother.

GROUNDED. JST CM N SEE ME BASTARD, ILL PAY TAXI she wrote. Moments later a bleep heralded his reply. CAN PAY OWN TAXI THANKYOU AM MAJOR STAR.

Not that he needed to pay a taxi: the next morning, having charmed the Festival organizer with ease, Francis turned up driven by that fluttering lady in her neat little red Peugeot. He left her to her own devices while he further charmed his way into the camp and the medical centre. The first Susie knew of his arrival was the sound of pattering feet and a high happy voice in the corridor, effortlessly beguiling the duty RAMC nurse.

'Well!' her brother said, plumping himself down on her bed. 'What goes on here? You storm through Basra terrifying the poor little Iraqis into submission, then one look at the bleak bitter Tyne and — whoops! You keel over.'

She smiled wanly. It was good that he was happy: his manner always became twice as camp when things were going well. She began to ask about his work, and Francis, divining that she really did want jokes and anecdotes more than soft sympathy, obliged with a highly coloured account of his recent travels.

'Middle England,' he concluded, 'loves and wants me. I should never have *squandered* myself on pubsful of yobs and feral poofs. I belong to the nation, like the Queen.'

'So you've moved upmarket?' said Susie, whose eyes were a little brighter in her pale face. 'More H. G. Wells and cultural observation, less of the stuff with the hips?'

'Mmm. Still have to do a bit of that. Doing the leatherwear queen tonight, rather against my will, but the thing is, there's this show I'm doing in Edinburgh . . .' He launched into an account of the concept he had worked out with Arnie in late excited writing sessions in his bedsit. It made little sense to Susie, and her attention began to wander. After a while Francis noticed, and broke off.

'Suse, are you all right?'

'No,' she said bleakly, surprising herself. 'Not even a bit all right. I wish I was dead. There's no point in anything, any, any more—' And she began to cry, great tearing sobs, her knees drawn up and clasped with whitened knuckles, her head down hiding her face. Francis looked at her with love and pity, thinking how childishly vulnerable was the white triangle at the nape of her neck where the dark tangled hair fell forward. He reached out a tentative hand and put it over her clenched fingers.

'Don't cry,' he said. 'He's not worth it.'

She looked up, red-eyed and wet-cheeked.

'Who said anything about sodding Callum?' she demanded with ferocity. 'I never want to hear his name—'

'Oh, Susie!' said her brother. 'It's not finished. You know it isn't. You're going to *have* to talk to him. He can't just vanish off to sea, it's not *allowed*, not these days. Even in bloody *operas* you get to say goodbye properly, even if it's with a knife in the ribs.'

Susie put her head down again and said indistinctly into the blanket on her knees: 'OK then. It is Callum. But—'

She began to cry again.

'But what?'

'Probably drowned anway,' said the muffled voice.

'What?' Francis was genuinely startled.

Susie raised her head and looked at him, not bothering to wipe away the tears.

'I said – he's probably jumped off the bloody ship. That's what he meant to do, I know he did.'

Francis was silent. He thought for a while, staring at the blistered paintwork, and then said carefully: 'Honestly, sweetheart, I don't actually think so.'

'Why?'

'Gut feeling. I saw the note, remember. It didn't have the feeling of a – a suicide. Not to me.' He was young, Francis, but his world was complicated and he had known two suicides. There was a bitter authority in his tone.

He had Susie's attention now. She looked straight at him, ignoring the tears still wet on her cheeks.

'What *did* it have the feeling of? To you?'

'A sulk,' he said flatly.

Three hundred miles to the south of them, it was not Callum who was sulking but Erik and Jez. *Miranda* had made good time across Biscay, but Stefan, having called the owner as soon as they closed the coast of Ushant, flatly refused to make landfall on either the French or British coasts. Instead he set a course up the centre of the Channel with the declared intention of dropping Maarten off at Ijmuiden, where he lived, and proceeding directly to Scotland.

'We haf a charter,' he said baldly. 'Out of Leith. Mackenzie is waiting. It is a good charter.'

'But we haven't got a bloody crew,' protested Jez. 'Not without Maarten. It's ridiculous!'

The Dutchman had improved a little in the past four days of relatively smooth fast sailing, but was still in too much pain to haul, lift, or move around other than slowly, with much wincing and bouts of sickness caused by the continuing pain from his ribs.

'He's broken more than one,' continued Jez. 'I worry about his breathing, too. He's puffed out after a couple of minutes.'

'So, he goes home,' said the captain. 'We can do fine without him.'

'Only because Callum's doing so much time on the helm,' said the girl. 'And he'll probably want to leave when we get near the English coast.'

Callum was out of earshot, at the wheel; Erik and Jez were talking in low voices as they crouched in the forepeak, passing tools and gear to Stefan as he fiddled once again with the troublesome generator.

'Ve do not go to England. Only Scotland. Does he say he vants to leave?' asked the skipper, applying force to a seized and rusted nut with a sharp grunt. 'Mmm – does he say this?'

'No,' said Jez unwillingly. 'But he's not one of the crew, he's paying his passage—'

'The new charter is necessary,' declared Stefan angrily. 'So, ve go to Leith. The Englander knows we go to Scotland. He has said this is OK. He owes more money now.'

'I don't think he should have to pay so much, now he's working all the time,' Jez objected. 'He's virtually crew.'

'He is disabled.'

'He is not! He's just a bit lame. You saw him sort out the sprit topsail on his own yesterday.'

'It is a light sail. He is not Able Seaman.'

'Oh, for God's sake, Stefan!' said Jez, whose own back was aching from the crouched and awkward position. She stood up, shaking out her cramped leg, and dropped on to the deck the spanners she was holding. 'You're really down on the poor bastard.'

The two men looked at her with matching leers. Erik made an obscene gesture.

'You are going down, like you say, yourself on him, yes, Jezebel?'

'Shut up!'

Callum heard nothing; it was a fresh bright afternoon and with one hand lightly on the wheel, responsive to the ship's tremors and purposeful plunges, he was keeping his mind blank. He focused on the moment, on the patch of warm sun on his shoulders and the gay driving motion of the vessel beneath her wide brown sails. He could stay like this for hours, deliberately barring himself from thinking about Susie or Jez, the Army, the past or the future. Off-watch, lying in his bunk by day or night, it was harder to keep troublesome thoughts at bay. And if he did manage to snatch a few hours' sleep, they transformed themselves into confused nightmares.

The easiest worry to tame, because the most recent, was the thought of his crewmate Jez. Since they had kissed beneath the moon she had made no further advance to him, but more worryingly she had adopted a quiet conspiratorial manner as if to suggest that something had been settled, something which could not be made public in their tiny floating world but which belonged to both of them. In apparently casual conversation she had asked about his life, his home, his mother. A possessive comradely hand would rest briefly on his arm when she passed him his food; and, foul as it was, he knew that he got more of the food than any of the others. Worst of all, he thought glumly, Jessica looked happy. She glowed. But where nothing is said, nothing can be denied.

Perhaps he should mention Susie, identify her as his fiancé. But that too was obviously impossible. He had abandoned

Susie (again, shame burned his neck and cheeks at the memory of it). So Callum filled his mind and his time by volunteering to stand ever longer watches; he whipped ropes' ends, swabbed the deck, wiped down the varnished coachroof in the dawn dew. Jez, however, merely gave her quiet approval to his solicitude for the boat, and loved him – he saw this plainly – all the more.

19

It was in Edinburgh, on the Royal Mile in drenching rain, that Francis first suspected that Arnie loved him. It was their second day in the city together, for Arnie had flown up with the blue costume-bag and two heavy cardboard boxes full of printed posters and flyers. Francis exclaimed at the smartness of the leaflets, and gloated over the mock newspaper headlines of his poster: FANNY POWER TO THE RESCUE AS ELVISES GO DUTCH. A moody monochrome shot of Fanny with a hat-feather curling round her cheekbone had pride of place. On the leaflet, he featured as a multi-headed cartoon monster, his three female characters sprouting from one torso.

'How the hell did you get this lot designed and printed so *fast?*' he said admiringly. 'I thought we'd have to have something pretty basic, at this notice.'

'There are ways,' said Arnie complacently. 'One has contacts in the graphic design field. Favours are owed. One is *such* a pro.'

'Cost a bit,' said Francis. 'Is Gigz stumping up willingly?'

'You've saved Maggie's bacon,' said Arnie, but there was something evasive in his voice. Francis suspected that Gigz was, at the very least, unaware of how much Arnie had spent. He would have been appalled to know for certain that £562.40 of the publicity costs had come from his friend's own pocket; but he never did find out, until years later.

Francis was still fretting about the show: although he had full confidence in the Fanny Fantoni segment and knew that Kelly would provide a rousing finale, the hula-hula interlude seemed to him to be weakly plotted and inconsequential, and the linking script not strong enough. With a kindly audience, like his community-centre gigs in the Midlands, it would be fine. With a sharp Edinburgh Fringe public, maybe seeing its third show of the day, it could be disastrous. It was part of Francis' burden that being verbose and articulate himself, he was more than able to write nightmare reviews in his own head before he even began performing. 'Jejune . . . ill-executed . . . skimpily prepared . . .' he thought. '. . . Only the most inconsiderate of last-minute letdowns could have put this under-rehearsed show on a Pleasance stage. Come back, Elvises – all is forgiven'.

Arnie steadied his nerves with banter, went patiently over the script with him, and took him out for a pizza. Over the pizza, and a bottle of Rioja of which Francis drank the greater part, they thought of a whole new joke to bring in South Seas Sadie, of a new verse about coconuts, and of a piece of business with the grass skirt and a borrowed pantomime cow's head which doubled them both up in tipsy laughter. Rushing back to the chilly flat which the Gigz agency had rented for its artistes, they typed and reordered the script on Arnie's laptop until three in the morning. They had to share a room with two hard, lumpy bunk beds for another night, and the Elvises got home extremely late and noisy after their final show, but the flat was reasonably positioned and reasonably warm. It lay over a parade of small shops and restaurants so that

they could at least eat without effort. They counted themselves lucky.

Through these few days, Francis went on letting himself
think that Arnie was merely a friend and colleague who,
through professional judgement, believed in his show. The
complicating revelation came only at noon the next day,
when the two of them had been distributing flyers up and
down the Royal Mile. They were nearly done, and planned
to walk back up over the bridge to the Fringe office to meet
up with their student poster-hangers and leafleteers. Maggie
at Gigz had authorized them to pay the requisite pittance
for this service, after Arnie told her that even if Francis were
not to be a success it was to be an investment in goodwill
to warn audiences that the Elvises were leaving town.

The two young men had been walking towards one another
from opposite ends of the street, thrusting their flyers into
the hands of the thronging passers-by, when suddenly a
violent rainstorm chased the buskers and jugglers and all the
happy idling crowds of tourists under cover. Every shop
doorway and patch of shelter in sight was packed with
huddling bodies; the two of them were marooned in the
downpour, classic Edinburgh rain hurtling down their necks,
soaking their hair in seconds and making them gasp as it ran
into their mouths.

Arnie, ever the more organized of the two, thrust his flyers
into a waterproof newsboy's shoulder bag which he carried
and ran over to rescue Francis' ever soggier stock. Then he
pulled from his anorak pocket a folding umbrella, deployed
it with a flick of his wrist and stood in the rain, holding it
over Francis.

It was at that moment that Francis knew beyond a shadow
of doubt how Arnie felt. 'The thing is,' he said to Susie much

later, 'he wasn't being kind. He was doing it for himself. He was actually more worried about *me* being wet than about *him* being wet.'

'Mmm,' said Susie, an expert in love. 'Yes, that's exactly it. Like mothers and babies. It's that dangerous moment when you stop mattering to yourself.'

Arnie had stopped mattering to himself some weeks before. Holding the umbrella over Francis' dark dancing grace, keeping him safe from the wet, was at that moment all he asked of life. And Francis suddenly knew it and was stilled. They stood close together in the rain, neither able to speak. Then Francis said: 'You're getting wet.' And Arnie muttered hoarsely: 'Don't care.' Then, with belated caution, 'You're the vocal artiste.'

'You need a voice too,' said Francis, trying to push the umbrella handle towards his friend.

'Not a singing voice.' Arnie moved a little away from Francis, and it almost hurt him physically to do so; he kept his arm outstretched, still protecting him with the umbrella.

They walked side by side, awkward and confused, up the hill and over the bridge which spanned the great chasm at the city's heart. For two days Francis had hardly looked up, so preoccupied was he with posters and flyers and scripts and costumes, so busy examining his proposed venue and its environs and scanning the faces of the crowds for signs of willingness to applaud him when his time came. Now, as the sky cleared from the east, he looked up and saw beyond the city a line of faint blue hills. Next to him Arnie was silent, walking in step, still holding out the umbrella at arm's length.

Nobody, thought Francis, had ever loved him first. He had

been in love himself, of course: hopelessly and unhappily, twice. At seventeen he had adored a girl a year older, a slim fair boyish creature in his school's sixth form. It was she, more sophisticated by far, who had pointed out to him that he was gay. She had done it lightly, laughingly, with sweet modern tolerance, but Francis had been mortified and vowed never to see Rhiannon again if he could help it.

Nonetheless, over the next few years he slowly came to accept that she was right, bang on the nail: he did not want what other young men wanted, or respond to what they leered at. What he *did* respond to remained a profound puzzle, about which he spoke to nobody. Then, inevitably, he found an object for his unfocused love: Peter, two years older, a brilliant baritone spoken of at music college as the next Terfel. And Peter was not gay. Not, at least, full-time. In the flippant parlance of their set, his status was, 'Well, he helps out when they're busy.'

His brief dalliance did not help Francis, but nearly sank him forever. First he found out that there was a girl on the other side of Peter's rails, and then, a little later, that there were two other boys. One of them took Peter far too seriously, and ended up with a Temazepam overdose. The other jealously attacked Francis with a bottle at an end-of-term party, while Peter laughed. It was after this final severance with Peter that Francis created his first female stage characters; the elegant elaboration of the costume soothed and seemed to protect him. If he would not do as a proper man chasing women, yet could not keep a man's affection either, then he would confuse the whole picture and be a woman: a diva, the cynosure of all eyes, applauded and beloved by the many-headed audience.

And when he was tired of that, he would just be Francis.

He never cross-dressed for fun, never went on the street in costume unless it was effectively part of the show with other performers. On stage, however, he would transform himself utterly, and delight his audience without stint or grudge. There was safety in numbers, yes, and a kind of love as well. He was good at it: good at comedy, good at making audiences like him and want to protect him, and above all good at music and able to write witty songs for his newly liberated female selves to sing. Thus a student prank, an existential joke against himself, matured into a sort of career; and here he was at twenty-seven years old, established with a small but satisfying degree of honour, preparing for a full-length show at the Pleasance.

But now for the first time that he knew of, somebody was in love with him unasked, uncourted, and unexpected. And it was somebody who mattered: a colleague and a friend, almost a manager. Francis felt as if within his breast a frightened horse was shying and jibbing and tugging away from this possibility. It was too complicating, too dangerous, too threatening to the fragile structure he had built up around himself since Peter. Friends he cherished, family he was quietly fond of; but Love, of the kind that sprang up fluttering and excitable under umbrellas in strange cities, was nothing but trouble. Even Susie had begun to find that, and he had always considered Susie and Callum as something completely different and safe, right outside his world and its temperamental troubles. Why, they were virtually *married!* And marriage, to Francis, was another planet. Parentworld. Not something he would ever know as more than a weekend visitor.

They delivered their instructions and payment to the band of student leafleteers and walked on in silence towards the flat. It was dry now, and the distant hills between the buildings were sharp and blue. Arnie had folded up his umbrella and was swinging it with a show of nonchalance, but Francis knew that he was aware of the change between them. Fear and pity gripped him. This wasn't another light-hearted flirtatious pass, like the ones he had batted aside a couple of years back. This was something less comfortable, more real. Poor Arnie, poor sweet, dear Arnie . . .

Dear, he thought. Yes, dear. Ever since the night his friend had driven him towards that ravening audience at the Frog in Waders, life had been better, less frightening, more full of hope and of jokes. They had fallen into a habit of seeing one another daily, talking about scripts, running along the Embankment, dropping in to the National Theatre for the £10 season of *Jerry Springer – The Opera*. Arnie had, he knew, championed and promoted him at the agency and personally engineered most of this summer's work. And, it occurred to Francis now and belatedly, in turning up at so many venues to watch and criticize and give him helpful notes, Arnie must have dropped out of quite a lot of his old social scene. One night, yawning his way home from the Soho theatre studio, Francis had echoed a refrain of his mother's and casually said, 'No peace for the wicked,' and Arnie had muttered sombrely, 'No bloody time to *be* wicked.'

Dear Arnie. They were almost at the flat; cautiously, Francis glanced sideways. Arnie's head turned too, and immediately Francis looked away. The devotion in the other man's eyes was too naked.

'Arnie—' he began, though he did not know what he meant to say. Luckily for him, at that moment the door was flung open and there emerged all three Elvises, none of them at

that moment looking remotely like the late King of Rock and
Roll. The two able-bodied performers were carrying the
wheelchair between them down the granite steps, while its
occupant shrilly enjoined them to be bloody careful. Chiff,
who was ambiguously dressed in a velvet cape, tight black
jeans and a corset top, was somewhat in need of a shave.
Sanjay, once he had put his side of the chair down, ran back
up the steps and returned with two large wheeled suitcases.

'Hi, boys,' said Francis. 'You off, then?'

'Mmm. Sheets are in the washing-machine,' said Sanjay.
'We got to go earlier because we found a direct flight from
Dundee, cheaper.'

'*Top* hotel in Amsterdam, it's in the contract,' said Alan,
from his wheelchair. 'No more bloody cockroaches and gas
leaks. Goodbye, Edinburgh, it's been disgusting.'

'Oh, it's not so bad,' protested Francis. 'We're lucky to be
so central.'

'Baby,' said Chiffon Elvis contemptuously. 'Edinburgh
virgin. Listen to him. Wet behind the ears. This is a grade-
six student let, top whack a hundred in termtime, for which
they are charging Maggie four hundred quid a week!
Edinburgh landlords are like bloody greenfly, milking
captive ants.'

'Other way round. It's ants,' said Arnie, 'who milk greenfly.'

He had not spoken before; his voice was not quite steady.
Francis darted him a worried glance, but the three performers were preoccupied with checking their holdalls and sharing
out the big luggage. Alan began to propel his wheelchair
down the uneven pavement, followed by his two friends with
their suitcases; as they crossed the cobbled street the noise
of the metal wheels was deafening.

'Why don't they get a taxi?' Francis asked, watching the trio struggle down the road.

'There's a bus. They lift Alan on to it. They're too mean for taxis,' said Arnie. 'Great players, though, those three. You can learn a lot from them.'

'I'm bloody grateful to them,' said Francis feelingly. Then all the strangeness of the last half-hour seemed to ebb away and leave a sense of increasing comfort and optimism: the sun had come out, the damp cobbles gleamed pale-gold, and he was with an amusing, familiar friend who maybe loved him and certainly would never let him down. Life was good, thought Francis. A great adventure. Whatever awkward feelings were complicating it, everything could be sorted out with a bit of goodwill. He bounded up the steps behind Arnie, humming.

20

Maarten was put ashore at Ijmuiden lock; Stefan had made him telephone ahead to tell the aunt and uncle he lived with to wait for them on the south wall of the main lock. Arriving at high water, he eased the little ship expertly alongside, made Jez throw a line round the rungs of the iron ladder and sent Erik up it with a thinner line which was made fast to a mast-climbing sling. Maarten hated being strapped into it.

'I can climb the damn' ladder,' he protested.

'I don't think so,' said Stefan coldly. 'If you fall you will be hurt seriously. I haf not got any time for such delays.'

So with Jez and Callum steadying him, the injured crew-man was hoisted, groaning, the few feet up to the quay. As he was eased to his feet by Erik and the anxious uncle, Jez swarmed after him with his sea-bag, and threw it on to the quay. Then she turned and shouted to Stefan: 'I have to buy some bread. Gimme twenty minutes.'

'Onboard, now!' shouted the skipper. 'We go now! The gates will close!'

'One hour won't hurt, will it?' said Callum, placatory. Stefan ignored him and yelled up to Erik, whose feet were on a level with his face.

'Erik, onboard! Now! And Jez!'

To Callum's horror Erik grabbed the girl, marched her to the ladder and manhandled her on to it. Jez looked briefly outraged, but jumped from the second rung on to the deck, landing with a thud and hissing at Stefan: 'You can do without any fucking bread, then, you ugly Kraut!'

Then she vanished into the saloon. Erik was untying the one line which held them to the ladder and Stefan putting the engine into reverse; before Callum could come to terms with his own bewildered outrage there was a metre of churning brown water between the rail and the wall. Then there were two metres, then more, and *Miranda* was turning her bows again to the open lock gates and the North Sea.

Still gaping with amazement and disgust, he found himself hurrying below to find Jez. She was sitting in the saloon, arms folded, face like thunder.

'What the *hell* was that about?' he asked.

'He wants to get back to sea before you can leave. He wants to get to somewhere in Scotland for this new charter, and –' she spoke with an air of reluctant fairness '– he's got a point. The boat's right out of money and with just three of us it might have been a problem sailing up the North Sea. We haven't got enough fuel to motor it, and sails need a crew, so he just went for it.'

'I wasn't *going* to get off!' said Callum. 'I *live* in Scotland!'

'Yeah,' said Jez. 'I told him that was probably right, but he likes to take a belt and braccs approach.'

'So I've been kidnapped?' said Callum, trying to make light of it; as he looked up through the hatch he saw that the boat was steaming out through the lock gates, and the Dutch harbour official standing beside them was howling some abuse at Stefan, who responded with a single, dismissive finger.

'Yup. And there's not much to cat either, so pray for a

nice fresh wind,' said Jez. There was something so brave and vulnerable and resigned about her that his heart turned over. He returned to her side, and sat closer than he had for days.

'Why do you put up with it?' he asked gently. And immediately he was sorry that he had moved close and sounded tender. She looked him in the eye so honestly and with such affection that he flinched inwardly for shame.

'Because I like to sail,' she said. 'I love to go to sea. And I'm a competent crew but I'm actually kidding myself if I think I'll ever be a skipper. I talk about getting a boat of my own, but I know I won't really. So I have to put up with skippers forever. End of story.'

'You'll find a better one,' said Callum. And after a pause, 'You deserve a better one.'

Her look of naked devotion drove him away, back on deck where Stefan, without a word of apology or explanation, curtly ordered him to take the helm while the others raised the sails. Jez was the last to come on deck, strolling with insolent deliberation towards her station by the peak halyard. Stefan, he noticed, did not hurry her along. Perhaps she had, after all, a bearable working relationship with the appalling man.

She began, with calm competence, to prepare the sail for hoisting. Watching her, Callum knew clearly the nature of his feelings for this girl. She was a comrade. A mate. She had been a good friend, working alongside him bravely, buffering him against the surly contempt of Stefan and Erik, asking no intrusive questions, and providing human consolation during this strange limbo of a voyage. She was a replacement for the comradely friends he used to have, friends like Harry Devine; but more than that, as a girl she could provide a female softness and empathy that he increasingly valued since his injury. He remembered how she had nursed

Maarten during the gale. She was a dear thing, a lion-hearted honest creature who deserved the best of the best. She was the daughter he hoped to have one day; the sister he would have liked. She was a sport, a brick, a friend for life.

She was not Susie, though. As he stood at the helm, full of warm feelings for Jessica, he realized with a dull desperation that the girl he loved, and always would love, was Susie Anderson. Love, the kind of love you married for and raised children with, was more than this affection he felt for Jez. It meant – he frowned with effort, for he was not a natural philosopher on such subjects – that something lay between you which could not be explained by comradeship or virtue, worth or liking. It was an affinity, a likeness, a passion. It was as if something in you was incomplete until you found the other half. It was forever, unless one of you deliberately set out to break it.

He had done just that. He had been a selfish, self-pitying idiot and had lost Susie for ever. Jessica had every quality he liked, and was not physically repulsive by any means, and yet he could never love her. Realizing that, he understood the full rare, fragile miraculousness of the love he felt for Susie. He had thought that losing the full power of his leg had been a grievous and irrecoverable loss: losing Susie was a thousand times worse, yet he had done that almost on purpose. He could not atone for his desertion, or for the note, or for his spiteful, dismissive, petulant, frigid behaviour in Portugal. He had shown her the worst side of himself, a side even he had never known he had. He had become less of a man, a coward and a whiner and a wounder. He was not good enough for Susie now. Even if she took him back, he would be too deeply in her debt for it to work. They were no longer equals. There was no hope.

The wind was freshening from the west. *Miranda* heeled to its power, plunging northward as the light failed; flecks of rain wet Callum's left cheek and ran down his neck unheeded. Jez came aft and stood by him for a while, watching the sails; but he said nothing, and exuded such threatening gloom that eventually she went to her bunk, cold dismay at the pit of her stomach. Perhaps, she thought sorrowfully, he despised her for letting herself be man-handled and ordered around by Erik and Stefan. Perhaps he thought she was a wimp for admitting that her dream of commanding her own boat would never come true. Well, so be it. She despised herself, too. There were tears on her cheeks as she finally fell asleep, and they were barely dry when she was woken for the midnight watch.

Callum, in his seafaring limbo, had lost all awareness of dates. His Commanding Officer had not. As *Miranda* left Ijmuiden lock with her cargo of short-tempered determination and sorrowful love, the Colonel was frowning at his desk over a note which reminded him of Captain MacAllister's due return.

'Where is he? He's two days late reporting. We haven't had a signal from the medics, have we?'

'No, sir. He was passed fit to go on leave, sir.'

'Well, find him. Ring his home.'

'Yessir.'

And so it was that Pat MacAllister, in a flap, later rang the Andersons and asked whether they knew anything; and with some trepidation, Marion rang her daughter's mobile.

Susie said that she knew nothing, had heard nothing and expected to hear nothing. She was out of bed but still shaky on her feet and relieved of all duties for a day or two. She went through the next few hours in apparent calm, stretching and walking and trying out some light hand-weights in the gym; but then was suddenly and violently sick outside the Officers' Mess and only just managed to clean it up herself before her brother-officers returned from their day's work.

'You're white as a sheet,' said one of them. 'Seen a ghost?'

21

With the Elvises gone, Francis and Arnie were able to give themselves separate bedrooms, and tidy up the little flat so that it was more habitable. Arnie rigged up a costume rail in the living-room, and stocked the fridge; Francis cooked. On the day of their first performance they ate scrambled eggs and smoked salmon at noon, then walked down through the city, across the bridge. Arnie swung his umbrella from his wrist and tried to conquer his nerves over appearing as MC and straight man; Francis looked tensely ahead of him, his lips mouthing the words of songs, giving an occasional skip as he tried to remind himself of a new dance step. His show was at five-thirty: not a prime time, but not a bad one either. He wanted to see the previous show from the back of the auditorium to gauge the acoustics and the atmosphere.

They had been warned of the impossibility of storing many costumes, props or cherished discs and tapes down at the Pleasance, but Arnie had hit upon an ingenious solution to this perennial Fringe problem by renting a small white van and sweet-talking an acquaintance of his who ran a souvenir business two minutes up the road. Mrs Apthorpe would let them use her back parking bay, where the deliveries came in, as long as they moved the van away on the two Saturday mornings.

'See? Our very own wardrobe and prop store. Nobody else has that,' he crowed. 'We can get the stuff to the dressing-room in five minutes, as soon as the Mini-Musical people get out.' There had been an additional energy about Arnie since that moment on the Royal Mile, a determination not to gaze or brood or let his lip tremble. It was enough, he told himself, to be useful to Francis and part of his show. Enough for now. He did not want to scare him off. Even as he thought it, Arnie was repelled by himself: *scare him off*. What was he, a stalker? He let his imagination veer off into possible, not too ambitiously romantic futures: success for Francis with Arnie working as his manager, caring for him, keeping the sharks away, making sure he ate properly. Or, if Francis didn't want that, just carrying on as a best friend, listening to his troubles, hearing about his weird Army sister and her runaway boyfriend, giving him an occasional chaste hug when he was low, but never moving in too far or presuming anything, making sure he ate properly . . .

'Perhaps,' he said gloomily to himself when this chicken-soup reflection went past for the second time, 'I just want to be his mother.' But Francis already had a mother, and seemed quite fond of her in an exasperated and mildly patronizing sort of way. No: Arnie was in love, no two ways about it. For all his philandering experience, it was only the second time he had felt such exalted and self-sacrificing passion, and the first was a very long time ago. He sighed, and glanced sideways at the preoccupied figure of Francis as they walked across the bridge. He had offered to get the van back earlier to drive them both, but Francis said the walk was necessary to calm him down. 'I love you,' muttered Arnie, under his breath as a noisy bus swept by, and the relief of saying it, albeit inaudibly, was immense.

Francis' mobile bleeped in his pocket, and he pulled it out and squinted, still walking.

'Bloody hell,' he said. 'It's Susie.'

Arnie sighed; Francis talked too much about this troubled sister of his, it was a distraction.

The screen said CAL IS AWOL – HIS CO CALLED PAT – TALK? Francis hit the button and held the phone to his ear.

'Suse? Can you talk now?'

'Mmm. I'm waiting for the doc. Going to be signed off fit today. What about you?'

'First show this afternoon. Not for a few hours.'

'God, I shouldn't be badgering you. But I don't want to talk to Mum, it makes me weepy. And there's nothing to say anyway.'

'Say it to me.' Francis stopped walking and leaned on the stone parapet, his back to Arnie. 'You said AWOL? I mean, literally? He was meant to turn up for the Army again?'

'Yup. Three days ago. They've rung Pat, which is a really embarrassing thing to happen. For an officer. I mean, it's what they do when they're trying to track down some squaddie who's got pissed and overstayed his leave.'

'Military Police on the doorstep, sort of thing?'

'Getting that way. Anyway, she's kicking up hell. Seriously upset, Mum says. Francis, what should I do? Yesterday I got in a panic and I was sick and everything, but now I've sorted myself out and I just think I owe it to him to find out what happened.'

Her voice wavered, despite her attempt at calm.

'What can you do?' said Francis, leaning on the parapet, looking over Arnie's shoulder towards the blue distant hills. 'His boat's late – boats always are, horrid things – he probably forgot the date – he'll turn up.'

'I mean, the other thing is, what can I do about Pat? She still thinks we're engaged. I don't want to tell her.'

'Then don't.'

'But should I ring her? I mean, she'll think it's odd if I don't.'

'Sweetie, you've been ill, you've been miserable, don't pile anything else on top of it. Pat'll be hell, you know she will. She's a fusser. Let her go and light candles and talk to the parish priest. Honest. Think of yourself.'

He was surprised to find how agitated he was at the thought of poor little Susie being keened over and further upset by her mother-in-law *manquée*. She had looked and sounded frail enough, physically and emotionally, when he saw her only a few days earlier. He frowned, and kicked the parapet base, and Arnie waited a little aside, stifling his irritation at the invisible sister who was upsetting his protégé.

'Tell you what,' said Francis suddenly, after a moment, 'he's sailing to Scotland, right? I'm in Scotland. I've got the phone books. I've got all morning tomorrow to try and not get nervous about the second show. I'll ring round the marinas and things then – it's too late now – and see if the *Mirabelle* is expected anywhere.'

'Not *Mirabelle*, *Miranda*. Francis, that's so brilliant – I should have thought of it but I'm all over the place with this stuff, honestly.'

She sounded on the verge of breaking down. Francis spoke soothingly to her, with a gentleness which made Arnie turn away, looking up at the Castle with tears of envy in his own eyes. Then Francis snapped his phone shut and put it in his pocket. To Arnie he said, 'You know I told you about the runaway fiancé? He's overdue. I'm now supposed to find his boat. It's called the *Miranda* and it's a Brixham trawler seventy feet long with brown sails. Apparently. And it might be in Scotland.'

'Shall I write that down?' asked Arnie, recovering himself and assuming the air of an efficient PA. 'You'll forget, and go walking the quays searching for a three-masted schooner called *Mirabella* with pink sails and a rude figurehead.'

'Sounds more like *your* idea of a good night out,' said Francis, and Arnie flapped his wrist in mock-indignation, and again they fell into step together and felt the better for it. But because Francis had a first night imminent, Arnie did pull a notebook from his pocket and write down the details. If Francis wanted the *Miranda,* he should have it. Arnie would lay it at his feet. He laughed aloud, entirely happy for a moment: exalted by the absurdity of his own passion. Francis, glancing round at his friend's delighted face and mop of white-blond hair, felt a powerful pang of affection. They would, he thought with a rush of confused but generous affection, find a way somehow. A way to be . . . whatever. Oh, dear, it was so difficult, there being no rules. But dear, dear Arnie!

Nine hours later, elated and enchanted with life, the two young men hared up the town again, skipping and giggling, sweeping deep bows to the dummies in the Princes Street shop windows. They had triumphed. Francis had triumphed. Arnie's brief deadpan narrations had proved the perfect foil to the songs, the dances, the jokes and breathtaking audacities of Francis' three imaginary women. One crisis had been averted when a prop was left behind in the locked van and Arnie had to run for it during the interval, arriving back with barely enough breath to cope with his few lines.

The audience had cheered and drummed their feet at the final number, and gone out chattering happily to spread the word. A terrifying, beaky woman in pointed red boots had swept up afterwards and congratulated Francis; when she was gone, Arnie crowed and danced in glee, for she was from a leading Scottish newspaper and counted as the most feared of all the Fringe reviewers. Friends with other acts in the festival crowded round them, calling the show a stunner, a truly original showcase, a joy, much better than the tired old Elvises. Drinks were put into their hands, appearing from nowhere as they emerged breathless into the mellow light of early evening and stood among their fans in the crowded Pleasance courtyard. A runner from the Nicholas Parsons live interview show, rather out of breath, demanded that Francis turn up the next day to talk about himself: in the mere fifteen minutes since the show ended his fame had been borne to the producer.

Francis knew that there were things wrong with *Take Three Girls*. Putting it in front of an audience had shown him where the flaws lay, but he knew how to put them right. When their exuberance had died down and they were walking quietly along the last stretch of road towards the flat, he raised these points, and they agreed to work on the script again next day, when they were soberer.

'Sleep first, sleep,' said Francis. 'God, I haven't slept properly for weeks!'

'Me neither,' said Arnie. But next morning he was up at eight o'clock, and, leaning against the worktop in the little kitchenette so as not to wake Francis, was telephoning every harbour and yacht marina he could find in the Yellow Pages, enquiring about the *Miranda*.

Nearing harbour, thought Callum, was a mixed blessing for any crew. The land beckoned, with all its variety and freedom and new company and far, far better food; but against those gains must be set a certain loss of simplicity. No more would they know the restful lack of choice, the addictive routine of interrupted sleep and the powerful, exclusive workaday bond which builds up between those who live in a small wooden world together for weeks on end. Losing Stefan would, for sure, be no sorrow; there was something about the captain's surly, shrugging rebuttal of every friendly overture which reminded Callum rather uncomfortably of the way that he himself had behaved towards Susie in Portugal. But he was going to miss Jez, and even the taciturn Erik. A new respect had built between Callum and Erik during the four days' sailing up the North Sea, for Callum had had to work hard once the wind shifted to the north-east, turning out on deck to helm through every tack, and going forward with Jez to hand the big jib when a brief gale threatened. He had become nimbler now, learning to use his defective leg better. The pain in his knee troubled him only when it was jarred or struck; otherwise he had grown accustomed to a dull, steadily fading, ache. Jez had, to his relief, backed off a little from her open affection: somehow she had come to understand in silence that the relationship was not going to develop.

On the last night, with the Isle of May lighthouse flashing before them in the distance and the bright line of the Forth Road Bridge approaching in a blaze of car headlights, he sat with her on the foredeck. Neither of them could bear to go to their bunk, sharing a rising excitement and foreboding at the voyage's end. The wind was light and fluky, and there was barely an hour's diesel left; it would be daylight before they got in.

'I've liked sailing with you,' he said, without preamble.

'Stefan is a bad-tempered git and Erik is an acquired taste, but I've learnt a lot from you. Thanks.'

'I don't know much,' said Jez, rather sadly. 'I know my limitations.'

'Bollocks,' said Callum robustly. 'You could perfectly well run your own boat. I think you ought to.'

She turned towards him, and there was pain and hope in her eyes.

'Do you really think so?'

'Yes,' said Callum. 'You're brave, you're intelligent, you're careful, and you care about the crew and the boat. But don't try and learn off arseholes like Stefan. Go on a course. Do a Yachtmaster ticket. Can you afford that?'

'I could ask my parents to lend me some money, ahead of the inheritance,' said Jez slowly. 'If it was for something in a proper college, they might. Do you think I should?'

'When you have your ship,' said Callum, laying a hand carefully on her shoulder, 'I will sign on your first voyage, with complete and utter confidence.'

Jez did not answer until he had taken his hand off her shoulder again. Then she said gruffly: 'Thanks.'

'Do it,' said Callum. 'I'm not joking. Bloody do it. Seize the moment.'

'I heard you first time,' said Jez. 'Look, that's the Port Edgar pier-end light. Must be.'

'Single red, four seconds.'

'Stefan's furious we can't go into Leith. He always went in there when he was on that Norwegian ship. Thinks a yacht marina is beneath him.'

'He's always furious about something. Stuff him.'

'Stuff him rigid,' agreed Jez, and turned to smile at Callum in the darkness. He felt a moment of danger again, and said prosaically: 'It dries out, apparently. Granton Harbour, I mean.'

'Has anyone looked up the tides for tomorrow?'

'I dunno. I'll have a look.' He heaved himself to his feet to go back to the chart table. 'What's the date?'

Jez told him, and with a choke of dismay he turned back towards her, wrenching his knee painfully as he did so, and blurted: 'Oh, bloody hell! I was due to report to my CO three days ago!'

'He should have rowed out from Lowestoft, then, shouldn't he?' said Jez equably. 'Or do you lot walk on water these days?'

22

Francis woke up with a start, wondering why he was so happy. The show! Of course. It had gone well! But there was still work to do on it. He rolled over and peered at his black plastic alarm clock. Eleven o'clock! And there was the Nicholas Parsons show to get ready for. Hooray, help, hurry, hurry!

He jumped out of bed, wincing a little as his feet touched the floor, for he had danced with inspired vigour in his high-heeled shoes the day before and afterwards walked the breadth of Edinburgh. Then he remembered that he also had a missing yacht to find for Susie – oh, God, Susie! Callum! Oh, let the silly bastard not be drowned! O world, O life, O time! Scuttling into the messy living-room, angelic in his white cotton kimono, his dark hair standing on end, he croaked: 'Arnie! I've got to—' but Arnie was emerging from the kitchen, mobile pressed hotly to his ear, pencil in his hand and Yellow Pages wedged under his arm.

'Shush!' he said, then into the phone, 'Sorry, not you, Mr Mackenzie. Yes, thank you, I'll hold on.' To Francis he mouthed silently, 'Found it!'

'What?'

'Your sister's pesky boyfriend's boat,' said Arnie aloud, holding the phone away from him then clapping it back to his hot ear. 'Mr Mackenzie, hello! It's about the *Miranda*, a

Brixham – er – sailing trawler, which I believe you own?'

He listened for a moment then began protesting. 'No, sorry, I'm not looking for a charter – no, very good of you and it's a very exciting idea, but it's actually a passenger on board I need to contact – name of, erm, Callum—'

'MacAllister,' supplied Francis, agog.

'Callum MacAllister.' There was a silence, Arnie listening intently, Francis hopping from one bare foot to the other. Then Arnie said into the phone: 'Sorry? There isn't? No charterers on board at all? Oh, well, thank you. But—'

Francis was mouthing, 'Where? Where? When?' and tactfully Arnie struggled to extract this information from the man on the other end.

'Granton Harbour, you said, getting in about two? Splendid – no, it's just that I've heard so much about the boat – she sounds magnificent – I'd love to go and have a look. Um – my company might be interested in a summer charter . . . no, I must have been mistaken about Mr MacAllister, easy to get things wrong on the phone, don't you think?'

Francis, trying not to be distracted by the delicious vision of Maggie from the Gigz agency taking a corporate charter party on some old tub, plied Arnie with questions.

'Why does he say Callum's not on board? Does he know who is? What's going on?'

'All I know,' said Arnie, rubbing the ear which had been pressed to the phone, 'is that Mr Mackenzie owns the boat and he says there are no passengers on board, just the paid crew, and the only UK citizen is a woman.'

Francis mused for a moment.

'It was all very sudden, Susie said. I tell you what, I bet Callum wasn't on board officially. It'll be some sort of racket the captain's running, cash in hand. Susie said it all looked a bit hippy.'

'Oh, bugger,' said Arnie, worn out from hours of telephoning marinas and harbourmasters from the Clyde to the Forth. 'I suppose I've dropped him in it, then. *If* he's on board at all.'

'We can only hope. If he isn't, Christ knows where he is. I hope nothing's happened.'

The two young men stared at one another in real dismay.

'It's due in just before two,' said Arnie.

'It's nearly noon,' said Francis. 'The show. The notes from last night . . .'

'The Nicholas Parsons thing,' said Arnie, 'Is at half-past four. And then there's Radio Scotland at four. They rang this morning in between the old salts. Oh, hell and damnation!'

'How far is Granton Harbour?' asked Francis after a moment.

'Granton. It's under the Forth Road Bridge.'

'Well, that's not far. Sounds quite scenic, really. Look, Arnie—'

'I know,' said his friend resignedly. 'Don't ask me because I might say no It's the last thing we ought to do, for the show's sake. But you won't be happy till we check it out, and we in the trade *love* our artistes to be happy. Sometimes it can be done with flowers and chocs in the dressing-room, which is convenient. Sometimes it involves nasty wet boats and wild goose chases for missing soldiers.'

'Well, the thing is—' began Francis.

'Just don't speak. And never, ever, tell anyone at Gigz. I'll call a taxi, we'll pick up the van and go like hell.'

'We can talk about the show on the way,' offered Francis, surprised and touched by Arnie's acquiescence.

'Get a notebook.'

'Oh, dear, but I do want some breakfast.'

'McDonald's!'

Francis threw on his clothes, T-shirt back to front, sweater inside out, and pushed his sore feet into unlaced trainers. Together they tumbled down the steep stone steps and into a taxi; as it sped towards the van's parking place Francis stripped off his top half again and adjusted his clothing.

'This is not,' he puffed, from deep inside his sweater, 'the way it should be on the morning after. Oh, God, we ought to buy the papers.'

Arnie dived out of the taxi at the first red light and snatched a copy of the *Scotsman* from a newsboy, thrusting a pound coin into his hand. Struggling to open it in the confines of the back seat, over the expostulations of the driver, he read out choice praiseful snatches as the car swerved down the hill.

'Well, that's a bit of all right,' said Francis happily. 'Must wave it at Nicholas Parsons.'

'And Radio Scotland' said Arnie.

'You're an angel,' he said feelingly. 'If we bag Callum, I'm going to tell Susie it was you who did it. Oh, bugger, we ought to ring her so she can tell Mum, and Mum can tell Pat . . .'

'Find out if he's on board first,' said Arnie. 'Oh, God, I do need something to eat.'

They paid the taxi, snatched a lukewarm hot dog each from a stand, and with Arnie at the wheel and Francis muttering changes to his lines, made for the banks of the Firth of Forth.

Miranda coasted into the yacht harbour under engine just after one o'clock, her brown sails loosely furled on their spars.

Jez and Eric handled the lines, tying her to heavy cleats on a low pontoon. Stefan reached down and turned off the engine, and for a moment there was silence. Jez, already on the pontoon, swayed a little as her legs adjusted to its stillness. Erik climbed on board and began coiling down the rest of the mooring-lines. Then Stefan said to Callum, curtly: 'You must pay the extra days. I take off one-third for your working.'

Callum, who had not slept at all on the last night, yawned vaguely and said: 'I'll give you a cheque later, when I pack up.'

'You pay now. You go now,' said Stefan. 'Now!'

Jez opened her mouth to protest, but Callum spoke first. The land brought an end to all the disciplined restraint which had prevented his dislike of this man from surfacing while they were at sea.

'I get it,' he said. 'Your Mr Mackenzie isn't going to see any of this money, is he?'

'You pay now and go now,' said Stefan, and, to a cry of astonished outrage from Jez, picked up a heavy iron belaying pin from the pinrail at his side. He swung it in his hand with slow deliberation. 'Now!'

'I'll go now,' said Callum stiffly, 'but I'm damned if I pay you another penny! I've worked like a dog on this tub.'

Suddenly he noticed that Jez was gone from his side. There was a commotion from below and she reappeared with his wheeled case, which he had never unpacked but used as a locker throughout the trip. She threw it on to the pontoon – even in that fraught moment he could not help admiring the strength of her brown arms – and said: 'There you go. I've chucked your wallet and your other stuff in. You push off, and Erik and I will beat the shit out of our beloved leader if he thinks different.'

Stefan scowled, but Erik, amused, had moved to stand massive and reassuring beside the girl. She spoke again to Callum, who stood by the rail, uncertain and unwilling to leave them.

'Go! It's fine. I'm leaving anyway, and Erik's here. As soon as you're gone the stupid bastard'll put the pin down and have a beer. He's all talk. He just wants you off before Mackenzie gets aboard. That's why he lied on the phone about our ETA. I did wonder.'

Callum swung himself over the rail, took the handle of his bag and, in a gesture which for ever after represented for him the ultimate in male emotional inadequacy, spread his free hand, palm up, towards Jez.

He should, he realized much later, have kissed it, and blown her one last token of his respect and affection. Instead he merely held it out, muttered ''Bye, thanks', and turned away to walk rapidly up the wobbling pontoons towards the solid land, trailing his noisy wheels behind him.

There was a Customs van on the quay, and cautiously he slipped round behind it, unsure of the regulations for an unlisted UK stowaway coming home from an EU country. Being back on solid ground felt strange, but also reassuring: he was immediately aware that his leg was steadier than it had been when he left Portugal weeks earlier. He was walking quite easily without his stick; Jez presumably had not noticed it tucked at the far side of his bunk. His limp was noticeable, but not, he thought with satisfaction, pathetic.

At the iron gate beyond the dinghy park he paused, uncertain what to do. He could go into the marina building and order a taxi into Edinburgh, then draw some sterling out to pay it and get the train home to Glasgow. But he was reluctant to go into a building so close to his unofficial landing. He did not want complications.

Indeed, a dangerous conviction was growing in him that perhaps this was the moment to discard all complications, and merely vanish. Nobody knew where he was, or even for certain that he had been on the *Miranda*. Stefan would deny it, Erik would follow his lead, and Jez would probably be gone herself before any enquiries could be started. In any case, she would not give him away if she had the slightest clue that he had not resumed his own life. He had enough credit to draw a considerable amount of cash; he could make for Stranraer, cross to Ireland, and thence to anywhere in the world. He would e-mail untraceable messages reassuring Pat that he was safe. She could tell Susie – if Susie still wanted to know, which, he thought bitterly, seemed unlikely.

No, that was unfair. She deserved to know that he was alive, and then she could write their whole history off to experience with no regrets. He would find an internet café, and send the messages today.

Meanwhile, hitch-hiking seemed the best option. He was shabby, but knew that the Scottish motorist was less suspicious and more generous with lifts than his nervous equivalent south of the border. He looked at the sun and the line of the Firth, and worked out which way to turn for the city. Then he pulled his denim cap down over his eyes and trudged on, alone, towards the next part of his life.

He had gone about half a mile, failing to attract lifts, when a white van with a hire logo on the side shot past him going the other way, then stopped in a screech of brakes, skidding slightly on the damp roadway. He turned, expecting to see an accident, and instead saw a dark-haired young man tumbling hurriedly out of the passenger door and staring at him, before turning to the driver and almost shrieking: 'It *is* him! It *is!*'

Then the figure ran towards him in the middle of the road as the van cautiously reversed along the verge, and he recognized Francis Anderson, erstwhile prospective brother-in-law and dedicated hospital visitor. Tears pricked behind his eyes, because the slim dishevelled figure in jeans and sweater looked, as it ran, exactly like Susie.

23

'What are *you* doing here?' It was, Callum knew as he said it, an inadequate greeting. Francis, still jigging nimbly on his toes in excitement, scored higher.

'Meet 'n' Greet facility for incoming stowaways,' he cried. 'All part of the service. This –' he indicated the white van which had stopped beside them '– is Arnie.'

'Hello,' said Callum stiffly. 'I don't see how—'

'Arnie rang the marina. They said you wouldn't be in until after two, though.'

'Our skipper lied because he wanted to get me out of sight before anyone found out he'd taken an unofficial passenger. But how on earth did you know it was today? We've been weaving up the North Sea with no fuel for days. *We* didn't know we'd be in till yesterday.'

'I dunno. Coincidence. No, not actually pure coincidence. Your mum's going ape-shit, that's what, because your regiment rang her in a wounded tone asking for you back. God knows why. That started us investigating. Well, Arnie did it all. He's amazing. I'm doing a show in Edinburgh, so don't flatter yourself we've come far. But honestly, why didn't you ring?'

'Couldn't. The skipper kept his Satphone locked up.'

'Well, anyway, get in the van.'

Callum glanced up and down the road, not best pleased

with this suggestion. After his half-formed fantasy of flight and changed identity, to be picked up by Susie's own brother and immediately spoken to about his mother and his regiment created an unwelcome triple surge of anxiety and guilt. But there were no other vehicles in sight, and he did need to get to Edinburgh. And it looked like rain. And it was a stupid idea, anyway, the disappearing. People never disappeared successfully for long.

'Where are you going?' he temporized cautiously.

'Edinburgh. Oh, just get *in*. I've got a show to do. And two interviews. I'm *working*. I'm getting *famous*. We just came out to get you because it seemed too good a chance to miss, and I'm sick of Mum and Pat and Susie all worrying and thinking you're drowned. I never thought you were for a minute. You don't have that romantic Shelley look about you at all. So just get *in*, for God's sake.' Callum moved towards the van door, but Francis jerked his head in an unaccustomed show of impatient authority.

'In the back. I'm sorry about that, but Arnie and I are working up our lines on the way. We need the middle seat to put scripts down on.'

Arnie's pale head was leaning from the window now.

'Francis! It's going to be nearly bloody half-past three before we get parked! The traffic could be bad, so get the bastard *in* or leave him be!'

Callum climbed in through the back doors of the van, feeling distinctly wrong-footed by these two elfin scolds, and settled himself cautiously among the white sacks of costumes and the boxes of props. There was a furry cow's head, with horns, lying flaccid on one of the wheel-arches in a clear plastic bag, and a tin box of CDs digging into his back. He was tired after his night spent sitting watching the lights of

Scotland from the *Miranda's* deck with Jez, and after a few moments trying to sit up in the jolting van, he meekly interrupted the pair in the front, who were manically exchanging show patter at double speed, and asked if it was all right to lie on the sacks.

'No problem, all easycare no-crumple fabrics for our girls,' said Francis lightly. 'Be our guest. You'll probably,' he added in a moment of kindness, 'find the wig-bag makes the best pillow. It's the blue pillowcase.'

The little van swayed and thundered along the road to the city, and within minutes Callum was fast asleep. After a while, glancing back to check his passenger was unconscious, Francis broke off from show talk and said to Arnie: 'What are we going to do with him?'

'He's your pigeon,' said Arnie reproachfully. 'I assumed you'd have a bright idea.'

'You're more expert at picking up random guardsmen than me,' said Francis flippantly. 'Ow, stoppit!' Then, more seriously: 'Oh, hell, though, Arnie. I suppose the first thing is to ring my mum, ask her to ring Pat and tell her that he's OK and say she'll get more news soon.'

'Your sister could tell Pat.'

'No. Not fair on her. Pat will go on and on about the wedding, she doesn't know anything that's going on at all really. I'll text Susie that he's alive and OK, so she can stop thinking about that aspect of it. Honestly. She was convinced he'd top himself, but I never, ever thought he would, he's too sulky.'

'Does she –' this time it was Arnie who glanced back to check that Callum was sleeping '– does she want him back?' He found himself unaccountably interested in this strange couple; the nature of love was something he had thought about a great deal in recent weeks.

'Love's a funny thing,' said Francis, echoing his thought. 'So I'm told, anyway. The thing is, I rather think she might want him back.'

'I wouldn't,' said Arnie sententiously. 'So mean, running away to sea without a word.'

Francis looked at him, hard. Arnie, eyes on the road, blushed as his friend said softly: 'You bloody would. Soft as a pudding.'

''S what you think.'

'Anyway,' said Francis, recovering from a brief blush, 'we don't know what *he* wants, do we?'

Recalling the main point of the discussion, he then pulled out his mobile and rang his mother. Marion, far away in her quiet sunny hallway, gasped with relief.

'Oh, Francis! How wonderful! He's OK, you say? Where did you meet him? Is he going home? Shall I tell Pat to expect him? And do you think I should call Susie?'

'Mum, I don't think I should say much. Just that he's all right. Tell his mother, tell her it's all OK and he'll turn up shortly, and he's not in any trouble or ill or anything. There was just a confusion about dates or something. Make it up. I'll let Susie know.'

'I think I ought to talk to her—'

'No, Mum, I know best. Honest. I'll text her, then she doesn't have to react till she's ready to.'

There was a pause; Marion was about to ring off with standard farewells when Richard appeared at the end of the hallway, and she mouthed 'Francis'. Straight away he said in a low voice: 'How did his show go?'

Marion's hand flew to her mouth, and hurriedly she said into the phone: 'Darling, how did your show go? I thought that would be why you were ringing, but then you said you'd

found that blasted Callum and it shot out of my head. Um
– *Take Three Girls* has started, hasn't it? We're longing to
know!'

Richard, in the shadows of the hallway, nodded gravely in
approval. Francis, happy and entirely fooled by his mother's
last-minute save, quoted a few lines from the *Scotsman*
review and gave a brief paean of praise to Arnie for his
organization and the brilliance of his prop-van scheme.
Richard came on the line for a moment, said 'I bet you're
better than those Elvis Presley chaps who ran off to Holland',
and Francis giggled happily and accepted parental good
wishes for the rest of the run.

Then he tapped a brief text message to his sister.

CAL IS FINE AND IN UK. ARRIVED TODAY. PAT
BEEN TOLD. MORE INFO WHEN I HAVE IT. CBW-
CBR. The signoff was an old joke between them.

He pushed the 'send' button and glanced out of the
window. It was, in fact, raining. With difficulty he wrenched
his mind back to the imminent show; the van had slowed to
a crawl in the approaches to the city, and the clock showed
half-past three already.

'Radio Scotland!' he moaned. 'Where are we meeting
them?'

'Outside Pleasance Above, that end of the bar. They've
got a quiet spot they can do it before Parsons, at the end of
his auditorium. Then you're in the right place for doing his
show. He knows you won't be in costume. It's actually classier
to do, the chat shows *not* in costume, anyway. We'll just make
four o'clock if you jump out while I go off and park the van.'

At a minute to four, Francis flung himself from the van
outside the university courtyard which led to the myriad
small auditoria named as different varieties of 'Pleasance' for

the fringe festival's duration. He ran toward the bar, and identified the interviewer by her BBC T-shirt and ostentatiously badged microphone.

'Sorree! Been rushing all day!' he said. 'Right, where do we go? If you want Arnie he'll be five minutes—'

The interviewer did not want Arnie, and led him indoors out of the hubbub of the young crowd which, undeterred by the drizzle, was happy to drink and laugh and queue beneath its umbrellas and cagoule hoods.

Arnie, meanwhile, was having difficulties. In the parking bay behind the souvenir shop was a large red van with a scuffed transfer of a tartan-clad pixie on the side, whose driver was offloading boxes of goods in a leisurely manner in between flirtatious asides to the girl behind the counter. Leaving his own van askew on the pavement, Arnie ran in to the shop.

'Sorry – the van – I have to park up!' he said. 'Mrs Apthorpe's letting us have the space.'

'Och, it'll be twenty minutes or so,' said the girl casually. 'Danny's had to bring the delivery today, because they're stocktaking at McAndrew's on Saturday.'

'Is there much? Can I help?' asked Arnie desperately. 'Only I'm in a rush, we're onstage at half-past five and we have to get the costumes and props and go through the CDs with the technical guy—'

'That's guid o'ye, laddie,' said Danny. 'There's six boxes right at the back.'

'It'll give you time for that cup of tea then, Dan?' said the girl, who clearly had a *tendre* for Danny in his van. 'Will ye take one with us, Arnie?'

'No – no – I mean, I'm in a *real* hurry,' said Arnie. He fled out to fetch the first box, and found a policeman prowling round his van, peering disbelievingly in through the back window at the sight of Callum, unshaven and filthy, his arm flung over a furry pantomime cow's head, fast asleep on a pile of sacks from which peeped rose-pink flounces and the odd tress of blonde ribboned hair.

'Ye can't leave this here,' he said flatly, when Arnie began to explain. 'It's an obstruction.'

It was half an hour before Arnie got the van into its space, having driven slowly round the block under the policeman's sceptical eye while Danny the deliveryman personally unloaded his boxes of tartan pencils and furry Loch Ness monsters, and defiantly drank his tea.

Callum, unbelievably, was still asleep, only uttering a peaceful groan when Arnie pulled out the first load of bags. He ran up the street with them, threw them into the dressing-room at Pleasance Oblique and begged the Mini-Musical cast not to abuse them, then crossed into the main court-yard and cautiously pushed open the double doors of the room where the Nicholas Parsons Show was due to begin at four thirty. Parsons, grey hair sleek, was into his opening spiel and from the angle he stood at, Arnie could just see the corner of Francie' face, peering whitely from the wings. Satisfied, he ran back to the van and shook Callum's foot.

'I have to take the other sacks,' he said. 'Stay asleep if you like, you look as if you need it. Here, have my coat to lie on. We'll be back by six-thirty. Don't go away, for God's sake, not after all this.' He grabbed the costume sacks, lashing them together with a short piece of rope kept for the purpose, and picked up the last box of props. Callum, still deeply dazed from his headlong attempt to recover a long sleep debt, nestled acquiescently into the anorak thrown to him by Arnie, and fell asleep again. Arnie staggered up the road, laden and red in the face, and delivered his load to the dressing-room just as the cast of the Mini-Musical were clearing out.

'Good house?' he asked politely.

'Shitty,' said its principal artiste, disgruntled. 'Hey, is Francis doing Nicholas Parsons as well as Radio Scotland? Someone said they saw him out there.'

'Yup.'

'Jammy bugger.' The star of the less than starry Mini-Musical stumped off, his accordion bumping despondently against his bottom on its Tyrolean strap.

Arnie sat down on the chair, faint and tired. He realized that neither of them had eaten anything but a bad hot-dog all day, and that Francis in particular needed fuel for his high-energy show. Nothing heavy: just some fruit and a sand-wich. Wearily, he glanced at his watch – nearly five – and picked himself up to plod devotedly down the road to the corner shop.

Francis would be back soon from his interview. Arnie wished he had been able to see it. He wished he had been there for Radio Scotland. He wished there was not a large problematical AWOL army officer asleep in the back of his hired van. He wished he could be sure that the said army officer would not vanish again, plunging Francis into further worry for his sister.

When he got to the shop, he wished there were some other sandwich on sale than cheese and pickle because he, Arnie, hated pickle more than anything except Marmite. Francis liked cheese and pickle, though. He bought four, and some pears, and trudged back towards Pleasance Oblique. No business like show business.

24

Susie's mobile was off all day; she was back at work, super-vising a high-spirited recruiting party at a sunny country fair outside Cheadle. With some difficulty, and in defiance of the doctor, she had persuaded her temporary Commanding Officer that she was fit for the job. Since the other officer detailed to replace her was wanted back at Catterick, her task was not difficult. Not for the first time, the uniformed discipline and structure of her day held her together; she carefully cherished the expanding chip of ice in her heart which froze out terror and pain. The stand did well, drew large crowds, and was packed up in good time when the day ended.

Upright and determined, she strode back to the vehicle and, relaxing at last as Corporal Kevin took the wheel, flicked on her mobile out of habit. In a minute or two it bleeped, and she read the message; her hand shook so badly she had to lay it on her lap while she read Francis' message again. CAL IS FINE AND IN UK. ARRIVED TODAY. PAT BEEN TOLD. MORE INFO WHEN I HAVE IT. CBW-CBR.

She was glad of the jokey sign-off. From childhood the two of them had picked up this phrase of their father's: *could be worse, could be raining*. They had used it when trains stopped for hours between stations, when holiday plans went askew, when Francis was expelled from school again, when ten-year-old Susie broke her arm falling off her pony right in front of a dressage judge. She had texted it to Francis from Kuwait before they took her mobile away. In this context it was clearly a code to confirm that Callum was not in grave trouble, not mad, not hurt any worse in his body and not, as far as Francis knew anyway, living with some hippy girl off the boat.

Susie had tried not to allow herself to dwell on this latter possibility, yet it had never quite left her mind. Callum was back and he was OK, even if he did have some hasty explaining to do to his Commanding Officer. He was basically all right.

The useful chip of ice melted. Terror receded. The pain of blighted love returned. All the way back to camp Susie stared silently out of the window, her head averted from her Corporal at the wheel, tears running down her cheeks. It was, she judged, safer not to wipe them away. Young Kevin would just assume that she was tired, or preoccupied with some deep officerly thoughts. She blew her nose once, and muttered something about hay fever. Finally, while the driver was engaged in showing his pass at the camp gate, she ran her sleeve across her face, blew her nose again and spent the last few minutes texting back to Francis.

THANKS. TELL ME MORE. HOPE YR SHOW IS FAB. TELLABOUT THAT TOO. I CD CM & SEEIT?

In the dressing-room Francis sat in tights and bustier, wolfed down cheese-and-pickle sandwiches with a can of lager, and talked excitedly about his interviews.

'I suddenly see why lots of people sound such pillocks on the media,' he said, 'it's a whole different skill. You feel weird answering questions for the benefit of a third party and not the person who's asking them. Because you've got to talk to intelligent people who might be listening, but meanwhile the person you can see, the one who's asking the actual questions, might be a complete wally – I mean, not Parsons, but the woman from the radio station, all she'd read was the one review. So she didn't quite get that it wasn't just a drag show. Parsons was brilliant though, terrific feed lines—'

'Ten minutes, Francis!' said Arnie. He was already in the tweedy jacket and half-moon glasses which were supposed to define his part as a rather bumbling historian introducing the girls. He had hung up the main costumes earlier, and now passed the Fanny Fantoni dress to his protégé in a way which brooked no disobedience. 'Get your kit on!'

'You sound like a PE master,' grumbled Francis.

'Where would you be without me?' said Arnie rather complacently. But five minutes later, when Francis had expertly applied his make-up and looked round for his wig, all Arnie's confidence evaporated in a shrill cry of: 'Wig-bag! Oh, my God!'

'Didn't you bring it? It was next to the costume bags.'

'No, remember, we let your soldier-boy use it as a pillow. Oh, God, four minutes.'

They looked at one another in dismay. Starting late was not an option, not with the remorseless timetable of shows succeeding one another through the day in all these Fringe venues. But the show opened not with Francis, but with a five-minute introduction from Arnie, accompanied by offstage sound effects of singers warming up and acrimonious quarrels between Fanny, Sadie and Kelly. A local student worked the sound effects, so Francis was free for nine minutes rather than four.

'I'll get it,' he said decisively. 'Gimme the keys!'

'No, we'll send the ASM.'

'He won't find the van, he'll bring the wrong bag, and I don't know how to do the tapes – I'll go!'

'You're in drag!'

'This is Edinburgh! Nobody'll notice one more chorus girl breaking into a white van. Just start a couple of minutes late, and I'll have plenty of time. But hang on—' He kicked off his red high-heeled shoes and thrust his feet into Arnie's discarded trainers, which were the nearest.

'Shoelaces!' wailed Arnie as his friend disappeared down the stone stairway. 'Oh, God, don't fall over!'

Francis paused to tuck the laces in, then hared down the road to the souvenir shop, thinking to cut through the shop itself to the parking bay behind. As he neared it, though, he saw the retreating figure of the shopgirl swinging her keys and realized that it had closed. He doubled back, ran up the sidestreet and round to the back, fished out the van keys and then realized that he did not need them; with Callum asleep in the back Arnie had not locked up. He wrenched the rear doors open and scrambled in. Callum woke with a start and grabbed him, clearly prepared to fight for his life; in a repetitious gabble of 'Sorry!' and 'Emergency!' Francis wrenched the pillowcaseful of wigs from under Callum's head and then said: 'Look, we just forgot something. Back in an hour or so – go back to sleep. We'll sort you out after the show. Don't run away!'

Callum sat up, confused and uncomfortable, suddenly aware that for the past half-hour he had been lying on the hard metal ribs of the van floor. 'I should go—' he began.

'Don't be stupid, we've got a spare room at the flat, we'll eat after the show, but I have to *go!*' said Francis, anguished, and vanished with a slam of the rear doors. For a moment he wondered whether to lock the vehicle and keep his valuable prisoner; commonsense prevailed and he merely shouted, 'Stay put or I'll bloody kill you!' considerably startling a pair of elderly strollers.

'It'll be part of a show,' said the man consolingly to his wife, who replied disapprovingly: 'It's a funny hairdo, though, with a dress like that.' The fugitive's hair, indeed, stood up in black spikes above the swooping décolleté of his dress and the sparkle of his necklace.

Francis ran back to the dressing-room, and heard through the makeshift Tannoy that Arnie was halfway through his introduction with the sound effects going to plan. There was laughter from the audience. He kicked off the trainers and slipped his feet into his shoes, carefully checking the elastic which kept them on during his dance. He looked in the mirror, noticed a bad smear of his eye make-up, probably caused during the tussle with Callum, and adjusted it. Then he went into the wings to steady his breathing and prepare for his dramatic lunging entry from the time machine.

What he did not do was to put on his wig. He never understood why, but in later weeks, when the shame had faded a little, he would explain it away loftily as 'a matter of Stanislavskian focus' – he was so intent on his character that he no longer cared about the external detail of his appearance. The repair to his mascara was something he carefully overlooked in constructing this argument.

The first he knew of it was Arnie's frozen face, wide eyes staring at the top of his head. Raising his hand to smooth his hair, always the first gesture of Fanny's landing, he found no ringlets there and understood.

'Lawks!' he squeaked, mugging at the audience. 'I've left me bloody 'air in 1896!' So saying, he rushed from the stage to leave Arnie alone and improvising. Arnie was not a perfomer by choice or by nature; only exigencies of time and money had pushed him into learning the lines which he and Francis wrote for the show's introduction.

Frozen in terror, he stammered a few nonsensical words, polished his glasses on his shirt-tail and put his thumbs in his jacket pockets in a way the two of them had agreed was theoretically funny. The audience, drawn by the favourable review and the rumour of a hot new talent, sat silent and disappointed. There had been a small laugh at Francis' line, but no goodwill remained for the flustered Arnie. Seconds stretched into centuries for the hapless young manager; rescue came almost too late when Francis at last sashayed back on to the stage, ad-libbed 'You still 'ere? Gettoff, I got a show to do', and signalled to the lad with the music to skip the slow start and give him the rousing overture to 'Only a Poor Little Country Girl'.

The audience relaxed, and giggled; Francis gave it all he had. When he dashed offstage to grab his grass skirt and coconuts and Arnie stumbled back to introduce South Seas Sadie, all went reasonably smoothly; the cow's head, indeed, went down better than the night before. But at the interval, when Francis according to custom drank a pint of water and lay flat on his back in the dressing-room, arms spreadeagled, Arnie's state was pitiable.

'It's totally my fault. I never picked up the wigs. It's my fault you had to run. It's a miracle you could even b-breathe, let alone sing! Could've wrecked everything. I *did* wreck everything, I d-dried. Oh, God, Francis. I am so sorry, so sorry . . .'

As Francis sat up, alarmed by his friend's tone, he saw to his horror that Arnie was weeping. His pale face beneath its white-blond crop was pink and distorted; his normally sharp features blurred, his straight shoulders slumped. He looked terrible. Francis loved him in that moment, and never afterwards stopped doing so. Pushing himself to his feet, he tottered over to Arnie and folded him in his arms; Arnie sobbed helplessly on his shoulder, and so the young men stood until the student stage manager, enthralled to witness another great Edinburgh Fringe moment, popped his head round the door and told them there was a minute to go to the second half. Tweed jacket, half-glasses, brogues, leather jacket and black boots were scrambled on in mute, panicky co-operation; the two stumbled towards the wings, and flew.

Callum, meanwhile, climbed over into the front seat of the van to find some comfort for his aching back, and sat for a while rubbing his head and staring confusedly into the mirror. He needed a pee, and achieved this, with some shame, in the drain sheltered by the offside front wheel of the van. Having no idea where he was, and no keys to protect the vehicle anyway, he then climbed back into the front passenger seat and continued rubbing his head for a while. All he could remember of Francis' nightmare crash into his sleep was an improbable décolleté, a jangling necklace, an injunction to stay put and the words 'spare room' and 'eat after the show'.

Those words had had a comforting sound; and indeed there was something generally comforting about the bossy good-natured atmosphere that the two young men carried with them. They had nothing to do with any life he had led recently; nothing military about them, and none of the dogged, solemn romance of the sea journey. They exchanged sharp pattering jokes, he remembered from the minutes before he slept; they spoke of wigs, and dragged bags of costumes from underneath one, and lived in brief exhilarating bursts of showbusiness panic. Yet Francis looked like Susie, was kind like Susie, was telling him what to do. He could obviously never face Susie again, let alone claim her, that was clear; but for the moment he was safe in the care of her brother. There was comfort in that. He would wait for Francis to tell him what to do.

25

'Right,' said Francis in the dressing-room, when he had taken his final bow and dragged a reluctant Arnie on to the stage to take one with him, gaining a final laugh by taking the half-moon glasses and putting them on with his Kelly costume, then whipping out the Fantoni wig from behind his back and putting it on the tweed-jacketed Arnie. 'Another one down. Another day, another dollar.'

'I am *so* sorry—' began Arnie again, but Francis put a finger to his lips.

'Shut up. You recovered. Your ad-lib wasn't so bad. You finished the show. They clapped. That's all that counts.'

'I shouldn't be on a stage though really. I'm a backroom boy,' said Arnie. 'The thing is, I honestly don't like it. I don't get whatever the buzz is that you lot get.'

'Fair enough,' said Francis. 'But this particular thing works better if you're a bit of a dork, see? It's how we wrote the part.'

'Hmm. Well, anyway, sorry about the wig—'

'Never mention wigs again in my hearing!' said Francis theatrically. 'I do not wish to hear of wigs.'

Arnie gradually recovered his equanimity, eventually managing to say, 'I thought we might keep that line in. About leaving your wig in 1890-whatsit.'

'No,' said Francis. 'I said, no wig talk. I may be brave, but I bear scars.'

They were walking towards the van again, slowly this time, the burden of bags and boxes divided amicably between them and Francis' shoelaces properly tied.

'Oh, I am hungry!' said the diva. 'And weary!'

'Let's go to Alfio's,' said Arnie happily. 'In a cab!'

'With Callum.'

'Oh, God, yes. Forgot Callum. Perhaps he's gone?'

'He'd bloody better not—' began Francis, but then he saw the distant shape of Callum sitting up, lost in thought, in the front of the van. 'Goody, he's still in the bag.'

'Why do you want him?'

'For my sister, of course. Don't be jealous, dear.'

'As if,' replied Arnie, now entirely master of himself. He was struggling against a tide of rising hope and joy, for he had no real confidence in it. The day had been too confused, too shocking, too much of a roller-coaster ride between humiliation and happiness. It was better to go back to brittleness, and laugh together. But Francis shot him a look so loving, so entirely new, that he could not stifle his hope, and looked straight back; the two of them with one mind slowed their step, so as to recover their emotional balance before they faced their guest.

'Hi, Cal!' said Francis breezily as they approached. Callum had swung the door open and was awkwardly climbing down into the yard. 'Don't know about you, but we are very, very hungry. Did you eat well on that boat?'

'No,' said Callum, relieved to have an easy topic of conversation. 'Rice, pasta, rice, onions, rice, pasta. The tins more or less ran out two days ago, we'd run out of bread and the flour spoiled in the bad weather—'

'Oh, God,' said Arnie, 'he's going to talk about ship's biscuit and weevils in a minute, I can tell. I'll be sick if I don't get some *food*.'

'Alfio's,' said Francis. 'Come on, dump the stuff and bring that wheelie-bag, we're going by cab. We're staying ten steps from Alfio's, so we can stagger home however drunk we all get.'

'Epic,' said Callum with an attempt at heartiness. He had taken his wallet from the side pocket of his bag – where, he thought with a brief pang of sadness, the faithful Jez must have stashed it in the tense moments before his departure. 'I've got fifty quid in sterling, but everything else is Euros that I ought to change.'

'Fifty quid will do nicely. At Alfio's,' said Francis. 'Oh, food, food!'

Three hours later, gorged and tipsy, the performers led Callum back to the rented flat and pointed him towards the lower bunk in the small back room. There was no possibility of any serious conversation about the past or the future. Over dinner Arnie and Francis merely relived their tumultuous performance and reviewed the two nights' audiences in detail, and Callum ate slowly, almost silently, taking unreflective animal pleasure in the sheer variety and tastiness of landsmen's food. By the time they got back to the flat none of them wanted to do anything but sleep, alone, on quiet beds till mid-morning; which they did.

Morning, however, brought a chillier wind of reality into their lives. Arnie's hangover was interrupted by an irritating call from Maggie at the Gigz agency, enquiring about some arrangements he was supposed to have made in Purley for one of their singers. By the time he had found his note-book and read the relevant telephone numbers, Francis was awake and wandering round the flat complaining about a new and troublesome pair of blisters on his toes.

'I knew I should have bought Fanny some new shoes!' he

mourned. 'It's the cheap bloody taps that do it, but the Anello ones cost so *much* – how was I to know that I was going to be an international superstar?'

'What do you mean, international?'

'Scotland's a nation now, innit?'

Then Callum got up, and having excavated his shaving gear and some cleanish flannels from his wheelie-bag, made a more formidable and soldierly appearance than yesterday. This dulled the spirits of the others, making them feel like exiguous Fringe butterflies next to his manly solidity. Arnie, still hungover, was faintly hostile; Francis began to flutter. Eventually, when Arnie went out for some tinned soup and fresh milk and bread, Francis broached the subject nearest to his heart.

'Cal, what about Susie? When are you going to ring her?'

Callum, who was sitting in the only comfortable chair pretending to read yesterday's *Scotsman*, looked up sullenly and said: 'I don't know what you mean.'

'You were going to be married, a month ago,' said Francis flatly.

'Yes, but – you know what happened. It wasn't working. She's far better off without me.'

'Yes,' said Francis satirically. 'You know that, and I'm beginning to agree, the way you carry on. But Susie ought to have some say, no?'

'That's not how it works,' said Callum stiffly. 'When a thing's broken down . . . anyway, everything's different now. I'll probably have to leave the Army.' He made a show of rubbing his leg.

'Why do you both have to be in the Army to get married? Is there some *law* about it?'

'Susie's better off without me,' said Callum, who was

becoming seriously embarrassed by this frontal assault. 'What passed between us is our own business. It's over. I'll write to her and apologize, obviously. I know I wasn't any kind of a gentleman about it.'

'Write to her? Creep!' said Francis pleasantly. 'Cowardy custard!' He, too, was hungover. Callum spoke not another word; when Arnie had returned with the lunch he ate with them in virtual silence, and then said stiffly: 'Well, thanks for the lodging. I'll be off now. Ought to go and see my mother. In Glasgow.'

Francis was angry with himself. He had gone too far. Trying to ignore his headache, and pulling together all his resources of charm and manipulation, he said: 'Look, Cal. Go home by all means, sort out your life, but we did rescue you and let you sleep on our wig-bag, so do one thing for us, soldier? Just one?'

'What?'

'If they let you out again, come back on Saturday night and come out on the town. A last farewell to the Anderson family. I don't want us to go out on a sour note, and we're all too shaken up and hungover and tensed up with the show to be civilized now. Just come back and have a jar or two, with me and Arnie here, and say goodbye properly. Then, if there are any family messages to pass on about the Army and stuff, we'll do that for you.'

Callum was too surprised to say no. When he had gone, Arnie asked Francis in some mystification, 'What was that all about?'

'Relationship counselling,' said Francis. 'I texted Susie, and she's got the night off on Saturday. Says she can stay over.'

'You really shouldn't interfere,' warned his friend. 'I think he's a bit of a Benny, frankly. Not all there. Your sister'll get over it.'

'One more push,' said Francis. 'Then I'll give up. Promise.'

His plan, in fact, was simple; they would take Callum to dinner, probably at Alfio's, meet Susie there and artfully abandon the couple alone together at a table. In a public place, with drink inside them, they would surely come to the beginnings of an understanding. At the very least, Callum would have to apologize face-to-face for his desertion and his cold letter, and Susie could express any remaining fury in her heart. Closure, that was what they called it. Closure, at worst.

At best . . . but Francis did not want to risk contemplating the best. He believed his sister to be still in love, and suspected that Callum, now his leg worked better and his cosmic sulk against the universe seemed to have abated, probably still loved her too. He felt particularly tender towards lovers just now; the unfolding of his own tentative passion for Arnie made that inevitable. But old Cal was never going to take the plunge himself. For a soldier, he seemed to be frankly a bit of a wuss. Not the kind of chap to spot what he wanted and go for it at all costs, guns blazing, death or glory. If he, Francis, were to mislay Arnie now in some Portuguese shenanigan, he would go straight after him and nag and beg and court any humiliation to see if things could be mended.

'He's actually scared of facing her,' he said to Arnie later. 'I wonder how he'd manage when the guys start throwing bottles, down at the Frog in Waders.'

'Well, he's a soldier,' said Arnie reasonably. 'He'd obviously have some intercontinental ballistic bottles of his own to throw back.'

'Mmm. S'pose so. It's going back out into the smoke with nothing to throw that's the hard bit,' said Francis. 'But he's gotta do it.'

Pat was tearful and grateful and maternal and, after a while, unbearable; once she began gushing about Susie and the wedding, Callum hastily collected his uniform and hugged her goodbye. His Commanding Officer was not at all maternal, nor tearful, nor grateful for his return, he was acerbic and damning. Overstaying leave without contact or excuse was not acceptable. It was time Callum considered his position. Given his continuing sub-optimal fitness, a medical discharge with gratuity would be granted, but not enforced. Otherwise a desk job would – for a period – be available. He had three days to think it over before reporting again on Monday. End of story.

The interview took barely ten minutes, and left Callum feeling distinctly crushed. By now it was Friday; he remembered that he had agreed to return, if he was released, to Francis and Arnie's flat in Edinburgh. He found himself shakily grateful for the invitation. He had no idea at all what to do; he had been as good as ordered to do his thinking off the base so travelled back north on the train overnight, sitting up in a cheap seat with a fuzzy, unclear head. The bar was open so he drank four miniatures of whisky as the night wore on, and arrived on their doorstep on Saturday morning unshaven and uncertain of step. Arnie, wearing Francis' white kimono, opened the door and surveyed him without enthusiasm.

'Your licentious soldier's back,' he called over his shoulder. 'Looks pretty rough to me.'

Francis emerged from the shower, wrapped in a threadbare

towel. 'Oh, come in, Cal,' he said vaguely. 'Yup. Tonight. Great.' Arnie's mobile rang and he vanished into the kitchen, slamming the cardboard door, to conduct an exclamatory, excited conversation which the two in the living-room could almost follow. Callum sat down and Francis went to dress; moments later Arnie shot through the living-room to Francis' bedroom, blethering about a cabaret.

'It's a fantastic chance! It's Duckie! They really pull in the interesting people! All they want is five minutes of Kelly, singing some words they've written for her – the producer was sitting in on our show last night and he says you're just what they need for a speciality act!'

'What time?'

'It's earlier than usual tonight – seven-thirty – all over by half-past nine because they have to get rid of the tables and the glitter-ball. You'll already be in the Kelly costume, so no problem changing. We can get a cab—'

'We're taking Callum out –' Francis lowered his voice '– and meeting Susie, remember?'

'No!' said Arnie explosively. 'You *have* to do this. You *have* to. It's big time. It's national press stuff. It's an amazing chance – and it's *now*.'

'They do it every night,' protested Francis.

'Yeah, but it's tonight that they've lost the speciality act. Green Giantess was doing it, but she's got 'flu.'

Francis made Callum a cup of coffee while they continued, *sotto voce* in the kitchen, to argue about the cabaret. It was, Francis knew, objectively true that this was too good a chance to miss. The unsettlingly original Duckie cabaret had been imported from its London base in Vauxhall to the Fringe for a week; it was a show Francis and Arnie had seen as customers. The audience sat at heavy round tables of eight, were given a menu, and after a louche dance overture ordered individual acts to come and perform in an intimate manner various bizarre burlesque performances: mildly obscene balloon modelling, high kicks in a variety of costumes, mimes, unexpected excerpts from classic novels (notably, and inevitably, Joyce's *Ulysses*). Its sheer absurdity and its teasing undercurrent of Weimar cabaret decadence had made it a surprise hit even among the more conventional audiences. 'Moulin Rouge meets *Viz* comic,' wrote one critic approvingly. 'So silly that it contains a sort of wisdom.'

And to be a guest star, thought Francis, you did not even have to dress in a body-stocking and frilly blue pants nor execute the bizarre fluffy duck dance which concluded each Duckie performance. You could just do your own thing – adapted to the close-up format – and depart with honour. Madame Galina had done it. Various singers and magicians had done it. It was hip, it was an honour to be asked; Arnie was right, he had to do it.

He began re-plotting the evening. Callum had asked if he could catch up on his sleep and vanished to the bunk bed. It was clear, though, that later on he must come to the cabaret to be kept under guard until the Susie-moment in the restaurant could be engineered. Susie, therefore, must be kept away until the cabaret was over at nine-thirty. Even Francis did not think that it would be ideal to create a surprise meeting over a table on which some lithe performance artist in knickers and an Aztec mask was miming girl-on-girl wrestling. It would be, apart from anything else, just too easy for the lovers to avoid one another's eye.

How could he dispose of Susie for two hours? She was coming to his own show at half-past five – that was the excuse for hauling her up to Scotland, after all, and she had no idea Callum was to be there – but that would be too early to break it to her, and if the former lovers met accidentally in the theatre it would all be disastrous.

'Arnie . . .' he began tentatively, when his thoughts had reached this stage.

'I know,' said Arnie glumly from the window. 'I'm like Sherlock Holmes. I just have to look at you thinking and muttering to yourself and counting on your fingers to know exactly where your awful thoughts are tending. You want me to field your sister until after the cabaret, so she doesn't see lover-boy.'

'Oh, would you *mind?*'

'I really wanted to come and see you do Duckie. I need to – professionally.'

'But there's nobody else.' Francis clutched his head. 'Oh, Arnie, you've put up with so much shit from me this last week or so . . . but she's my sister, and she's so sad . . .'

'I don't have a sister,' said Arnie, 'so clearly I don't understand this compulsion to micro-manage other people's pathetic love affairs.' He sighed. 'It won't work, you know. It's just screwing up your Edinburgh career for nothing. Having said that, where shall I take her?'

'She might enjoy the show after ours at Oblique. The Laurel and Hardy tribute thing.'

'I was afraid you'd say that. If she *does* enjoy it she is not a girl I want to spend time with.'

'It's not so bad!'

'It is, it's worse than the Mini-Musical.'

'It's the last awful job I'll ask you to do. Ever.'

'Believe that when I see it! Your sister, what's she like? Apart from thinking a Laurel and Hardy ballet might be a good idea? She's a soldier, isn't she?'

'Yes.'

'Oh, God. Habit of command. Click heels. Salute your senior officer. Look, Francis –' there was a real note of appeal in his voice '– how'm I supposed to control her, if she decides she wants to stay with you instead? I'm just a poor feeble poof – I can't take on a lady soldierine.'

'She's sweet. Really. We'll tell her I've got a meeting with a TV guy, we won't tell her about the cabaret at all. So she'll happily stay on with you.'

'Well, Callum will tell her about the cabaret, won't he?'

'If we get them talking at all, that's a victory. They could gang up on us for being deceitful manipulative bitches. That'd be *good*.'

'And if they don't, and your sister's staying over and Callum's staying here too, what sort of night do you think we're all going to have?'

'I don't think. I hope. Once they *see* each other it'll be fine. Probably.'

Callum slept on until they woke him at four with instructions to meet Francis at the cabaret venue, later in the evening.

'I'd rather like to see your *Three Girls* show,' said Callum politely. 'I thought I might come down with you, and not be asleep in the van this time.'

A shrill chorus of protest made it clear to him that they would rather he didn't. Mystified but obedient, he went for a rainy walk around the granite city instead, his thoughts circling helplessly round his lost Susie, the Army, the impossible future.

If he took a discharge, what else could he do? Tramp round the City looking for a desk job? Sell himself to some arms dealership? Retrain as a geography teacher? In the old days, he thought, people in his position went to America or Australia, or planted stuff in Africa, or did a bit of light ruling in India. But none of those places wanted washed-up Brits with gammy legs any more. They had grown up. He hadn't. He was a useless anachronism. He didn't even have a manual skill, like gardening. Perhaps he could be a delivery skipper, like Stefan? The thought oppressed him still more.

His mood grew bleaker, but he resolved to have a civil evening with Francis, who seemed at least to care a little about him. Nice boy. Decent. He felt a pang of extra sorrow, on top of his constant burden, because he would never now be part of the same family as Francis, and had never appreciated him properly when he was. He had always liked Marion and Richard, but it was strange that he had never seen how decent Francis was before. His showbiz friend was a bit of an oddball, but live and let live . . .

Francis, meanwhile, was assembling his sister a cup of coffee in his dressing-room and making her laugh with a highly coloured account of the wig disaster, carefully leaving out the reason why the bag was left in the van in the first place. Arnie popped in and out, enthusing exaggeratedly about the Laurel and Hardy tribute show which he would take her to between seven-thirty and nine. Susie, unsuspecting, went along happily with all their arrangements. It was restful not to be in command; like Callum before her, she rather enjoyed the bossiness of the pair. Unlike Callum, she spotted straight away that her brother was in love, and happy, and set to remain so. She was glad for him.

She did ask Francis about Callum once, where he had actually seen him and where he had gone. Her brother replied with an unblinking facility for fibbing which had always stood him in good stead.

'To Salisbury Plain, I think, sorting out his CO. Only saw him fleetingly when he got off the boat. He had to make a run for it.'

'As long as he's alive,' said Susie with a pretence of indifference which almost convinced herself. 'They'll sort him out. I'm over all that nonsense, by the way. Sorry I got a bit stupid when I saw you in the medical centre. Had a temperature.'

'Forget it,' said Francis, and pulled on his wig.

'You know something?' said Susie, diverted. 'You look just like that picture of Mum when she was in the Wrens.'

26

---•◆•---

The C'est Vauxhall Cabaret by the organization calling itself Duckie has become legendary, in circles where such entertainments are prized. Emerging from its beginnings in the gay pub subculture of South London, its verve and wit and solemn silliness turned it into a cult. Arriving in his taxi in full Kelly make-up, Francis hurried round to the back-stage area and found a full complement of performers: three tall, athletically built women and an equally willowy man called Chris, all insouciantly adjusting their tight flesh-coloured outfits and absurd frilly blue pants, and fiddling with hairnets and eyeliner.

To conventional chaps like his father they would be, he supposed, figures of decadent nightmare (he was wrong, in fact: Richard Anderson had seen the world in his time and didn't mind its ways a bit). The wickedness, however, seemed to be merely superficial: the young people's workaday back-stage good-nature belied their appearance. They were discussing the opening dance, when a group of apparently ordinary tables rise and gyrate on long human legs. One of the girls had already fixed a flat gold-draped miniature table on her head, complete with wineglass.

'Oh, it's much better now,' said her voice from beyond the opaque veil that formed the tablecloth. 'It was really slipping last night.'

'Five minutes' said a lesser performer, costumed this time as a waiter and cultivating – with judicious use of eyeliner – an epicene, faintly threatening manner designed to put the nervous customer in mind of a 1930s continental nightclub. 'They're all in. Full house.'

'The guy I told you about, did he turn up? The one with the house ticket?' asked Francis, who was fretting with his eye-black in the only vacant corner of the big mirror.

'Yes. Big, blondish, Viking-looking chap? In a sailor-type sweater?'

'Mmm, yup.'

'He's here. I put him on a table with some of the press people and Maddy and Louise.'

'Will they be nice to him?'

'Everybody is nice here. *Tout est permis*,' said the false waiter with a knowing leer.

The producer came to find Francis and check that he was happy with the new words for Kelly's song, 'Devilgate Drive'.

'You might want to do a few of the extra orders, too,' he said. 'Any ideas? Fancy an emotional striptease?'

'Dunno,' said Francis, honoured to have it assumed that he would ad-lib with the same insouciance as the four regulars. 'Haven't thought of anything.'

'Well, play it by ear.'

Francis found that all other thoughts, even thoughts of Arnie, were now swept from his mind by the need to adapt to a new format. He considered his options. The system for the evening was that tables consulted together on how to spend their toy-money, 'Duckie dollars', by ordering a menu of acts to come to their table; this happened in a random order, with each table suddenly spotlit when an act was looming, and temporarily inactive tables craning incredulously to see what on earth was being done to their neighbours. Then, in a brief free-for-all as the dollars ran out, just after Francis' short explosive performance was scheduled, various other possibilities were offered. You could opt for one of the performers to come and insult you each personally (or, rather more embarrassingly, to praise you) or you could order an 'Emotional Striptease'. This was popular among the cast, who after an evening of exhausting dances, contortions, high-kicks on the table and generally subversive parodies of the lapdance genre, quite enjoyed sitting down in their alarmingly bare costumes among giggling customers, and permitting the punters to question them for three minutes by egg-timer on such topics as 'Me and My Make-up' or 'Coming Out'. There was always the possibility of an outbreak of emotional honesty in these sessions which would startle the cast as much as the customers. Francis thought, on the whole, that he was not ready to subject himself to it.

Callum, sitting in his worn sweater at a tableful of strangers, was in a curious and unfamiliar state of mind. He should, he thought, be uncomfortable: the chattering journalists seemed to have nothing in common with him, and the two girls he sat between, identified as Maddy and Louise, were apparently local Scottish friends invited by one of the technical staff. Talking across him, they mainly exchanged compliments on one another's clothes and inside knowledge about the low-hanging nightclub lights over each table, which would power up into the ceiling and become spotlights when the show began.

The girls were pleasant enough to him, firing off a few questions about how he knew Francis ('He got fantastic reviews on his first show! I mean, *so* lucky!'). He evaded these, mumbling something about 'just an old friend I ran into'. The girls convinced themselves that the two had been at school together, and moved on. They did not seem to have noticed his limp, nor did they show any curiosity about what he did. Perhaps, he thought hazily, there really was a whole new world out there, a macrocosm of the wooden world of the *Miranda*, where people would not be interested in Iraq, or the Army, or care that he had run out on a devoted fiancée. Perhaps he had lived for too long in too narrow a trench. Perhaps he was a bit of a bore. Perhaps he really had done Susie a favour by moving out of her ambit. Everything came back to Susie now; every thought, every regret.

The group at his table now had their heads bent over the performance menus, and the journalists – three men and two assertive young women – were shrill in their insistence.

'Have to have Nacho Snatcho. It's astonishing, barely legal.'

'And the Mexican wrestling. And Miss High Kicks of the Six Cocks . . . they're only balloons, don't worry, Tim.'

'Who's worrying?'

It all seemed silly to Callum, but harmless. Francis had given him a brief outline of what to expect; he had been to enough nightclubs to understand what was being parodied. The only mystery to him was that anybody in this youthful, ironic British audience should be expected to be aware of the overpriced, outdated *boîte de nuit* culture the show was sending up. He supposed that they had seen the film of *Cabaret;* that might do the trick. But on the whole they looked to him more like modern clubbers, swiggers from bottles and tablet-taking ravers; very unlikely customers even for the lapdance clubs to which chaps like Harry Devine dragged friends in London.

'Colin here hasn't chosen anything,' said the girl called Louise kindly. 'Go on, you choose.'

'I ought to see my friend Francis,' said Callum. 'But I'm not sure what his act's called.'

'He won't be on the main menu,' said Maddy, the bossy voice of experience, 'if he's not one of the four regulars. He'll be a special. I daresay he'll come round all the tables anyway. What's he doing?'

'No idea. I know it's a song, and he's going to be in costume.'

The girl looked at him as if she were a jaded primary school teacher and he the most unpromising of her remedial class. But her sense of justice remained strong.

'Well, though, you choose something. You haven't had your go.'

'Er – no, you know the score, you do it for me. I'll just sit back.'

'If you're sure? I think we ought to have the swivelling guy who reads your aura – Thomas says it's great.'

Some fairly terrible champagne had arrived; Callum drank deeply, and paid for another two bottles to keep the table going. This proved a popular move with the journalists, who began digging for information about their quiet benefactor.

'Are you in the biz? Scouting out talent, sort of thing?' asked one of the women. She was, he saw, rather older than he had first thought in the dim light; plump bare shoulders beneath thin gold straps had deceived him. She had a wide mouth like a dogfish, and pale lecherous eyes, and she swore a great deal. Callum felt a shrinking horror of her, but resolved to be polite.

'No,' he said, peering round the dangling lamp. 'I'm nothing to do with the theatre really. Just a friend of—'

The lamp between them abruptly brightened, and swirled up into the ceiling. The dogfish woman forgot him instantly, clapping her hands and uttering a pleased obscenity. A loud chord introduced a harsh voice though the sound system, welcoming the company, and a hitherto unnoticed curtain swished aside, revealing on a makeshift stage a group of four round tables each with a gold cloth and a champagne glass on it, like a smaller version of the room where the audience sat. The tables rose and began to dance in an absurdist parody of eroticism. Four sets of excellent legs manoeuvred beneath the wavering, swaying tablecloths; heads and torsos were invisible, but to Callum's startled eye it was soon apparent that one set of legs was male.

Ah, well. This was Francis' world, not his, and the audience was giggling in surprised delight. He himself felt his spirits rising, for no reason. So, result! Success, thought Callum with a shaft of surprise, must surely be measured only by what you set out to do, and whether you do it. He hadn't. Francis, and these curious friends of his, clearly had.

An hour earlier, Susie too had been happily impressed by her brother's professional efforts. *Take Three Girls* was witty, it was likeable, and it was too well done to seem in any way undignified. It was, she thought, a minor but genuine piece of art, especially the poignant first section with Fanny Fantoni. She liked the songs very much too, and wondered whether at the end of this flamboyant phase in his life Francis might settle into being a singer: his high light tenor was more attractive than ever, and the numbers he wrote himself, pastiche though they were, had real beauty. He might be capable of writing a musical; she saw the beginnings of it in what he had done tonight.

Whatever he did, she thought with sisterly satisfaction, he was on his way now. A well-reviewed Edinburgh Fringe show

– and virtually a one-man show at that – took a performer into a different league. She looked forward to telling their parents about it, and showing them the *Scotsman* review and any others which came out. Even the London papers might review him now; if they signposted him as worth seeing, and especially if he got a television airing, his stock would instantly rise higher among the parental friends. There would be no more patronizing remarks from the likes of Marjorie Hampton and the ghastly Rupert. Yes, he was on his way. There was real, warm comfort in the knowledge.

When the show ended she went to the dressing-room and told him so while he caught his breath, packed a small bag with his day clothes and waited for his taxi. She also, most punctiliously, congratulated Arnie on his part in it all. He flushed, insisting that he had done virtually nothing and that the talent was entirely Francis' own. He was stuffing costumes into a sack as he spoke, and explained the van routine to Susie. There was something hurried and furtive about him, she thought; perhaps it was just the embarrassment of having to look after a female stranger.

'It won't take me long, couple of trips, we'll be in plenty of time for the Laurel and Hardy thing,' he said, shaking down the wig-bag and avoiding her eye.

'Well, look,' said Susie, 'that's daft. I can carry half the stuff down to the van with you, and then you won't have to do two trips. Then we'll both have time for a drink before the other show.'

She was not without guile in this suggestion; as they went, she could ask him about Francis, or at least probe gently into what was going on between them. 'Come on, give me those sacks.'

Francis blew her a grateful kiss, and slid off to his waiting taxi. Arnie, only his eyes visible above the box of CDs and the wig-bag, said as he left, 'Good luck, Francis! Hope it goes a storm!'

Susie followed him round to the back of the souvenir shop with her load, and on the way managed to catch up with his scuttling progress and ask curiously: 'Why did you say "good luck"? Is this meeting really important?'

'Meeting?' said Arnie, forgetting himself. 'Oh, yes, Francis' meeting!' He unlocked the back doors and tumbled his burdens into the back of the van. 'Yes, a meeting with an – er – TV man.'

Susie put her load down and stared into the dark belly of the vehicle. She said nothing. She stared for so long that Arnie followed her glance to see what she was looking at. It was a hat.

It was Callum's denim hat. She had bought it for him in Portugal, because of all things he hated to have the sun in his eyes. Since he also hated baseball caps because they reminded him of the US military, and she herself disliked the cotton Christopher Robin sun-hats worn by middle-aged British tourists, she had been particularly pleased to find this hat. It was unexceptionably boaty, with a decent but not exaggerated brim over the eyes and no embarrassing logos or cheeky buttons on the top. It was also quite a nice colour, faded denim, and had a small elasticated section at the back which made it unlikely to blow off. There were not many hats like it. It was more faded now than when she had last seen it; but it was, undeniably, Callum's hat.

Arnie looked at it too, and although he had no particular memory of it on Callum's head, he recognized that given the personal styles of himself and Francis, there was no way he was ever going to pass off this grubby object as the property of either of them. It looked like something that Donovan might have worn on a 1965 album cover.

'You had him in the van.'

It was a statement, not a question. Susie was still looking at the hat; it affected her strangely and not at all for the worse. There was something very personal about it. It was a link to Callum's real physical being, and the longer she stared at it, smiling slightly in spite of herself, the less able she was to hold on to her more recent mental construction of Callum: an unloving, deserting, careless, probably unfaithful and – she now saw – largely fictional figure. The man who had walked beneath that hat was wholly real. The face which that peak had sheltered was known to her in every mood; its troubles and joys were her own. She knew the spring of his hair, the set of his ears, the glance of his eye. She could smell him, feel him in her arms, forgive him.

'You did, didn't you? You had him in the van?'

Arnie nodded mutely, then rallied a little and said, 'Yeah, like we – um – said. We saw him briefly, gave him a lift before he went to – um – the army place.'

Guilt was written in every line of his slight body. Susie looked at him consideringly; what he said might perfectly well be true, but there was something about his manner which was all too familiar from her soldiers' occasional attempts to pull the wool over her eyes.

'He's still here, isn't he?' she said. 'He's in Edinburgh. You've got him. This is all a set-up, isn't it?'

Arnie began to protest, but her steady officer's eye overmastered him.

'I told Francis,' he said sulkily. 'I told him it was a rubbish idea.'

'What was? Come on. Give me the whole plot. No – I mean it.'

She stood by the white van doors, one hand on the handle, her foot tapping almost imperceptibly: her authority, thought Arnie helplessly, was unbearable. She was such a slight sweet-faced little thing, wholly feminine in her soft blue skirt and tight sweater; a walking echo of Francis with her vivid expression and wide green eyes. She was rather endearing. Yet, with that look on her face, she made the formidable Maggie the agent seem like a Barbie doll in comparison. Generations of Field-Marshals spoke again in her clear calm voice. Thank goodness Francis did not seem to have inherited this power, thought Arnie in his helplessness, or life would be impossible . . .

'Arnie, tell me the truth. It'll save time.'

'He *did* go to his horrid army camp,' said the young man sulkily. 'But then he came back here. Francis says the Colonel-man told him to go away and consider his position. And since you were coming up to see the show, Francis thought——'

He quailed beneath her eye, and the sentence tailed off.

'You were going to throw me together with him, acciden-tally on purpose?'

Arnie looked down. 'Yes.'

'Does Callum know I'm here?'

'No. And like I said, I told Francis it was a rubbish idea.'

'Perhaps it wasn't,' said Susie. Suddenly her manners returned as she realized she had been treating this inoffen-sive, kind and polite young man as if he were a troublesome soldier. 'I think it was a very kind thought.' She paused, and glanced back at the hat.

'But the thing is, Arnie, you probably know a bit about

love –' he inclined his head silently '– so you know that it doesn't work that way. Life isn't like some schlocky movie where kids bring their divorced parents back together. One of the two people has to make the first move deliberately, especially if there's been a break-up. Things don't just mend by putting the two halves near each other, like – like mercury running into one blob. Do they?'

'They might,' returned Arnie, still sulky. Loyalty flared in him. 'Francis really thinks it's wrong, you two splitting up. He goes on and on about it. He's obsessed. I tell him that you can't influence people in stuff like that, but . . .'

'He's right. I was wrong. It *is* wrong, us splitting up,' said Susie calmly. 'Which is why you're going to tell me, right now, where the hell Callum and Francis are. We are *not* going to watch a Japanese ballet tribute to Laurel and Hardy, or whatever the hell it is. We are going to find them, and sort this out. Now.'

A wonderful lightness possessed her. The hat had done it, she thought triumphantly; the hat had shown her the way. Callum was not a deserter and a betrayer and a cold fish. He was just Callum. She loved him, for better or worse. He probably loved her too, poor sod. He had had a bad time with his leg, and felt guilty and angry and helpless; well, she knew a bit about those feelings now.

She too had felt guilty and helpless and resentful and definitely spiteful towards the world after she collapsed on the PT demonstration. She had shared a little of that unique double humiliation, of feeling herself despised by the Army and patronized by the doctors. It did not take too much imagination to see how useless she must have been to Callum in Portugal, with her springing fitness, her forced bright optimism, her nurselike fussing. Callum, with his shattered body, must have felt in treble measure the same useless irrational sense of shame and anger at his body's betrayal. And it was a mistake to cart him off to that creepy old man's villa in Portugal, away from home and friends and normality and surrounded by depressing churches and black furniture. Harry Devine and Rachel must have been the last straw. It had just been bad luck that there was a boat to tempt him, lying alongside the quay. Perhaps a boatful of strangers was what he had needed all along, to recover his balance.

As far as Susie was concerned, in that simple moment of seeing his poor abandoned denim hat Callum was forgiven everything. He always had been; with a sense of inward flowering and release she understood how much proud but futile effort she had been pouring into the pretence that it was otherwise. She remembered her own voice saying in the dressing room 'I'm over all that nonsense, by the way', and blushed. Francis must have seen through her pretence from the start. She must have been obvious, so obvious that the dear boy set up this ridiculous plot to throw her together with Callum in Edinburgh.

Her exaltation and reborn love did not depend on hope. Even in this moment of epiphany she realized that Callum might not want her back. Or, at least, not yet. Strangely, having realigned her own feelings, she found she could accept that awful premise too. When she had asked Arnie whether Callum knew she was coming and was in on the plot, she had entertained a brief flash of hope that it might be so, and that all she would need to do was capitulate. But it could not be; if there was one thing she was sure of about him, it was that he would not involve himself in such a ridiculous, Francis-devised ambush. No, Arnie was clearly telling the truth: Callum did not know. The planned *coup de théâtre* by her all-too-theatrical brother was set to be as much of a shock for him as for her.

It still would be. He might flee, or continue his dismissive, defensive coldness. If he did want to mend their engagement it would be wonderful: life-giving, perfect, the best of all worlds. But even if he didn't, thought Susie bravely, it was still up to her to step towards him, make the first move, forgive. He had been a pain in the neck in Portugal, but he was the hurt one. She had been a pain in the neck to him, all unwittingly, but she had been the stronger. Anyway, it was her job to walk towards him now with arms outstretched, and hope, and risk rejection. Not to be loved was a sad thing, but one could get over it. Not to give love was worse.

'I'll take him his hat,' she said, and dived into the van to get it. With this talisman thrust deep into her shoulder-bag, she turned back to Arnie.

'So come on: where is he?'

'I'll take you,' said Arnie, meekly.

27

---◆---

It was a grey evening; the lights were coming on, gold and mellow, in the granite city. Taxis were scarce and Susie's bag was small, so the pair walked with fast, light steps up the road and through the self-conscious Gothic of the Royal Mile. A walking tour was assembling, with much nervous laughter, for the Ghosts 'n' Graveyards outing; a group of schoolchildren dressed in immaculate RAF wartime uniform handed out leaflets publicizing their school play. A stilt-walker in a top hat and tails lumbered past, flanked by two pleased acolytes carrying flaming torches which hissed as scanty raindrops fell on to them.

'We might get wet,' said Arnie.

'Who cares?' said his companion blithely. 'Do you know, I've really learned to love British rain after that time in the desert.' After a moment, as they came in sight of the bridge, she asked with apparent casualness: 'So, how's Francis been?'

'His shows are doing really well. Not just here, he did a few gigs on the way up which were fantastic. All that work's paying off now. He really puts in the practice, and the great thing is, he *thinks*, he's intelligent, he's perceptive about the mood in the room. He doesn't just treat all audiences as if they were the same animal. I think he's really going to go all the way. He's just so inventive too, and that's rare. Often these acts get stuck in a groove, but with him you just push a button, make a suggestion, and Francis comes up with wonderful new ideas.'

Susie smiled, enjoying the sudden outburst of enthusiasm from this hitherto reserved, nervous young man. She began to see what it was that Francis saw in him, beyond the cheerful flippancy. And Francis, she thought a little sadly, had not had very much understanding praise heaped on him in his life. He knew that his parents were a little disappointed in him, in their fond way, and although she had always taken his part loyally, she had not – until tonight's performance – ever really understood what it was he was trying to do with his apparently silly acts. This lad understood him, and was fired up by him, and wanted him to win. Francis, she thought, deserved such a cheerleader.

'What about that pub where he got things thrown at him?' she asked curiously. 'He said he was going back'.

'He did. He knocked 'em dead. He was petrified – they were throwing things at the act before him, complete bloody Neanderthals. But he did it. He had them yelling for an encore.'

There was such warm pride in Arnie's voice that Susie went straight on to her next question without hesitation.

'And he's happy?'

'I think so. Yes. We—' Arnie's breath caught audibly in his throat, but after another sharp, authoritative look from Susie he finished in a low murmur: '*We* are very happy.'

'Thought so,' said Susie. 'Good.'

Something in her eye was still compelling him, though, and after a moment he muttered: 'It's new for me too,' and flushed scarlet, looking away from her and up towards the Castle lights.

'You're not—' Susie hesitated now, and rephrased her question. 'He's not going to get hurt?'

Arnie stopped walking and turned to her, with an access of indignant courage.

'I'd rather die than hurt him.'

Susie smiled, ducking her head and looking away in turn; Arnie, breathing with difficulty, understood that she believed him and was grateful. They had gone too far, though, for restrained British comfort, and said no more until ten minutes further up the town she asked if they were nearly there, and which restaurant it was. Whereon Arnie began to explain to her the nature of the entertainment they were heading for, and admitted that he was worried they might not be allowed in until it ended. 'No late admission, even with tickets, and we don't have tickets, because the idea was to meet at the restaurant . . .'

'OK,' said Susie. 'We'll play it by ear. Stake them out. Advantage of surprise. All I want is five minutes with Cal.'

'Good luck,' said Arnie. And, finally recovering his lost carapace of shining flippancy, added, 'At least he'll be really, really pleased to get his hat back.'

It was just after Francis' electrifying rendition of 'Devilgate Drive' on rollerskates, and during the final table performance of the Nacho Snatcho, that Callum finally and firmly decided to stay in the Army.

A tall and virtually naked girl was balancing on the table, resting on her shoulders and elbows in the position once favoured by gym mistresses demonstrating air-bicycling. Between her elegant splayed legs was balanced (though not, Callum's practical eye noted, without benefit of Velcro) a pot of salsa. With her immaculate toes she passed nachos to each guest in turn, deadpan.

The journalists hesitated for a moment, then with shrieks

of joy at their own daring, began dipping their crisps in the salsa. Looking across the room, which at his eye level was oddly framed between the dancer's spreadeagled limbs, Callum saw other performers at work: one twisting a final balloon into a comically biological shape, another wearing a curious grey granny-wig and doing high-kicks with a Zimmer frame, another sitting down with a shocked-looking group of blindfolded guests, telling them their shortcomings in a low but carrying stream of heavy sarcasm.

'. . . dress code said *smart*, or can't you read – yes, you, mutton dressed as lamb. You think you're so *cool*, don't you, coming to see the gay weirdos do their performance because you read about it in the *Guardian* . . . ooh, get you, how *brave*. And you, I've just got two words to say, you know who you are – those words are *bad breath* . . .'

As Callum watched, the girl's manner changed to brisk friendliness as she whipped off the guests' blindfolds and chirped, 'Time's up. Thank you, ladies and gentlemen. I hope you enjoyed your insults. That'll be two dollars.'

They were good, thought Callum. All of them. They were keeping up their act, making it serve its purpose, exercising the mysterious immemorial authority of the stripper. He remembered a holiday in Turkey with Susie, when a scrawny, tawdrily dressed belly-dancer had been brought in by the beach club management on barbecue night. The British contingent had been shamingly loud and loutish, and he'd braced himself to defend the poor child if it got nasty. But that little Turkish girl had needed none of it. She held absolute authority during her brief performance, and would no more have called on his chivalry than would a heavyweight boxer in the ring. She sized up the company in seconds and targeted certain truculent but easily embarrassed men. She threatened them with a flutter of her veil and a thrust of her jewelled navel; she whisked away from groping hands, but a moment later reappeared behind the offender, laughing and trailing her spangled scarf across his chest in a manner which directly and deliberately impugned his virility. She controlled the group utterly; Susie had just passed out of Sandhurst and after the girl's performance said to Callum, not entirely in jest, that that young woman would go a very long way as an army officer. 'Definitely a leader of men,' she said. 'Though where she'd lead them I hate to think.'

There was the same sort of confident authority here, wielded by this group of jokers in their fake nightclub. As the nacho girl eased herself gracefully off the table with a smile as serene as the late Queen Mother's, in the moment the spotlight dimmed above their table at her going, Callum suddenly knew for certain that he was not yet done with his own profession. For the first time since his injury, he found himself thinking calmly about Basra.

He saw again the hot city in the few days before he was invalided away from it. Whatever the rights and wrongs of the war itself, he thought with a spurt of pride, they had been doing all right, his army. The area was virtually secure, food was starting to be organized, there were clear plans for restoring the water supply. The Iraqis were shocked, afraid, confused, often angry; but a growing number of them were visibly learning to believe that the invaders were not trigger-happy tyrants.

He remembered being out with Simmonds and McNair singing 'Ally Bally Bee' to the children, and being bollocked afterwards for not wearing a hard hat and showing off to the TV camera; but he also remembered how a group of them had sat around that evening and agreed that fraternizing, especially with the children, was something which would work to the benefit of all. He remembered the careful searches for weapons, and the exhilaration he felt on the occasions when they were given up quietly by thin, suffering men who made it cautiously clear that, all things considered, they were happy to see the end of their dictator. He remembered the patrol on that last night, the glimmer of the moon and the smell of the cooling earth; and – for the first time – he recaptured the brief adrenalin moment of absolute certainty, absolute rightness, when he had understood that there was another child in the burning house and had ignored every natural terror to plunge in and save it.

He tried not to remember any further: he had done that, God knows, often enough and for far too long. The horror would never quite leave him, but he could find it a safe dwelling-place, a context in the story he held in his head. He could control it. It helped when he called up instead another memory: of Jez in the galley, faithful and dogged and uncomplaining, kneeling and pumping as the water swirled around her legs and the gale howled in the rigging overhead.

These elemental battles, he thought with wonder, ought by rights to make him feel disgust at the frivolous skylarking all around him tonight. He had, after all, just watched his once putative brother-in-law doing the splits in tight leather trousers and a pair of jutting false breasts while playing an electric guitar.

Yet it did not disgust: rather the opposite. In this strange place, and this strange moment, all the effort and nerve and calculation and risk and professional daring in the world seemed to come together around him, and stiffen him, and make him resolve to go back to his CO on Monday in a different frame of mind. He would stand upright, apologize for his earlier sullen demeanour, deny all he could of his lameness and apply to go back to duty. Maybe, one day, even to Basra. Hell's teeth, why did an officer need to be super-fit? He didn't need to dance, did he? He could walk fast enough now, he could think and decide and give orders, he could even drive. He would go back, and let the Army get some bloody value out of him.

And he would write to Susie and tell her so, and apologize for being such a bad-tempered wimp. As time went on she might not think so badly of him, for he would have returned to the vocation and the values that they had shared so long ago.

'Good evening, ladies and gentlemen,' lisped a voice at his elbow. 'I believe you ordered the Lazy Susan?'

'No, not you,' said Louise indignantly. 'We ordered the other man, the one who lies on the table and—'

'Kindly remove your glasses and bottles. I am also licensed by the authorities to lie on the table,' reassured Francis, who had taken off his jacket and stood neat as an acrobat in leather trousers and a spangled vest. He was as good as his word, promptly flipping himself on to the table and lying, knees up, ankles crossed, his face looking upwards at Louise's chest. 'This is a very *special* counselling facility. You are aware of the swivelling serving aid known as a Lazy Susan, normally provided by Mr Chris Green, but tonight available equally from myself, who am also psychic.' Callum stared down at Francis, who had taken off his wig and gelled his short hair into black spikes like Dennis the Menace. 'I will revolve to each of you, and offer a personal but discreetly whispered analysis of your aura. Please respect the confidentiality of the persons sitting next to you and do not listen.'

The journalist group liked this, and began giggling and nudging one another with tipsy knowingness. Louise, who was first, leaned forward with her ear to Francis' lips and then jumped back with a squeaky laugh, saying, 'Ooh, that's not true!'

Francis smirked and swirled on, spending fifteen or twenty seconds whispering to each of the journalists and producing squawks of 'Dear, oh, dear!' and 'No, I am *not!*' and 'Denial? – it's a river in Egypt'. None of them managed a very witty reply; whatever Francis was saying about their aura and their personal qualities was clearly well-judged to shock or amuse them out of any ability to resist.

With a cry from Maddy of 'Ooh, you've got a nerve!' Callum became aware that he was the next, and last, of the revolving Lazy Susan's victims. Francis swivelled until his black-rimmed eyes were looking straight up into Callum's from his upside-down face. Obediently, the soldier dropped his ear to catch the creature's words.

'I see a beautiful woman. In battledress,' whispered Francis. 'I see a complete mutt, blowing his chances. I see a happy ending just waiting to be grabbed as it flies past – oh, fucking hell!'

The last words were spoken not in a whisper but a shriek. Everyone at the table jumped in shock, and the dogfish woman dropped her glass to the floor with a tinkling crash. Susie was standing behind Callum, her hands on his shoulders, her gaze boring down at her dishevelled brother lying on the table. Arnie, clutching his strawlike hair with both hands, stood just beyond her, shrugging violently in the direction of Francis, his palms upturned, mouthing, 'It's not my fault!'

Susie's clear cool voice cut through the tipsy fug of the room.

'Francis, what *are* you doing?'

Callum turned at the sound of her voice, although he had known who it was from the moment her hands fell on his shoulders. He managed a reply, speaking for Francis.

'He's working,' he said. 'He's terribly good at it.'

The music for the finale struck up, deafeningly amplified, and a procession of dancing fluffy human ducks swayed on to the little stage. The music was so loud that several merciful minutes passed before anybody could speak again. Callum and Susie spent them in smiling, with almost idiotic joy, into one another's eyes.

28

---◆◆◆---

'We fixed it, then,' said Francis to Arnie, as they trailed up the hill to the flat. He yawned. 'God, I'm tired.' The rain had cleared; a pale, almost full moon was rising over the crags. As they passed below the Castle Mount they could just hear the thudding of military drums and the skirl of pipes from the finale of the Tattoo. 'Looks as if those two are sorted. Good day's work we did there. What a team!'

'You have no idea,' said his friend, equally tired and limping a little from too much walking across Edinburgh, 'how terrifying your sister is. She flattened me, and then she walked straight into C'est Vauxhall, past the most *snubbing* waiter, without even breaking stride.'

'Oh, she's a softie really,' said Francis. 'It's all just an act. Useful for quelling mutinous soldiery. Come to that, every-thing—' he tossed his costume bag joyfully from hand to hand '—absolutely everything is an act. We strut and fret our hour upon the stage . . .'

'I hope Alfio's is open. I am so hungry.'

'He will be. I rang up this morning and booked a table for four, but we're only two so we ought really to eat twice as much, so as not to damage his profits, poor Alfio.'

'Well, the lovebirds are better off down in posh old Princes Street,' said Arnie. 'Callum'll find his way back to the flat, won't he?'

'Yeah, he's trained to cross trackless deserts. I said we'd leave the door on the latch.'

'Bunk beds again for us, then,' said Arnie. 'Still, it's in a good cause.'

'Oh, aren't we *clever!*' said Francis. 'We did it, we did it! The prince and princess walk off, hand in hand, into the sunset!'

'Except they won't, will they?' said Arnie wonderingly. 'They'll get married and then promptly march off to completely different bits of the Army.'

'It's their chosen world, weird as it may seem,' said Francis sententiously. And then, his mind veering back to practical matters and the morrow, 'Hell! I was so excited I forgot the hair-bag and chucked the Kelly wig straight in with the jacket. It'll take hours untangling it from the zip again.'

They quickened their step; the warm, steamy golden window of Alfio's shone before them, the broad white moon above.

Francis sang at the Christmas wedding, twice. Once in irreproachable hired morning-dress in the church, calling for the wings of a dove; once at the reception, in a red silk sheath dress and a Dietrich wig, adding some startling new words to the old tale of lamplight and barrack-square. His parents were very proud; Harry Devine was seriously annoyed when Rachel was so overcome by the latter performance that she ran up afterwards and gave Francis a tipsy, lipsticky kiss, and then came back to inform him that he, Harry, had no soul.

Jez was a guest, Susie having insisted on tracing her; she arrived rather surprisingly hand-in-hand with a slightly cleaned-up Erik. They were on the way to Antigua to look at a likely boat for the charter business. Pat was very, very shocked by Erik's pigtail. Arnie said that he itched to set fire to it, to see if it was dipped in tar like the pirates used to do.

Callum eventually served again in Basra, and so for two months did Susie, although their overlap there was barely a week. Within two years, though, Callum's increasing interest in aid work saw him resigning his commission; within three, Susie made a parallel decision that it was time to start raising children.

'It'll be interesting,' she said at the Sunday lunch when she announced this onward move in her life, 'to see whether the next generation turn out military, or theatrical, or take up something else altogether.'

'They'll be tax inspectors,' said Francis lugubriously. 'Bent bookies. Speed-camera designers. Government spin-doctors.'

'We will learn,' said Callum piously, 'to accept their vocations with grace.'